Just My Luck

EMILY WOOD

RISING ACTION

This book is a work of fiction. Any references to historical events, real people, or real places are used fictitiously. Other names, characters, places, and events are products of the author's imagination, and any resemblance to actual events, places, names, or persons, is entirely coincidental.

Distributed by Simon & Schuster

ISBN: 978-1-998672-08-0
Ebook: 978-1-998672-09-7

FIC027660 FICTION / Romance / Small Town & Rural
FIC027020 FICTION / Romance / Contemporary

#JustMyLuck

Follow Rising Action on our socials!
Twitter: @RAPubCollective
Instagram: @risingactionpublishingco
Tiktok: @risingactionpublishingco

For Tyler.

Meeting you was the greatest stroke of luck I'll ever have.

Just My Luck

Chapter 1

Call me unorthodox, but I think I've fallen in love with a brick wall. I'm not even mad about it, because I know my followers will too.

"Put the phone down, Sloan."

"I can't help it. I am Leonardo da Vinci, and this is my *Mona Lisa*." I snap three more pictures of the exposed brick I've been obsessed with since I found the online listing for this charming former café. I bask in Lyla's laughter as she rolls her eyes and then sticks her head in the empty glass display case for the third time.

She teases me again, "Seriously, how is your storage not full?"

"We should keep the tables on the other side, so this wall is clear for photos," I say, ignoring her as I mentally furnish the space. "Ooh, what if we decorate it with vintage picture frames? All gold could be pretty. Or maybe painted in mismatched colors?"

"I'm leaving the decorating up to you, my friend. I'm just the flavor guru."

"Yes, but your delicious cupcakes are the hook that will pull people in. The smell of them alone will have the whole town leaving a trail of drool all the way up the block and right up to that counter. *Our* counter," I correct myself.

Lyla scrunches her nose. "We'd better buy a mop to avoid slip and fall lawsuits, then."

By now, she's emerged from the display case and glances at her phone before tucking it back into the pocket of her bright yellow pea coat. Running a hand over her straight blonde hair, she looks around the room.

"Heard from Adam yet?" I ask.

"Still waiting to hear. He texted me a little while ago to let me know he was going into the meeting. I'll call him after we sign the papers, and then we can all celebrate this promotion together. Get your earplugs ready, people!"

Our realtor emerges from the kitchen, arms wide. She's almost as pleased as we are, and I don't blame her. It's been six months of painstakingly combing through real estate listings and visiting every vacant storefront in town, and I'm sure she was beginning to share my fear that we would never find the perfect place. Somewhere that was more than four walls and a kitchen, but that had real character, a charm you can't fake with a coat of paint. We've seen more than a few great places, but Lyla has been harder to please than expected.

But this place ... this is *magic*.

I felt it the first time we stepped inside. I can *see* us here. Me, running calligraphy workshops in the front, with twinkle lights strung up against the brick, and Lyla's elaborate cupcakes filling the glass display cases that double as a counter. The exposed red brick offsets the full front wall of windows, so the vibe is bright but private, with faux-wood laminate flooring and black and white checkered tiles in the kitchen. It's everything we've been searching for and more.

"Alright ladies, are we ready to sign some papers?"

I contain my squeal (because, professionalism) but squeeze Lyla's arm tightly to convey my excitement. The smile she returns is tinged with nerves, but I get it. This is a big step. Plus, she's been distracted all day with her husband's impending promotion. We follow Elaine to the kitchen, where she has the paperwork spread out over one of the (*three!*) stainless steel worktops. I can already picture Lyla baking up a storm back here underneath the bare bulbs—a far cry from our tiny apartment kitchen back in college when she first turned her baking hobby into a modest side hustle. Honestly, even the light fixtures in here are Instagram-worthy.

"Did you remember to bring the champagne?" Lyla asks.

I lift a hand to my chest, pretending to be hurt. "After two long years of dreaming and planning, do you honestly think I would forget the celebratory bubbly?" I reach into my oversized purse and pull out the bottle, setting it down with a clunk on the worktop.

"Sorry! But you're not exactly known for your follow-through. Don't blame yourself; you're a Pisces. You can only do so much."

"That's why we make the perfect pair. I have the ideas—you bring them to life. Speaking of, have you ordered the business cards yet?"

"Oh ... um, not yet. I still haven't picked a favorite," she replies, brushing invisible dust off the countertop.

I bump her hip with mine. "Now who's the one who can't follow through?"

I'm teasing, but it doesn't make her smile like I expect, and the guilt settles in my stomach like a bowling ball. I'd given her ten different business card options and begged her to choose one for me. Like she said, I'm not known for my decision-making skills. Having designed them myself, I was already worried that Lyla wouldn't be completely honest with me if she didn't love them. It's unlike her to put off making a decision, but maybe in all the excitement, it just slipped her mind. Either way, I don't want to add any undue pressure.

"Crap. I forgot cups!" I say.

She waves her arms dramatically. "Look at the size of this place, there has to be at least one cup in here."

Elaine is holding out a pen for one of us to sign the paperwork, but I don't take it; crossing instead to the cupboards and opening them one by one because this is it—this is our moment, and it has to be perfect. We'll sign the papers and make each other tear up with toasts to our future as business partners, about hard work and dreams coming true. We'll take a boomerang of us clinking our glasses together, and it'll be the first post on our new Instagram account. Elaine will take a photo of the two of us hugging, capturing the moment when we're both elated and terrified, and in ten years we'll look back on it and say: look how far we've come.

Lyla digs through the pantry for the elusive cups, or anything that will hold liquid—glasses, mugs, or hell, even measuring cups would do. In fact, that would be pretty damn cute on our feed. The previous owners have mostly cleared everything out, but I strike gold in a forgotten drawer filled with paper cups and plates.

"Aha!" I yell, holding up my treasure.

Lyla's phone rings, and she reaches for it instead of a cup. "It's Adam. Do you mind if I …?"

I shake my head and motion for her to answer it.

"Adam, honey? How did it go?" She holds up a finger (polished, like mine, in preparation for the aforementioned boomerang) and ducks out to the front of the store.

"Did you want to get the ball rolling?" Elaine asks, extending the pen to me a second time. Under the blonde highlights of her angled bob, her dark-lipped smile falters.

"I kind of want Lyla to be here for the whole thing," I say, thinking about the photos that would be missed if I started without her. We've waited so long for this moment, for our dream to become real; I don't want it to feel rushed. So instead of signing the papers, I fluff my hair, checking my loose, copper waves in the shiny surface of the counter, then line up three paper cups on the counter and start to undo the wire around the champagne cork so it's easier to open when the time comes.

And then Lyla's back, but she's not smiling anymore.

"What's wrong? Is Adam okay?" My words are rushed, but I'm frozen to the spot as I take in the crestfallen look on her face.

"He's fine," she says, her words shaking around the edges. "But ... you'd better not open that champagne."

I don't mean to. Really, I don't. But it's like telling someone not to think of a purple elephant wearing a tutu—your brain does it anyway. So, the cork pops, shattering the exposed bulb above me (and *whose* idea was bare bulbs, anyway?). Champagne overflows down my jeans and brand-new boots in a sticky waterfall of endless bubbles that pool at my feet.

Along with all our hopes and dreams.

Chapter 2

My throat burns from the vodka shot I just tossed back as music pumps through the club, but I relish it. At least it's something real I can resent. Slamming the shot glass on the bar top, I signal the bartender for another while wincing over the first.

"Someone came to party tonight," Caleb says, slipping an arm easily around my waist. "That's my girl!"

Nope. Just wallowing in my reality of being a thirty-year-old woman who lives with her parents and has wasted the last two years pouring my heart and soul into a business that may never happen. No wonder my parents tried to talk me out of trying in the first place. I should have listened to them when they told me to stick with my communications degree, but nooo, I had to follow my stupid heart and switch to a business major, all because I got too wrapped up in a *side hustle.* My parents were right—I should have left it at being a hobby.

Another shot appears in front of me and I slam that one back too, hoping it washes away the aftertaste of my hopes and dreams.

"Come on, babe, let's go dance." Caleb tugs my hand, already searching for his friends, but I stay where I am.

"I don't really feel like dancing."

"Sure you do, this vibe is popping," he says, his phone suddenly out as he records a quick video of the mass of bodies jumping up and down to the thumping beat the DJ is churning out. He turns the camera back on himself. "Let's gooooo!" he shouts at the phone to be heard over the music, grinning ear to ear. The same beaming, unreserved smile drew me to him when we met on New Year's Eve. Usually, I'm a fan of his optimism, but for once, I wish he could press pause on the persona he uses for his followers and be real with me. In dating an influencer, I've learned that you're never in a relationship with just one person—Caleb comes as a package deal: him and his sixty thousand followers.

"Can we go home soon?" I ask, the vodka swirling in my gut.

He gives me a knowing smirk, but sex is the last thing on my mind right now—way down the list after wrapping myself in my most comfortable pajamas and curling up under the covers with a pint of ice cream for at least a week. Pressing a kiss to my temple, he says, "Wish I could take you to my place, but you know I'm working, babe."

I nod because I get it, and I don't want to ruin his night just because I had a bad day. Our jobs are similar—both in the realm of social media, the only difference being he's the face of the products and clubs he promotes, whereas I hide behind other people's accounts, keeping myself out of the spotlight. My family—and even Lyla—have never really understood the demands of the job, or how stressful it can be, and I don't like to complain to my parents after pushing so hard to switch my university major in the first place. I need them to see that it was the right choice; only now the doubt creeps in. Caleb is the only person who understands, but lately it seems like all we have to talk about is work.

"Cheer up, buttercup," he says, pinching my chin and giving it a playful wobble. He gives me a sympathetic lip pout. "I don't like seeing you so bummed."

I try for a smile. "I'm sorry, I'm such a downer today. I probably shouldn't have come."

Especially not when this night out was *supposed* to be a celebration. Instead of being here with us, though, Lyla is at home with Adam, trying to figure out the bombshell they got dealt today with Adam's unexpected layoff. (So much for the promotion he thought he was getting.)

As if summoned by BFF telepathy, my phone buzzes in my back pocket and I pull it out to find a text from her.

"It's Lyla," I tell Caleb, who's bobbing beside me to the music, his attention back on his own phone. "Apologizing *again* and checking in to see how I'm doing."

I roll my eyes, despite the gratitude that manages to push through my bad mood as I text her back.

Me: Please don't worry about me, I promise I'm fine.

Lyla: Proof please.

I show Caleb the text and gesture for him to come in for a picture. He fixes his hair quickly, then bends to tuck his chin over my shoulder and flash his perfect white teeth as I snap a photo and send it to her. There. Proof that I'm alive and doing well. So well that I'm partying at a club. She doesn't need to know that I'm doing the mental math of how long I need to stick it out before I can ask Caleb again to take me home.

Me: Happy?

Lyla: Your smile is as fake as Caleb's hair color.

Me: Be nice.

Caleb's never been her favorite person, but she's a worrier who can't help but watch everyone's backs. As the oldest of five siblings, her mother-henning comes honestly.

Me: Go worry about your husband. I'm fine, promise.

Lyla: How many 5-minute wallows did you do today?

Me: I'm going through a tunnel.

Lyla: That's what I thought.

Me: Our entire life plan just went out the window. Give a girl a break. You're allowed to freak out about this too, you know.

She doesn't answer, and after a minute, I slip my phone back into my pocket to find Caleb filming himself taking another shot of something. I spot a couple of his friends headed our way with a bottle, but I don't want to share him right now. It's silly, but I need some comfort, so I grab his hand, pulling him around the dance floor's edge to the hallway leading to the restrooms where the music isn't quite so loud.

"You look so sad, babe," he says, brushing my hair out of my face, his blue eyes peering down at me. "Want me to get you a ride home?"

My childhood bedroom flashes through my mind, and I almost groan at the thought of going back there.

"Can I go to your place, and you can meet me there when you're done?" I ask. "I love my parents, but I know they're going to have a million more questions if I go home, and I don't have any answers yet."

"But it's just business as usual for you, right? Nothing has to change. You haven't quit on your clients yet."

"Don't remind me," I say, pressing my face into his chest. "My resignation letter is already in my email drafts. The only reason I haven't sent it is because my dad insisted I wait until the ink was dry on the lease. It's just one more thing for them to say they were right about."

He frowns down at me. "But you like what you do."

I pull my lip between my bottom teeth. "I did. But I've spent so long helping other people build their brands ... I was looking forward to finally building something for myself, you know?"

"Then don't let Lyla stop you. Just go for it."

I frown. "Setting aside the fact that I can't afford the space alone, this was always mine and Lyla's dream. Doing it without her feels wrong."

"So, what will you do?"

I shrug, biting the inside of my cheek as that feeling of helplessness from earlier washes over me again. "I honestly have no idea what's next."

He rubs circles on my back. "Don't worry, babe. You'll figure it out."

"Maybe ..." I say, but I'm doubtful. "I didn't realize how badly I was counting on getting the storefront and apartment until today when everything exploded."

My parents are great, but they've kept my bedroom the same since I moved out almost ten years ago. As supportive as they are, they're already hinting at me backtracking to find a different career path that's more stable and dependable, and the last thing I need as I try to figure my life out is them pressuring me to do it their way.

The vodka shots are catching up with me now. Along with the vision of what living with my parents indefinitely would look like, they make me blurt out my next thought without running it through the filter.

"I could stay with you," I say, tipping my chin to peer up at him.

He grins. "Sure, babe. You can spend the night."

"No, I mean—what if I move in?"

His confident grin flickers, and the alcohol starts to sour in my stomach. *Oh. God.*

"That's ... kind of sudden. Don't you think?"

I take a half step back, hating that I sprung this on him. "No, no. I know. You're right." Maybe it's the loud music making it hard to hear my thoughts, or maybe it's the buzz, but instead of leaving it at that, I keep talking for once. "It's just ... we've been together for almost a year."

Caleb's eyebrows lift. "Well ... it's only been eight months."

"Some people get married after less time than that."

"Whoa. Sloan, I—"

I wave away his instant panic. "I'm not saying *we* should get married. I'm just making a point."

"Okay."

He starts looking around again, subtly shifting away from me, and my anger flares.

"I can't believe this," I say, laughing at how blatantly he's avoiding the question. "I'm basically homeless and you won't let me move in with you."

"That's not true," he argues. "Your parents said you could stay with them as long as you needed, and you'll be more comfortable there anyway. My condo is tiny, and if I'm going to start this podcast—"

"You're picking a *podcast* over your *girlfriend*?"

For the first time, the understanding expression on his face wipes clean, his eyes turning hard and determined. "No, I'm picking me, Sloan. This isn't just some stupid podcast; it's the next step in my *career*. Which you should know better than anyone, most people don't take seriously, but I do. And I thought you did too."

The hurt in his eyes makes me reach for him, but even though he doesn't pull away, he doesn't lean into my touch either.

"No, that didn't come out how I—*ugh!*" I run my hands through my hair, squeezing before I look up again and try to backpedal. "I'm sorry. I take you seriously, Caleb, I do, but everything I've been working towards for the last two years just imploded before it even started, and I need ..."

I pause, not used to making selfish demands of anyone, even Caleb. I'm low maintenance, the farthest thing from needy. Only right now, that doesn't feel true. My heart is so fragile it feels like it might crack at the slightest gust of wind, and I'm not sure I can keep it intact. My best friend feels guilty enough without me piling on, and my parents can only be so supportive when every sympathetic thing that comes out of their mouths is followed by I told you so. Caleb is the only person I can lean on right now, and I need to trust that he'll be there to catch me. So, I take a deep breath and ask for what I need from him.

"I need to know that I'm not in this alone. I need a real partner."

His expression softens into something more like pity. Taking a step back, his arm slides out of my fingers. He takes my hand in his, but he may as well be standing on the other side of the dance floor for the gaping void between us.

"I'm not sure I can be that for you, Sloan." He runs his fingers through his hair, puffing then releasing a long breath. "Maybe we shouldn't talk about this right now. You've had a long day, I'm working—let's hang out for a bit, then get you something to eat on the way home and we can talk about this tomorrow when you're back to normal. There's a great fish and chips place around the corner that I want to post about."

I grit my teeth. "Hi. Have you met me? I'm a vegetarian, remember?"

"See, this is what I'm talking about. This lashing out, this anger—it isn't you."

"Maybe it is!" I say, tipping my chin up. "Maybe this is me when I react to stressful situations."

He shakes his head, frowning like he's seeing me for the first time. "It's not the Sloan I know."

I swallow. He's right. I'm freaked out because things are falling apart, and I'm pushing too hard. Normally, I'm a chronic people pleaser; it's not like me to make demands like this. But for the first time since I can remember, I'm mad. Self-righteous, blood-boiling mad. At myself, at Caleb, at Adam's company. At the universe for dealing me this shitty hand.

The rage inside me threatens to hit the boiling point, and I take a deep breath, doing my best to think clearly over the incessant *thud thud thud* of EDM.

I shouldn't be here. It isn't my scene, and it hasn't been for months. I only come to places like this because of Caleb. But Lyla has Adam now, and I don't fit into her settled, married life, and I *definitely* don't belong in my childhood bedroom with my parents across the hall. I need someone to want me as I am. Someone who cares enough to make room for me and all my drama in their life—not just their Uber. The thought of Caleb telling me he doesn't want that makes me feel sick to my stomach, and this time it's more than just from the alcohol.

"You're right," I say, trying to steer us back to safer, neutral territory—my specialty. "We don't need to talk about this. I'm just buzzed and depressed. Let's go dance."

"Sloan, wait." He catches me as I try to walk away. I follow his gaze to his boat shoes, staring at the strip of bare ankle exposed under his rolled-up pant legs. "I don't think I can do this anymore." His gaze meets mine again, and though it's not unkind, I recognize it for what it is—he's putting himself first. "You of all people know what my family's like. They've never taken what I do seriously. I need to be with someone who does."

"I told you, I do—"

He shakes his head. "And—I need to be around positive energy, or this podcast will never work. I have sponsors who are counting on me, and this could be the launch forward in my career I've been waiting for, but I need to stay focused. You obviously need time to figure out what's next for you, and that's fine, but..."

"But what?" I manage, trying and failing to keep my bottom lip from trembling.

He squeezes my hand gently. "Sloan, you know I care about you. But I'm beginning to think we're on different journeys."

"Different journeys?" Lyla spits in disgust. I glance behind me to see one hand propped on her outraged hip. "What a grade-A douchebag."

"I know. Who talks like that?"

"Influencers with overinflated egos, that's who. I hope a rabid squirrel steals his favorite beanie."

I snort, and God, it feels good to laugh. It feels even better to have an ax in my hand, and I send it hurtling towards the target where it sticks with a satisfying thwack. Lyla got the details over FaceTime after the breakup a week ago, but this is the first time I've seen her in person since Adam got fired and we had to bail out of the shop lease. Since then, she's been busy focusing on damage control of her life, but this morning she showed up on my parents' doorstep with an itinerary that would put a camp counselor to shame and insisted on getting me out of the house to help purge my frustration. I know what she's doing, and I love her for it, but feeling sorry for myself is pathetic given what she and Adam are going through.

Honestly, I'm more upset about losing the business than Caleb, which proves he might have been right about us after all. Instead of feeling comforted, though, it only makes me feel worse. I haven't missed him once in the last week, and if that doesn't scream wasted time, then I don't know what does.

"I spent eight months with him and have absolutely nothing to show for it. I don't even want to think about what that says about me."

I send another ax flying with a powerful *oomph*.

"That you were willing to give him a chance. Or ... that deep down you knew it wouldn't work, but overlooked the obvious red flags because you don't do well with confrontations."

The third ax slips as I let go, missing the target and clattering to the floor as I turn and raise my eyebrows at my best friend.

"I didn't realize we were doing the brutal honesty thing today, or I would have packed an extra pair of underwear."

She holds up her hands, and I can tell by the firm but determined set of her eyes that she won't let me deflect this time. "I love you, and I mean this in the nicest way possible, but ultimatums aren't really your thing, either. Maybe he was surprised?"

He wasn't the only one. But speaking my mind like that, not holding back, felt *good*. The *only* good thing to happen to me in the last week. And I'm not about to apologize for it.

She waves her hand. "Regardless, he showed his true colors last night. Forget Caleb. You should get back out there. I can set you up with one of Adam's friends. Someone who's *not* a Gemini," she adds with a mumble.

"Hello, I'm an unemployed thirty-year-old living with her parents; I'm a walking turnoff. Who's gonna want to date me? Besides, with my luck, it would end in disaster."

Lyla *tsks* as she trades places with me, adjusting her stance and lifting the ax above her head. "It's not bad luck. I told you; Mercury is in retrograde right now, which helps *no* one."

She sends the ax soaring down the laneway before turning back to me. "Have your parents changed their tune at all?"

I sigh and sip my grapefruit beer, propping an elbow on the chest-high wall separating us. "They keep reminding me that I don't need any distractions while I focus on what's important," I say, using one hand to make air quotes. "They mean well, but it's stressing me out. Meanwhile, Tabitha is trying to set me up with some guy she has working for her."

Lyla perks up, eyebrows waggling. "Hot farm hand?"

"I wish. You know Tabitha. She has a bleeding heart and a knack for finding the people who know how to take advantage of it. If history indicates anything, I'll be shocked if he's still there by this weekend."

We wrap up our game, and Lyla drags me across the street to a little café and bakery. There, she insists I wait at a small iron table while she treats me to a drink and a donut. A few minutes later, she sets everything down on the table, and I pull the drink towards me and take a sip, instantly destroying the foam art.

"Whoa," she says, face grave. "No picture of the first pumpkin spice latte of the season? This is worse than I thought."

I sigh, turning to face the sunny street through the café window. The leaves on the trees lining the street are just starting to turn, the bushy green canopies edged with shades of orange and red that normally mark the beginning of my favorite season. The dead leaves already dried and crumpled on the sidewalk are just a reminder that I'm coming to the end of another year, no closer to getting my business off the ground—or my life together—than I was last year.

"Do you ever feel like you're taking one step forward, three steps back?"

"Constantly," Lyla answers without hesitation. "Did I tell you Aiden decided *not* to change her major after all that, even though she hates her courses? And Simon still hates me for forcing him to take the football scholarship instead of following his high school girlfriend to the other side of the country? If my siblings would listen to me for once, they'd see I'm right."

"You're not responsible for them, you know," I remind her gently.

"Except I am," she says, falling back in her chair. "Trust me, I wish I could turn it off. I have enough problems to deal with right now," she admits, a rare spark of heaviness to her words. "Mom almost didn't let me come back to work."

"Wait, *what?*" Lyla's been working at the office of her family's landscaping company for years. When she initially told her parents she wanted to work for them, her mom cried with relief. Lyla knew the expanding business was getting to be too much, especially since her parents didn't have the tech savviness to modernize how they managed things. Still, it wasn't until that moment that she realized how they'd barely been managing to keep their heads above water before she got involved. How could they possibly not want her to come back? "Are they having money problems again?"

"No, business is booming, thank *god.*" Lyla hadn't been working for them yet when they almost had to close their doors for good, but that was the summer she had to practically take over taking care of her younger siblings and managing the house, dinner, homework—all of it—while her parents worked around the clock to save the business they'd put their life savings into opening. I met Lyla two years later at college, which she'd put off for a year to stay behind and help at home, making her a year older than everyone else on our residence floor and the default mother hen there, too.

"Mom's being very cagey about the whole thing," Lyla continues. "She keeps saying it's time for me to spread my wings and do something for myself."

"And your dad?"

She makes a face. "You know how he feels about change." I make a fond noise of acknowledgement. Her dad is a man who has always and will always prefer to work with his hands. He still calls scans faxes and braces himself whenever he has to do work on The Computer Machine—watching him sit down to do it is not unlike watching a scuba diver taking that first breath and tumbling backwards off the edge of a boat. "He's about as excited about Billie being in the office as she is."

Though I don't say it out loud, I can admit it's an odd visual picturing her sister in the role Lyla held for years. Billie is the second oldest and left home the minute she could to go to college across the country and travel the world. She's not one for staying in the same place for too long, and I hope Lyla isn't wasting her time training her to take over for a job she might not stick around for.

"What does Adam think about everything? Is he doing okay?" Lyla filled me in on the details the day after Adam got cut in the downsizing, but since then, she's changed the topic as quickly as possible whenever I try to bring it up. I'm not surprised. Lyla has always had an independence I've admired.

"He finally changed out of his sweatpants yesterday, so I'm considering that progress."

"Yikes. I hope you washed them immediately."

She makes a face. "Are you kidding? I burned them. They were about to become permanently fused to his body."

Lyla seems back to her usual self, but she's always been a silver linings kind of person, while I'm more of a type of brace-for-impact gal, which is why I've been keeping my head down, trying to get through the rest of the day without stepping in dog shit a second time.

Because yes—that *already* happened today.

"Any luck on the job hunt?"

She sighs. "Nothing yet, but we should be fine for a while between his severance and our savings. Enough about me. When are you leaving for Vermont? Did you finish packing? Oh, and don't let me forget to send you the list of podcasts I put together for you to listen to on the bus ride."

"Yes, and tomorrow morning," I say, draining the last of my latte. The kernel of excitement I have over seeing my aunt lets me enjoy the flavor of pumpkin spice. A week in my favorite place couldn't come at a better time. "I feel bad that it's been so long since I've been to visit Tabitha. You and I were too busy this summer with ..." I trail off. We'd been too busy with preparations for the shop for me to take my usual two-week holiday at my favorite aunt's farm, making this the first time in my entire life—or at least as long as I can remember—that I'd missed my summer visit. I'd also missed Easter this year, and even though the farm isn't as much fun in the spring with all that mud, I missed my aunt. Apart from my parents, Tabitha is my closest relative—closer even than my parents. She's the person I've always been able to be completely honest with, judgment-free. As the only other artist in the family, she was the most supportive of me turning my calligraphy hobby into a side hustle and switching majors to pursue it as a legitimate business, making me believe it was possible. When my parents went through the roughest patches in their relationship, she's the one who took me in, letting me stay with her for the entire summer when I was seventeen. Thankfully, my parents worked things out, but Salem Stables will always be my happy place.

My best friend's face falls. Her gaze drops to her hands, clasped on the table before her. "Sloan, I—"

"If you say sorry one more time, we're no longer friends," I say sharply.

She scoffs. "You'd throw twelve years of friendship out the window, just like that?"

"If it means you'll stop apologizing, then yes. Seriously, Lyla, this isn't your fault. It's like you said, this wasn't the right time, but we'll try again. We can still do this."

Something like uncertainty crinkles her features, but it disappears just as quickly. "In the meantime, are you sure you don't want to get back out there and try to meet someone? The rest of it might not be in your control, but your horoscope says that your love life is something you should focus on right now."

"Caleb and I just broke up," I remind her. "Besides, with everything else that's happened, dating is the *last* thing on my mind." My phone buzzes in my pocket, and when I see the text message, I can't help but laugh. "Between you and Tabitha, I can't believe I haven't been married off yet. Listen to this: 'One more sleep! Clock emoji, pancake fixings are ready to go, clapping emoji. Can't wait for you to meet Parker finally, I think you're going to like this one, raised eyebrow emoji.' Subtle, right?"

Lyla lifts her eyes to me, smirking. "I guess she finally learned how to use emojis, huh?"

I shake my head fondly. "Last week she sent me a message from the grocery store with an eggplant emoji and I almost died."

She gasps, covering her mouth as her eyes open wide. "Did you *tell* her?"

"I'm waiting until I see her in person so I can see the look on her face."

We dissolve into giggles, and for a few seconds, it feels like old times, when we thought we'd be able to spend every day together. Remembering that's not going to happen—at least not for a long while—causes my mood to dip again.

Lyla pulls my phone from my hand and taps the screen a few times before placing it face up on the table between us. Our eyes lock over the screen, where a timer starts counting down, and she squeezes my hand.

"You have three minutes to wallow. Make the most of it."

I suck in a breath, fighting the sudden pricking sensation behind my eyes. Normally, this is where I would be bluntly honest about everything I'm feeling: devastated that the last two years of planning have gone nowhere. Hurt that we got so close to finally opening, only to have yet another obstacle thrown in our path. Scared that we haven't devised a plan on what to do next. Embarrassed at being seen as a failure by my parents, who tried to warn me that this would happen. Only ... I can't say any of it. The words dry up in my throat as I stare at Lyla through blurry eyes, because I'll hate myself if I say anything to make her feel a sliver more guilty than she already does over what happened.

"I'm okay, really," I lie as I blink back the tears before they can fall, stopping the timer.

"Are you sure?" Lyla asks softly.

"Absolutely," I say, pretending to check my text notifications. "Ready to head out?"

She doesn't answer immediately, but eventually says, "Let me go to the bathroom first. I swear, my bladder's getting smaller."

She disappears to the restroom, and I'm left to stare at the increasing notifications on my social apps. I know I should check them, since I'm responsible for engaging with any activity on my client's accounts, but I can't do it; instead, I dip into my email, thumbing through the messages. There are a few from referrals asking if I'm taking on any new clients right now—hard pass, seeing as how I'm not even managing my *current* workload—and the usual newsletters from other calligraphy accounts and marketing tips. They used to be useful, but now feel like junk mail since I can't apply any of the information anyway. One email stands out though. The subject line catches my attention.

It's time to Discover Yourself.

Before the blood completely drains from my face at the strange omen, I remember that *Discover Yourself* was the name of the company Lyla and I sent away for a DNA test at the beginning of summer.

"Hey, my results for the ancestry thing came in," I say when Lyla returns to the table, holding my phone up.

"Finally! I got mine three days ago, but I've been waiting so we could go through the results together. Come on, let's go back to your house and see which celebrities we're closely enough related to that we can brag about."

I raise an eyebrow at her.

"What?" she asks, the picture of innocence.

"This wouldn't be another attempt to distract me from my problems, would it?"

She flashes a self-assured grin and hitches her cross-body bag over her shoulder. "Besides the fact that this was my birthday gift to you, it's in your best interest to be nice to me if I'm related to a Hemsworth and you want me to set you up."

It's something we've talked about doing ever since college, where I walked in on Lyla watching an episode of *Forensic Files* in the dorm's common room and discovered our shared love of true crime; it quickly became the basis for our friendship. Despite everything else crowding my thoughts, I'm excited to see the results. Finding out I'm the descendant of some badass female pharaoh could be just the boost of confidence I need to dust myself off and keep moving forward.

We head outside, the wind blowing with a hint of the crisp September air. Lyla's parked on the street out front, and I climb into the passenger side.

"I thought you were doing the DNA kit as a public service in case we're related to a serial killer and can help catch them," I say.

"Originally, yes," Lyla concedes, pulling away from the curb and heading west on shop-lined Main Street towards my parents' house. "But after the week we've had, I'm hoping I have deep connections to some rich and generous old lady looking for a loveable young woman to be the daughter she never had to share her fortune with."

"Is there any chance these results could be mixed up with someone else?" I say, frowning at my screen.

"Hey, no peeking!" she shouts, letting go of the steering wheel to smack me. "I've waited three days, and you can't wait another five minutes?"

"I'm serious," I say, dodging her before she can swipe my phone from my hand. Something twists in my stomach as I comb through my connections for several quiet minutes, that same tingling sensation that came right before Caleb dumped me slowly growing in my chest like heartburn. I scan the results of my immediate family tree, confusion washing over me. "Lyla, I don't recognize a single one of these names."

"Really?" Lyla glances at my screen before turning her focus back to the road, a line forming between her light eyebrows as she senses my playfulness evaporate.

By the time she pulls into my parents' modest red-brick bungalow's driveway, I'm convinced there's been a mistake.

"Seriously, there's ... no one on my dad's side that I know."

"That can't be right," she says as I hand her the phone. "Didn't you say Serena did this one last year? She's your cousin on your dad's side; she at least has to be there."

But she's not.

After saying a distracted goodbye to Lyla, I go inside to ask my parents to make sense of it. The look on their faces after I ask tells me that sick feeling in my stomach wasn't a fluke or the pumpkin spice latte not sitting right. Turns out my instincts are much more reliable than my horoscope, after all.

Chapter 3

My stomach lurches violently as the bus pulls off the highway, which is either from a) the three-hour-long charter bus ride, b) the body odor coming off the man in front of me, or c) dread over having to look my aunt in the face in about five minutes for the first time, knowing she isn't the person I thought she was. Or rather ... that I'm not who she thinks *I* am.

That, and I have absolutely no idea how I'm going to break the news. I almost wish the smelliest bus ride of my life was an hour longer so I could have more time to figure it out. Maybe I should have planned this out more before leaving home, but after that sit-down with my parents yesterday, I need some space and time to figure out ... everything. I don't even know how to feel about this. My dad is not my real father. That in itself was enough for me to try and wrap my spinning mind around, all while my parents kept insisting: *This doesn't change anything.*

Maybe it doesn't. It's not like there's any big scandal behind it. They used a sperm donor when they couldn't get pregnant and decided not to tell anyone to keep things simple. I might not know who my biological father is, but I've always had a dad in my life who loves me and who I love.

It does, however, mean that I'm not biologically related to Tabitha, my favorite person on this planet. All the traits I've always thought we shared—our green eyes, sense of humor, creativity, love of snack foods, and less-than-critically-acclaimed movies—have been nothing more than my imagination playing tricks on me. Which only makes me wonder ... what *else* about our relationship have I deluded myself into believing? Are we really as close as I think? And if we are, what if that changes once I tell her the truth?

As it turns out, I'm not the only one my parents kept in the dark. They didn't tell *anyone.* I have to give them credit because once Mom and Dad knew the secret was out, they answered all my questions and offered even more details, not holding anything back. They told me all about how difficult it was for them both, dealing with the infertility. It was easier to keep what was really happening to themselves. By the time they finally managed to get pregnant with a donor, they decided to keep it that way. Dad was there for me growing up in every way a father should be. They didn't want to give anyone a reason to doubt his love for his child—least of all me.

I'm not angry. Being angry with them doesn't feel fair. In fact, I can't help thinking how lonely it must have been for them to go through all that without any support from their family and friends. But I am confused. It feels like I've been lied to, but the betrayal that's settling in my chest only spawns guilt for holding any resentment towards the two people who brought me into the world at all, the ones who have given me everything I've ever needed, including a loving and supportive environment. Honestly, I don't have a clue what to feel. I haven't lost anyone, exactly, but I can't help feeling like I have lost a kind of connection with the most important people in my life.

I'm shaken and nervous about seeing Tabitha for the first time. Will she look at me differently? Will things change between us? I hope not, but the doubt sits heavy in my chest. The closer I get, the bus grows more confined with every mile. My parents agreed to let me tell her. It's not that I *want* to be the one to share the news with her. What I really want is to see her again before she finds out ... just in case.

If I hadn't done the stupid DNA test, I would have remained blissfully ignorant for the rest of my life. Why had I cared so much about finding out if I was related to some stupid serial killer? Of course, it would be just my luck to do something like that on a whim for a laugh and end up rocking the foundation of my family and my sense of identity. I wish I could go back in time and undo the whole thing because learning this was like pulling the first thread that unravels the sweater. Except instead of a sweater, it's my life.

Before I know it, the bus pulls to a stop in a small plaza on the outskirts of the tiny town nearest Tabitha's farm. The uneven, cracked parking lot is home to a four-pump gas station, a general store, and an empty, boarded-up storefront. My heart leaps into my throat as restless passengers clamber to their feet to use a restroom that isn't on wheels, with only a few others getting off at their destination. I shove my phone into my bag, ignoring the ridiculous number of notifications from Lyla checking in yet again. I'd answer, but what is there to say? This information changes nothing about my life except how I feel. Meanwhile, she's wondering how she will make her mortgage payments in a few months. How can I complain about this to her, or anyone?

Despite my nerves, the telltale excitement I always get when I'm about to see my favorite person bubbles in my chest like champagne. It's the September long weekend, and I haven't seen her since Christmas—eight, almost nine months ago. I've had an entire relationship start, crash and burn since then.

Squinting, I step out from behind the tinted windows into the sunlit parking lot, craning my neck to scan for Tabitha, willing myself not to burst into tears at the sight of her. I've been holding it—mostly—together until now, but the minute she wraps her arms around me in one of her classic bear hugs, I'd bet money that's the key that will unlock the floodgates. I don't see her, though. There's nothing but the quaint downtown strip of shops we're at the edge of and grassy fields in every other direction. The autumn air is crisp, so I pull the zipper up on the ugly-as-sin Juicy Couture tracksuit I'm wearing, imagining it's a reassuring hug from Lyla, who gave it to me as a practical joke in college. The pink velour material is not my style at all. I'll be damned if it's not the most comfortable thing I've ever worn—perfect for hangover days and traveling, and comfy enough that I can *almost* forgive the word *juicy* being stamped across my rear-end in public.

I crane my neck, peering around the parking lot for Tabitha. A few people are waiting to pick up other passengers: a middle-aged couple waiting with hands clasped, an older woman waving excitedly as she bounces on her toes, and—

My eyes snag on a guy leaning against a beat-up green Jeep slightly farther back. It must be a popular choice of vehicle around here, since Tabitha has one that looks just like it. But I'm more focused on him than the car. The entire man is in shadows. Dark eyes stare straight ahead, buried beneath rigid eyebrows and a dark head of short, slightly messy hair. His jaw is lined in dark scruff, and I can't deny he's cute in that rough-around-the-edges way, but I'd hate to be the one he's picking up. Whoever they are, he does *not* look happy about it.

Since Tabitha must be running late, I can focus on collecting my luggage. The driver, a woman with short, graying hair, lifts the bus's hatch for undercarriage storage. I point, and she hauls out the first of my rolling suitcases. A few other passengers cue up behind me, chatting happily with their greeters. The only one still there is the broody-messy-hair-green-Jeep guy, who is now watching me, staring at me, somewhat expectantly. His arms are crossed, his knee bent with a muddy work boot resting against the door.

"Are you finished?" someone asks behind me.

"Sorry!" I say, jumping back even though I've only collected one of my three bags. I'll grab the rest when they're finished.

While I wait, I feel a weight on my neck and turn around to check. Yup. He's *still* watching me, now with an impatient frown etching his scruffy face. I turn away, scanning the parking lot again for Tabitha.

"I think I'm your ride."

My head jerks up at the deep voice calling from across the parking lot, the guy who was watching me before, though he still hasn't moved. Like he can't be bothered. His dark eyes, however, are zeroed in on me. I check behind me before I answer, sure he must be talking to someone else.

"Uh ... thanks, but I'm good." I turn back to the bus, intent on ignoring Mr. Wannabe Uber.

"Are you Sloan?"

Slowly, I lift my face again, trying not to be too concerned that this perfect stranger somehow knows my name. This is a small town, not the city I'm used to. Who knows, Tabitha probably told one person and word spread like wildfire from there. "Yes ..."

"Then I'm your ride."

I frown. "I already have a ride."

His eyes drag up to the clear blue sky above. "I know, *I'm* your ride. Tibby sent me."

For the first time, I realize the green Jeep looks like Tabitha's because it *is* Tabitha's. Oh my god. This must be the Parker she's been texting me about. Her newest stable hand isn't quite so rough around the edges as the usual deadbeats she hires, and he's younger. *Much* younger; I'm guessing early thirties. Whatever interest had sparked during my earlier appreciation for his appearance is doused by a bucket of freezing cold water.

"She sent *you*?"

I cringe inwardly as I hear how those words must sound to his ears, but I can't help it. Tabitha's always been the one to pick me up when I visit. We'd grab donuts from the coffee shop and eat too many on the drive home, gabbing the whole way and spoiling our dinner. It's our thing—or at least, *I* thought it was. Maybe it was never something she planned or looked forward to the way I have been ...

I haven't even told her yet, and things are already changing.

I whip around so my back is facing Parker, willing my lower lip to stop trembling as I fight the tears off.

"If you'd rather walk, just tell me so I can leave," he calls. "I have other things to do."

Someone beside me gives me a dirty look, as if I'm somehow responsible for the man shouting across the parking lot, so I sniff and pull my suitcase over to the Jeep. The others are digging around, trying to find their luggage anyway, so it'll be a minute or two before I can grab the rest of mine. May as well sort out my transportation while I wait.

"Tabitha sent you to get me?" I ask when I reach him, dubious. Tabitha knows I'm not as trusting as she is of the people she usually finds to work for her. "Where is she?" I'm trying for confident, but a gust of wind chooses that moment to rush up and send me a face full of my hair. Sputtering, I pull the copper strands out of my mouth.

"Busy. Need help with that?" He reaches for the suitcase, but I grip it tighter and take a half step back. He tosses me a frown. "What's the problem?"

I let out a small laugh. "I don't know you; I'm not getting in your car."

"I told you. Tabitha sent me."

A bitter spark ignites in my chest. If last week has taught me anything, it's that people say a lot of things. *Let's open a business together, yes, we'll move in together, of course, I'm your biological father.* Saying something doesn't make it true.

I fold my arms and shrug. "Prove it."

His back straightens, eyes narrowing at me like he can't believe I'm serious. I stand a little taller too, jutting my chin to show I am.

"I'm driving her Jeep," he says, tossing a hand towards it.

"I have better things to do than memorize license plates."

"And I have better things to do than play chauffeur. In or out?" He lifts his hands in surrender. "I'm more than happy to leave you stranded."

"Why should I believe you? You could be a deranged ax murderer for all I know."

His frown deepens. "Ignoring the fact that you think I look like a murderer—thanks for that, by the way—how are you planning to get to Tabitha's, then?"

"I'll call her." I pull my phone out of my pocket.

"I already told you." He fires back, impatience creeping into his tone. "Your aunt's busy. That's why she sent me."

That can't be right. How could she be busy on the day she knew I was coming? We've been counting down to this all summer—it was supposed to be the trip to make up for months of lost time, and to soak up as much of each other as we could before I got sucked into the life of business ownership and working weekends and holidays, getting another chance to visit her who knows when. At least ... that's what it was to me. Maybe ... this was just a standard old visit to her. Nothing special.

My heart cracks a little under the pressure of that thought. Tabitha, her farm—it's always meant so much to me, and it's been the safe place where nothing bad happens. It's the one place that's always felt like home—and not just in the childhood home sense, the kind of home that calls to you, deep in your bones. Where you long for, and it feels like it's longing right back. It's the one place I've always felt like enough. Is that a fabrication of my imagination, too?

"Can we hurry this up?"

"No, we can't *hurry it up*," I say, bristling at his tone and the expectation that I'll snap to. If this guy thinks I'm hopping into his truck no questions asked, he's got another thing coming. There's no way I'm letting him pressure me into doing it by making it seem like *I'm* inconveniencing *him*. "If you're telling the truth, Tabitha will confirm your story; if not, then I'll avoid being the subject of an episode of *Forensic Files*."

"*What* are you talking about?"

I ignore him in favor of holding my phone above my head, spinning and stepping toward the grassy area surrounding the parking lot, trying to get a decent signal. Finally, I get two bars—enough for a call—and quickly pull Tabitha up in my contacts. The phone rings once before another sound catches my attention—the bus. The engine roars to life behind me and I whirl around in time to see it pulling away from the gas station—my last two suitcases still tucked away in the storage compartment.

"No! Wait!" I run after it, waving my arms. "Stop!"

When I reach the road, the bus is already too far gone to catch. If this were a bigger town with more than two streetlights, I might have a chance.

But it's not, and I don't.

Instead, the Greyhound rumbles to the end of the road and turns towards the highway, before it disappears. Of course. *Of fucking course.*

Chapter 4

"You don't have to look so smug about it," I grumble from the passenger seat.

He says nothing, but his lips stay tipped up, making me want to wipe it off his scruffy face. I don't, since he's driving and that would be dangerous.

"You never introduced yourself. It's Peter, right?" I know that's not his name, but he deserves it since he didn't bother telling me what it was back in the parking lot.

The muscle in his jaw clenches. "Parker."

"See, that wasn't so hard, was it?" I ask, even though saying it seemed physically painful for him. He doesn't respond, and my instincts to smooth things over kick back in the longer we ride in awkward silence. This really will be easier if we can be civil to one another. "Look, maybe we should start over," I say grudgingly. "I'm Sloan."

Maybe he's more forgiving than he looks. He's smiling, so that must be a good sign. He glances over, his hard eyes rake over my face, lingering. My usual instinct would be to make friendly conversation. Still, there's something about him that prevents me from employing my usual good nature to diffuse the situation, and I refuse to break eye contact first. No matter how much those deep brown eyes make me want to squirm.

Finally, he turns his attention back to the dirt road ahead, adjusting his grip on the steering wheel as amusement dances in his dark brown eyes.

"Sloan, huh?" he says, though his tone is too flat to sound like a question. "That's not what your name tag says."

Name tag? Irritation gives way to confusion. And then, when his eyes flick down to my *Juicy* track pants, the cold horror of realization washes over me. So much for nobody seeing me in this outfit.

Oh *god*. If only Lyla could see me now.

"It's a travel outfit," I say, as if that's any excuse, but it only deepens that smirk.

For several minutes, Parker does a convincing job of acting like I'm not even in the car. I take the opportunity to study him more closely, my gaze trailing over the hard line of his jaw underneath dark stubble, the slope of his slightly upturned nose. Irritated, I pull my eyes away, letting out a huff.

"Something wrong?"

I cross my arms. "Yes, actually. Thanks to you, I have to figure out how to get my luggage off the bus, which is headed God knows where." Screw being civil. Being civil is overrated.

He casts a glance my way, a crease forming between his dark brows. "It's in the trunk."

"I mean the rest of it. I left two more bags on the bus because you distracted me."

"Jesus, I thought you were only here a week. How much stuff do you need?"

I bite my tongue, facing the window.

"You *are* only here for one week ... right?"

The way he asks the question makes it crystal clear what he wants my answer to be. I don't need to explain myself to him, though. I *will* need to run it by Tabitha at some point. When she and I made these plans, I was only supposed to visit until next weekend. That was all I would have been able to afford before diving into renovations and setting up the shop, drumming up business with an aggressive marketing plan to get the doors open and customers flocking in by the holidays. Now, though, I have no business to go back to, no boyfriend waiting for me, and I've been living in my parents' house. Not exactly the ideal place to wrap my head around the fact that my dad isn't really my father ...

I'm not angry. I need some space to figure out how I feel about everything and decide what to do next. Salem Stables is the only place I've never had someone breathing down my neck with expectations.

"Are you at least going to tell her?"

My head snaps back to Parker, whose jaw is clenched as he stares through the windshield. "Excuse me?"

"If you're going to squat at her place, you should at least give her the courtesy of a heads up."

"It's not *squatting*. It's just an extended visit, that's all. It's not like it's permanent."

For as far back as I can remember, Salem Stables had been my second home, something Tabitha isn't shy about reminding me. Still, a tiny kernel of doubt is worming its way inside me. Once she finds out the truth, will the door remain as open as it once was? Staring out the window, I chew at my polished red nail. I would never have hesitated before asking to stick around indefinitely, but I can't shake the fear that she'll treat me differently when I tell her the truth. I've never felt like an intrusion before. Now, it claws at my insides, making me doubt everything about our relationship. Like it or not, thanks to the results of that stupid DNA test, things will be different now.

I glance back at Parker, who's still frowning. He looks like he's not quite done giving me a hard time.

"Does Tabitha know that?" he asks, a bite lacing his words.

I squirm in my seat. "It's ... a surprise." Truthfully, I'm no closer to deciding how to bring it up. I'd hoped to figure it out on the three-hour bus ride, but here I am, nearly at the farm and officially out of time.

He scoffs under his breath.

I throw a glare his way, doing my best to burn a hole in the side of his head. "Is there a problem?"

"Nope."

"Really? Because there's a judgy vibe on your side of the car, which is pretty ironic, if you ask me."

He arches a brow. "Where did you say the judgy vibes were coming from again?"

"I'm just stating facts. I've seen a million freeloaders like you come and go at the farm."

The way his jaw twitches, I can tell immediately that I've struck a nerve, but he recovers quickly enough to spit out, "I'm not the one showing up unannounced on her doorstep expecting her to put me up for a handout. Sorry, *extended vacation*."

"This is *not* a vacation," I argue.

"That's true. Generally, you have to pay for a vacation."

I gape, unable to believe my ears.

"Must be nice to take a spontaneous trip with no responsibilities waiting for you," he continues, gaining steam. "So, which Kardashian *do* you want to be when you grow up?"

"It's a *travel* outfit!" I cry, waving a helpless hand over my clothes. Though with the rolling fields passing us in a blur beyond the dusty windows, I have to admit that I do kind of look like Paris Hilton from *The Simple Life*. Not that I'll admit it out loud.

"Whatever you say, Princess."

"Don't call me that," I snap.

I'm almost grateful that he isn't trying to play nice. I'm used to being the people pleaser, but so much happened last week that my mind is fried. Not having to filter myself is kind of a relief. I didn't intend to take my anger out on him, but he's being a dick. I'm giving back what I'm getting.

"So, how long *have* you been scamming off my aunt?"

"Unbelievable," he mutters with a shake of his head. "You know, when someone goes out of their way to help you, the bare minimum you can do is say thank you. But I'm sure that's not in your vocabulary, so I'll try not to hold it against you."

His tone suggests he is very much holding it against me.

A flare of guilt burns hot in my belly as I realize ... he's right. I was so focused on being braced to see Tabitha for the first time that Parker's presence had thrown my brain into an inconveniently timed software update.

The easiest solution would be to apologize and thank him now. If there's anything my mom taught me about thank \-you cards, it's better late than never. But ...

All everyone has told me for the last week is that I'll get over it. Nothing's *really* changed. The business never got off the ground, so it's not like we lost it. I didn't live with Caleb, so the break-up can't hurt that bad. The DNA test doesn't change anything.

They all want me to carry on without feeling anything. But I do. I feel ... *angry*. I can't explain why, but I'm done letting people tell me everything is fine.

"You," I drag out the word, stabbing a finger towards Parker, "don't know the first thing about me. I happen to be going through a crisis, so I'm sorry if saying thank you is low on my priority list when I thought I was about to get murdered by a serial killer in the middle of Nowhere-seville."

Okay, mad or not, I sound ridiculous. I'm being dramatic, and I usually would rein it in (like, *way* in), but what's the point? It's not like this guy will still be working for Tabitha when I return for my next visit. Heck, based on the ones I've met in the past, there's a good chance I'll outlast him on *this* visit. My chest is heaving and I feel fierce for standing up for myself for the first time in ages. I can't tell from his baffled expression if he wants to rip my head off or ask me what I'm talking about.

"You need help," he tells me.

Before I can sever his carotid artery in response, I spot the *Salem Stables* sign up ahead, swaying in the fall breeze. The words dry up on my tongue as we pull into the long driveway, the familiar crunch of gravel under the tires. I was so wrapped up arguing with Parker that I didn't have time to stress out as we got closer.

I feel his eyes on me again, like he's surprised I'm letting his insult slide, but I'm too busy staring out the window at the canopy of towering, hundred-year-old maple trees flanking us, the green just beginning to give way to tinges of rich orange and yellows and reds. A dozen horses graze in fenced-in fields on either side, their heads popping up to investigate the sound as we bounce past on the narrow, slightly uneven driveway. My heart climbs into my throat as we roll up to the soft yellow farmhouse. Beside it sits a long black barn with white trim, the big door wide open like a pair of awaiting arms.

Welcome home.

The Jeep jerks to a stop between the house and the barn, pitching me forward. If the sight of the farm hadn't already rendered me speechless, the sight of Tabitha waving wildly from the front porch would have done it. Her frizzy, brown hair is loose and wild around her face; nothing is reserved about her. The front porch yawns behind her and the same wooden swing I used to curl up on to read Nancy Drew mysteries is swaying on its chains as if waving too. I probably spent as many hours on that porch as I did inside the house, back when everything was much simpler.

"If you're waiting for me to open your door, you're going to be here a while," Parker grunts beside me, snapping me out of my thoughts. "And trust me, Princess, the chauffeur service was a one-time thing."

I barely hear him as I fumble out of the Jeep and rush forward, legs moving on autopilot. I fall into her at the bottom of the porch steps, practically tackling her. I could weep at the feel of her arms looping around me and squeezing tight, for dear life. She hugs me exactly like I knew she would. She smells like green apple shampoo and paint; I know she's been in her studio. As she describes it, the farm is her hobby, but art is her career. Like my dad and their brother, Tabitha grew up here but she was the only one interested in taking over the farm when my grandparents passed away. Since then, she's made it the best of both worlds, boarding horses to earn money and fill the gaps when her pottery and art sales are slow.

Digging deep into whatever willpower reserves I have left; I manage not to burst into tears as we rock back and forth excitedly. Finally, we pull back enough to look at each other with watery laughter.

It's a touching moment—so of course, Parker ruins it.

My suitcase lands with a thud next to my feet, and I jump.

"Careful with this one, Tibby," Parker says over my shoulder. "She's itching to leave a bad Yelp review. We have to hope it's not high enough on her list of priorities."

The condescending curl of his lips makes my blood boil all over again.

"Does the Welcome Wagon know about you?" I snap, rising to the bait. I'm faintly aware that I'd be even more annoyed if I wasn't grateful to have an outlet for all my feelings finally.

"I see you two have already gotten to know each other," Tabitha says, as if we were trading compliments instead of insults. She keeps one arm around my shoulder. After everything, I can't help but lean into her comforting grip. "I can't tell you how happy it makes me that you're finally meeting! I knew you would get along. I just *knew* it!"

"Definitely. I left my friendship bracelet in the car," he deadpans. "I've got some stuff to do in the barn. You need anything else, Tibby?"

It doesn't escape my notice that his tone is much softer with her, with a warmth that's almost ... friendly.

"No, just the one emergency favor today," she says as she rubs my arm. "Thanks again, Parker. You're a lifesaver."

He shakes his head. "No problem."

My eyes practically bug out of my head. *No problem?* He told me no fewer than three times how much of a problem it was for him to go out of his way to pick me up. Suddenly, for Tibby, he's all stop-and-smell-the-roses?

Without another look at me, he strides towards the large black barn, hands in his pockets. I watch him go, suddenly less sure than I was on the ride over that he'll be gone within a couple of weeks.

Tabitha bumps my hip with hers. "What do you think, same place, better view?"

I snort. "Hardly. I was trying to see the loose wire. He's defective."

She shakes her head. "Trust me, they don't make 'em much better than that. Come on," she says, hauling my heavy suitcase up the steps herself. "Let's get you settled in."

I follow her inside, feeling more at ease than I have in days. I like the sound of that.

Chapter 5

"When are you going to finally start listening to me and stop dating those boring city boys?"

Tabitha's smile is wide as she shakes her head at me, and I can't help but grin back. We're curled up in the living room on opposite ends of the couch, where we've been since dinner, catching up on ... well, everything. Or *almost* everything. The uncovered windows have gone dark with the night sky, like someone's turned off the rest of the world. If I try hard enough, I can almost forget that anything outside this perfect yellow house exists.

"Woooowww," I drawl, peeking at the antique grandfather clock in the corner of the room. "I'm impressed. It took you all four hours and ... eleven minutes to try setting me up with him."

She gasps, feigning ignorance. "I don't know who or what you mean." She stands and pads to the kitchen in her knitted socks, no doubt made by someone she knows. "Hot chocolate?" she calls over her shoulder.

"Mmm, please."

She continues talking to me from the kitchen, raising her voice so I can hear her over the boiling kettle.

"Listen to me, Sloan, I'm wise beyond my years. What you need is not some carbon copy, AI-generated hipster. You need a real man."

"Is that so? You seem happy enough without one."

Sharp laughter rings from the kitchen. "Oh no, not you too! You sound like my friends." She comes back carrying two steaming mugs and hands me one. "I'm just saying, you keep dating the same kind of guys and expecting different results. That's the definition of insanity."

She sets her mug down and heads back to the kitchen.

"Fine, I can admit that Caleb was not the guy for me. But ignoring the way it ended—"

"Which you shouldn't!"

"We *did* have fun together," I say, a little louder. "Do you know how hard it is to find someone who respects what I do for a living?"

"Hello? I'm an artist. I've heard some variation of the 'but you don't know what it's *really* like to work' line more times than I can count."

"Fair point, but at least people can wrap their heads around what you do. Most people think social media brand management is a fancy way to say I'm an influencer, and all I do is sit in cute coffee shops taking pictures of foam art." I wish it was that easy. I haven't done a lick of work in three days, and I know I will have a mountain of it when I finally manage to crack open my laptop, but that's a problem I can deal with tomorrow—one thing at a time.

"Speaking of adorable cafés..."

I stop blowing on my hot chocolate to stare at the white cardboard box she places between us on the couch. My eyes prickle. "You remembered the donuts," I murmur, almost to myself.

"Course I did," she says easily, like it's a given. She reaches over to tug the end of my braid. "It's our thing."

A giant lump in my throat makes it very difficult to say anything—or take a bite of one of the delicious-looking donuts. I could tell her right now. *Tabitha, I have to tell you something.* But I can't make the words come out of my mouth. Because once they're out, it will feel real.

"Hey," she says, voice filled with concern. "You okay?"

I nod quickly, taking a big sip of my hot chocolate to avoid speaking, but an unexpected sting hits the back of my throat, making me choke.

"Did you ... *spike* my hot chocolate?" I sputter in disbelief.

Grinning, she shrugs. "You're old enough, it's not that scandalous."

I laugh. Now that I'm ready, the next sip goes down much easier before I trade my drink for the donut. The thread of easy conversation that's been flowing for hours drops off, and suddenly all I can think about is what I haven't told her.

When everything went down with my parents, they reluctantly agreed not to say anything to Tabitha. After everything, they didn't want to put that on me. But it was too big a conversation to have over the phone, and I wanted to be the one to tell her in person. My visit here was already planned, and honestly, I could use the space from my parents. They warned me this would happen—that dreams don't pan out in real life like they do in our heads. I can't let them watch me struggle to come to terms with the fact that they were right. And if I hadn't put myself out there like that, I would only be dealing with one crisis right now, instead of a total identity shift of everything I thought I was or would be.

I haven't even been here a full day yet, but I'm already starting to feel better, like there's a dividing line between Salem Stables and the rest of the world that lets everything outside this place ... melt away. I could tell Tabitha what I know now. But what's the harm in letting myself enjoy another day or two of *these* versions of Tabitha and me?

Unsure what to say next, I glance at the clock in the corner again, surprised to see the hands at quarter past eleven.

"Hey, is the clock broken?"

Tabitha grins like the Cheshire cat. "Nope. I finally managed to fix the damn thing so it wouldn't bother me every freaking hour."

"You're kidding? No more chimes?"

She barks out a laugh. "Calling it *chimes* is far too generous. That thing sounds like a cupboard of pots and pans collapsing every sixty minutes. Or at least it did."

Tabitha has hated the chime on that clock since she was a kid, but it was built by her great-great-grandfather, and when she inherited the farm from my grandparents, the clock came with it. Even though she hates it, she's too sentimental to part with something that's been in the family for generations. She's always joked that she'll pass it to her least favorite relative when she dies as a parting gift.

"How...?"

"Parker. That man can figure out just about anything, I swear."

My smile fades. She seems so comfortable with him. Based on the people she's hired before, I'm not sure that's smart. He might be a whiz with a clock, but I still don't trust him as far as I can throw him—and I'm not one for organized sports. I've seen too many people take advantage of my aunt's kind heart and generosity. She has a soft spot for the nomads passing through town, the down-on-their-luck people looking to make easy cash before blowing right on through. From one visit to the next, I've never met the same farmhand twice. Besides, if he's making her life as easy as she claims, why does she look so tired?

"Sorry, I didn't realize how late it was," I say before nudging her with my foot. "Isn't it way past your bedtime?"

Mornings have always been her time. She loves being up before the rest of the world, at her most creative when the world hasn't filled with noise yet.

Something passes over her face. "Not lately. If you don't want this, I'll have it," she adds, reaching for my hot chocolate. "Who knows, maybe it'll help."

"You're not sleeping?"

"It's nothing." She waves it away like an offhanded comment. "A lot on my mind lately, that's all."

Great, and I'm about to make it ten thousand times worse.

It's enough to solidify my decision to wait a few days before I tell Tabitha what I know. Which means I should probably hold off on mentioning my extended stay ...

She yawns, leaning back on the couch. "If I'd known how much work this farmer's market committee would be, I never would have let Debbie talk me into it. Serves me right for letting her bully me into making new friends."

I chuckle. "You have friends."

"Thank you!" she shouts. "Can you please tell Debbie when she comes over for book club next week?"

"Will do. Need any help getting ready for it?" I may as well offer, since I've got no intentions of doing any of my own work tomorrow, and I've got nothing but time.

"No, but I may need a hand with dinner tomorrow. I've got another committee meeting in the afternoon."

"I thought the market started on Thursday?"

She nods. "It did. Usually by now it's self-sufficient, but based on last week's turnout ..." she trails off, and I notice for the first time how tired she looks. "Let's just say last year's poor attendance isn't looking like a fluke anymore. So, we decided to try something new for the final market of the year to make it special. End with a bang, you know? Only problem is, it's a little over six weeks away and we haven't figured out what that is yet."

She laughs, but it's not her typical breezy one. Usually, my brain would already be filling with ideas, but instead, it stays strangely quiet. I guess getting knocked down three times in the span of a week is enough to make me want to sit this one out. Before I can say anything, she's waving it all away.

"Here I am boring you when you probably want to get some sleep. You've had a long enough week, and you're here to relax."

I drop my gaze as the weight of everything I'm running away from catches up to me, crashing down hard enough to leave me breathless.

She sets down her mug. "Honey?"

"I did everything I was supposed to," I mutter, partly to myself, finally letting myself admit everything I've been keeping to myself. "I'm not a risk taker; everyone knows that. I take the safe road, usually the one someone tells me to take. I go with the flow, not against it. And that was fine. I had a job, an apartment, and a boyfriend. I should have left well enough alone."

"But were you happy?" she asks softly. "When you were playing it safe, when you had those things, were you truly happy?"

A vice tightens around my ribcage.

"I've always felt like something was missing. I'm sick of promoting other people's businesses and helping everyone else make it big. The shop was different. It finally felt like I had ... I don't know. A purpose. Something to offer."

I finally look up and her soft eyes offer the sympathy I didn't know I needed.

"Then playing it safe isn't all it's cracked up to be."

Chapter 6

Murder always clears my mind.

Not in a literal sense or anything, of course. I mean stories about murder. Investigations. There's comfort in knowing that there are detectives, family members, and friends who refuse to give up the search and, because of them, answers are found. Killers are caught. And then, lucky for me, podcasts are made, ones that keep me company in the middle of the night when I get tired of tossing and turning, waiting for sleep to finally pull me under and help me forget the mess my life is for a few measly hours. Hard to think about anything else while listening to those types of stories, making them the perfect distraction.

I listen to two full episodes while the sky outside my window turns from dark to hazy grey with the dawn before I give up on sleep entirely. Four hours is plenty. Grabbing my laptop from the bag beside my bed, I open it and stare for a few minutes at my emails, not responding to anything. I've gotten many new requests from clients to help with upcoming campaigns, and even two new clients wanting to set up calls, but nothing appeals to me like it used to. I'm good at my job and know how to help people establish and maintain their brands online. I'm proud of what I've been able to do, but the truth is, I'm sick of focusing on brands that aren't my own. I didn't realize how important it was to build something for myself until I lost the chance. The thought of returning to what I was doing before ... seems exhausting.

So naturally, I do what any sleep-deprived, directionless thirty-year-old would do. I get dressed and head for the barn for some good old-fashioned manual labor.

Unusually, Tabitha isn't already up, but I'm grateful that I don't have to come up with an excuse for why I'm not sleeping. The landing groans under my socked feet, my sneakers dangling from my fingertips as I tiptoe downstairs. My steps falter as I take in the black-and-white photographs lining the entire staircase, an entire family tree memorialized. It's one of my favorite parts of the whole house. I touch a hand to the photo of my late grandparents, surrounded by their kids. My dad and my uncle are teens and Tabitha is a young girl with wild, unruly pigtails. Two days ago, I thought I belonged on this wall and was connected to them. Something twists in my chest, and I force myself to keep moving.

I slip out the front door, closing it gently behind me. It's a short, albeit chilly, walk to the barn across the foggy lawn. When I tug open the large door, my low mood evaporates at the sound of ten horses calling out with friendly whinnies, eager for their breakfast. I'm hit by the scent of fresh hay and sweet manure as one by one the horses pop their heads over the chest-high stall doors, ears pricked with interest. Most people I know—Lyla included—would pinch their noses and recoil, doing their best not to touch anything. Not me. I inhale as deeply as I can, like it can make up for all the months of being away from this place. For the first time in a week, the clawing weight on my chest begins to lift enough that I can finally breathe.

Coming here was the right decision.

Nearest to the door, a bay with a white blaze nickers at me. I step forward, stroking down his long face. He leans into my touch—I'd bet money on it being a gelding, since the mares are usually less friendly—and I reach up to scratch under his forelock.

"Hi, handsome," I murmur. I peek at the name on his stall. "Nice to meet you, Fargo. I'm Sloan. Sorry, it's not time for breakfast yet. I'm housekeeping this morning, not room service."

He nudges my armpit and I chuckle, letting myself stroke his velvety muzzle one more time before I head for the feed room for a wheelbarrow and pitchfork, then pull open Fargo's door. He seemed friendly enough that he wouldn't mind the company. I toss him a flake of hay and block the door with the wheelbarrow, then get to work cleaning his stall, as promised.

In no time, the familiar task, along with a fresh podcast episode in my ears, lulls me into a meditative flow as I dump one pitchfork after another. I leave the lights off; each stall's open door and windows are enough to see what I'm doing as dawn settles in an hour reasonable enough to call morning. By the time I move on to my third stall, I'm breathing heavier from the workout, and warm enough to ditch my hoodie. I pause for a second to catch my breath. Damn, I'm out of shape. I used to be able to do the entire barn without breaking a sweat.

My calm is shattered when a hand clamps down on my shoulder.

"*Aaargh!*"

The pitchfork slips from my grasp and clatters against the wooden wall. I yank my earbuds out, cowering against the wall.

Zeke, a gray gelding, jerks his head up and snorts in alarm. Thankfully, the oldest horse in the barn is about as bombproof as they come, and while his neighbors spin and stomp in the wake of my scream, he shakes his head and dips his nose back into the hay I'd tossed in the corner for him earlier.

Standing in the doorway, arm drawn back with an expression I can only describe as consternation, is Parker.

"What is the matter with you?" I exclaim, clutching my pounding heart. "I thought you were a serial killer!"

His eyebrows somehow creep higher, nearly disappearing under the fringe of his short, dark hair. "Why?"

I plant my hands on my hips, faintly registering him tracking the movement before he wrenches his eyes to my face. "One, it's dark in here. Two, I'm a woman alone in a barn in the middle of nowhere. And three, because of what I'm listening to!"

Dark eyebrows furrow over his deep brown eyes, not looking tired despite the early hour. He's dressed the same as yesterday; the only sign that he slept at all is the slight muss on one side of his hair, making his angry face look adorable until he opens his mouth. "Okay, one: you could have turned the lights on. Two, you're not in the middle of nowhere. There's a Walmart twenty minutes from here. And three—what are you listening to, death metal?"

"Hardly," I say with as much dignity as I can muster as I retrieve my pitchfork from the dirty shavings. "It's a murder podcast. Which I've lost my spot in now, thanks to you."

"What the hell is a murder podcast?"

"It's—never mind. You shouldn't sneak up on people."

"I called your name three times."

Oh. My volume wasn't turned up that high. I must have been more zoned out than I thought. Then something else registers. "You remember my name?"

He stares at me for a second, then the edge of his lip quirks up into something sinful. "Yeah, I do. It started with a J, right?"

My face heats. I swear I am going to burn that freaking tracksuit. At my seething glare, he tilts his chin to the ceiling and lets out his own exhale of attitude, his rare flash of humor evaporating as quickly as it came.

"It's not hard, Sloan," he growls. "You really do think I'm an idiot, don't you?"

I blink, my face softening in surprise. Where did he get that idea? Annoying, yes. Antagonizing, absolutely. But I never thought he was stupid. Besides, he's not exactly innocent of making snap decisions about people.

"No more than you think I'm an entitled princess," I argue, stabbing at the ground with my pitchfork and tossing a fresh heap of soaking wet shavings that he sidesteps at the last second. "And I never thought you were stupid. Grouchy, definitely."

He's quiet long enough that I glance over my shoulder at him. He's watching me curiously, and my stomach flips under his scrutiny.

"You're here early," I remark. It's barely seven, and according to the feeding schedule on the chalkboard by the office, the horses don't get their morning grain until eight.

"It's not a long commute."

There's a small, single-room cabin towards the back of the property that Tabitha has used off and on to offer room and board to her staff. We've also had some epic sleepovers when it hasn't been occupied. I'd seen Parker's truck leave the driveway last night while Tabitha and I were watching TV and catching up. I assumed he lived in town, but I guess not.

"You seem to know your way around a stall," he says, interrupting the realization that he will be here a lot more than I anticipated. We're practically living together.

"I've always helped when I'm here visiting."

"You don't need to anymore. I'm here every morning by eight to feed, turn out, and muck the barn. That's the routine. I've got it covered."

"Sounds great."

His eyes narrow. "You're still planning on interfering, aren't you?"

"Listen, Peter—"

"It's *Parker.*"

"When I stay here, I help out. It's my way of saying thank you to Tabitha for having me, but it's also because I enjoy it. You couldn't pay me to stay out of the barn. It's a big part of the reason I'm here. Like it or not, you're going to have company. The old me would have let you scare me off, but I dare you to try and come between me and my happy place and see what happens." I've been stabbing the ground aggressively with the pitchfork and finally pause long enough to catch my breath and look up. "What?"

He's leaning against the stall door, frowning. "I figured you were more the breakfast-in-bed type. I didn't expect to see you getting your hands dirty." I pause, waiting for the actual apology to follow. "Although ... FYI, it is easier to take the horse out of the stall first, then clean it."

I roll my eyes and jab at the ground again.

"And yesterday you lectured me on the importance of saying thank you. Aren't I doing *your* job?"

His expression drops back to flat and cold in an instant. "So, you're trying to get me fired?"

"I won't have to. I just have to wait you out long enough."

"Hate to break it to you, Princess, but I'm not planning on going anywhere."

"Wanna bet?"

His jaw ticks. "I don't gamble."

There's an edge to his words, but for some reason, with him, I don't default back to my people-pleasing ways. I already have more than enough on my mind without feeling guilty for giving him a taste of his medicine. "Whatever. I know what kinds of people Tabitha finds to work here. You'll be gone in a month, tops."

That does the trick. His face flickers from pissed to neutral, and he pushes off the door and walks away.

He calls his parting words right before I can relish in my victory. "I'm curious, does Tabitha know that you'll still be here in a month, or are you just going to hope she doesn't notice she has a squatter?"

I'm just grateful he can't see my cheeks turning red.

I hadn't necessarily planned on mucking out as much of the barn as I had but watching Parker's annoyance grow every time he walked past me was motivation to stick it out. Besides, I wasn't in any rush to do my real job. I finally returned to the house when my stomach could no longer be ignored. Tabitha and I made our usual first-day brunch feast, then headed into town for a few errands before she dropped me back at Salem Stables and headed off to her committee meeting. I don't even bother to open my laptop; instead, I turn on the TV until it's time to start dinner.

I keep the meal—my go-to vegetarian stew—simple, since Tabitha hasn't been in her studio all day, and I'm sure she'll be itching to get to it when she returns. I'm slicing the carrots when the back door creaks open and Parker strolls in.

My hand pauses mid-chop. "Can I help you?"

"No." He holds my gaze as he toes off his muddy boots on the mat.

"What are you doing?" I snap, jumping out of the way as he strides towards me and reaches for the sink.

"Washing my hands after a long day's work. Though I see why that would be confusing," he adds as he lathers. "Hard work is probably a foreign concept to you."

The water comes out dark brown, making my nose wrinkle.

"As is bathing to you, apparently," I toss back with a sickly, sweet smile. "And don't forget I was in the barn doing *your* job this morning."

He scoffs. "You only mucked half the stalls. I don't think I have anything to worry about."

A cow-shaped oven timer goes off behind me. Oh, yeah—there are cows *everywhere* in here. Cow head cookie jar, cow-print apron hanging by the stove, cow figurines lining the shelves. It's a borderline bovine obsession, yet the woman has a barn full of horses. But that's Tabitha, and I wouldn't change her for the world; cows and all.

I grab a cow print oven mitt and angrily pull the crusty bread I dug out of the freezer earlier from the oven. Dropping it on the stove with a clatter, I pretend to busy myself with it for a beat longer than I need to, schooling my expression.

I will not *let him get to me.*

"Where's Tibby?"

"Not back from her meeting yet. I'll tell her you stopped by."

He doesn't move to leave, his gaze taking me in. Up close, he's a good head taller than me. I tell myself not to read into the prolonged eye contact, that it isn't a power move. Maybe he's socially awkward and that's why Tabitha has taken pity on him. There has to be *something* wrong with him if she hired him. He folds his plaid flannel sleeves over his broad chest, his dark brown eyes studying me. "Did you tell her that you're staying yet?"

"Why do you care?"

"Because I don't like lying."

"No one's asking you to."

"Really? I guess you won't mind that I mention it to her, then."

"No!"

His lips tip upward in a satisfied grin.

I roll my eyes. "I haven't figured out how to bring it up yet, okay? But it's not because I'm hiding it from her, it's just ... complicated." His smile slips, and I rush to fill the silence before he asks any questions I don't know how to answer. "And just so you know, I'm not planning on *telling* her anything. I'm *asking* her if I can stay longer while figuring things out.

He opens his mouth, but the sound of a car door closing outside stops him from saying anything else.

"I'll stay out of your way," I say, figuring he needs a bit more incentive to keep his mouth shut until I can speak to Tabitha myself. "I promise."

"Then I'll stay out of yours. As soon as you tell her the truth."

I glare at him. He reaches past me to pinch a piece off the bread and I smack his hand. He lifts his eyebrows, and I offer a sweet smile in return. If riling me up is what he wants, I will not let him see how much it's working.

"Now, now, you two. Play nice."

We both jump at the sound of Tabitha's voice. I didn't even hear the front door open. For some reason, she looks pleased as punch—then I realize how close Parker and I are standing.

Parker steps back before I can, and Tabitha hands him the bottle of wine.

"Would you be a doll and open this for me? I swear, this farmer's market might kill me."

"I take it the meeting wasn't as productive as you'd hoped?" I ask.

She shakes her head and grabs a couple of glasses, holding one out to Parker, who makes a face. "There's iced tea in the fridge," she tells him, chuckling.

"He's staying?"

"Did I not mention I'd invited him?" she asks innocently.

"You must have forgotten." I make a show of setting an extra place for him, earning myself another over-the-top eye roll. But he hangs back to let Tabitha and me serve ourselves before he does. We eat in silence for a few minutes, Parker quietly chewing away and darting the occasional glance at Tabitha, then me, before staring back at his meal. Tabitha, meanwhile, seems to be waiting for one of us to do the talking. She gives me an encouraging look, but I shake my head, and with a look of exasperation, she caves.

"So, Parker. How is Mason doing? You haven't brought him by in a while."

"Cass found a new babysitter to handle after-school pick-up, so that's helping a lot. He's doing good in school, though."

"Third grade, right?"

"Mhmm. They're doing art this year and he's got all kinds of stuff he wants to show off to you."

"You tell him I can't wait to see it."

I lift my wine and zero in on our uninvited guest. "So, where did you drift into town from?"

Tabitha coughs. She takes a sip of wine while Parker slowly lifts his eyes to me, unbothered.

"Sloan, that was a little rude, don't you think?" she whispers.

"It's fine, Tibby," he says amiably. "She's probably not used to dining with the help."

I open my mouth to argue, but he cuts me off with an answer to my question.

"I grew up not far from here."

Huh. Just specific enough to raise zero flags.

"Sounds nice. You've painted quite a picture for me."

He ignores this, reaching for another piece of bread. I glare at him, communicating a simple message telepathically through sheer force of will. *Leave.* Sadly, it does nothing to hurry him up.

"I have a talent with words," he says.

"And people," I add, sarcasm pooling under the table at my feet.

"The right people, yeah."

I shake my head slowly, smiling in disbelief. Who the hell *is* this guy? He lays into me the moment I arrive, and somehow, I'm the villain in this story?

"Actually, Parker's real talent is with the animals."

Our heads snap back to Tabitha, like we've forgotten she was there. Her eyes flit between us.

"You know, I believe that," I say. "It's probably comforting for them to be around something that smells so familiar."

"Sloan!" Tabitha gasps.

I'm the picture of innocence. "What? I'm only saying he smells like he's been in the barn all day."

"I *have* been in the barn all day."

"See? I'm just stating a fact."

Tabitha lets out an exasperated breath, but (annoyingly) Parker seems completely unruffled.

"Okay, I'm changing the subject. Sloan, your dad called today."

My hand jerks, nearly knocking my wineglass over. I lurch for it and somehow bump my spoon with my elbow, sending it clattering to the floor. My cheeks are warm when I retrieve it and emerge from underneath the table, ignoring Parker's curious stare.

"H-he did?" My voice squeaks, so I clear my throat. "What did he say?"

"Not much, he was just calling to say hi. I don't know why he didn't call your cell, but hey. I've never claimed to understand how my brother's brain works."

I force a laugh, and from the weight of Parker's stare, I'm almost positive he can tell it's fake. *Could be because of the three unanswered calls I've gotten from him since I got here.* "Oh ... I'll call him back tomorrow."

Luckily, Tabitha seems so relieved that Parker and I are no longer bickering to pick up on anything strange. "Parker, how is *your* dad doing?" she asks.

He goes stiff, his spoon pausing in midair. He darts a glance my way before offering a response that can only be described as curt. "Fine."

So much for unruffled.

"Any better since the last time you saw him?"

He shrugs; eyes fixed on his bowl. "No worse than usual."

My stomach twists with guilt as Tabitha looks on sympathetically. Is his dad sick?

"I know it's tough, but recovery isn't a linear process—"

"Tibby." He shakes his head. It's enough to stop her in her tracks.

"You're right, sorry." She gestures to the two of us. "I talk to you both every day, so it's easy to forget that you two don't know each other at all yet. Maybe the two of you could go to the movies or something?"

I make the face I'm sure Parker would if he wasn't busy choking. "Why?" I demand.

"Don't sound so scandalized, it's only an idea," she says breezily. "I think you two could be friends, is all. You both work so hard, so you should let yourselves have a little fun once in a while."

Parker and I exchange doubtful looks. Of all the things I hope will happen on this trip, getting to know Parker is not one of them.

Still chewing, he stands to take his dish to the sink. "Thanks for dinner, Tibby. I'd better go shower before Princess lodges an official complaint with management."

The kitchen rings silent once the door clicks shut behind him and Tabitha fixes me with a pleading look.

"Honestly, Sloan. Would it kill you to at least *try* to get along? This isn't like you at all."

I know it isn't. I wish I could tell her why. But the longer I spend in this mixed-up place, the harder it is to feel like I'll ever be able to find my way out of it.

"Can you blame me for not trusting him? Tabitha, I love you, but you don't have the best track record when it comes to hiring staff who aren't ... what's the word? Shady."

She tuts and takes her bowl to the sink. "They haven't been that bad."

"No?" I say, joining her beside the sink to dry while she washes. "What about Tony, who kept forgetting to close the paddock gates when he put the horses out? Or Mitch, who sold your trailer without you knowing and took off with the cash? Oh, and then there was Lucky; he was a treat. He's the one who used a crowbar to break into the barn locker and stole all the purses, wallets, and laptops from the corporate team building group, remember?"

"Trust me, I remember."

I look up, surprised to find her smiling.

She shrugs. "They can't all be winners. But that doesn't mean you stop giving people chances."

I sigh, wrapping my arms around her shoulders from behind and squeezing, my chin resting on her shoulder. "Tabitha, I love your big, giant heart. I hate that you're the one who gets left to pick up the pieces alone when people let you down, that's all."

I release her to help with the dishes and she bumps my hip with hers, handing me a bowl.

"Parker isn't like any of the others. For starters, he's already been here longer than anyone I've had work for me. If you got to know him, you'd see he's a decent man. So maybe lay off with the hazing, young lady?"

I hum in vague acknowledgement, though I don't mean it. "I'll do my best."

"You'd better. Because you're going to be spending a *lot* of time together."

"Why?" I ask slowly, eyeing her with suspicion.

She grins, looking positively evil. "I'm going to have you help out in the barn while you're here—every day. Starting with night check tonight," she adds as my mouth drops open to protest. She washes the last of the cutlery and grabs another dish towel to dry her hands before smacking my butt with it. "Off you go."

I've always loved helping with the horses, but I don't love the idea of being trapped in the barn, tripping over Parker. Still, I'll avoid him at all costs, even if being forced to work together makes that even harder. I can't seem to activate any sort of filter when it comes to him. Then again, after our verbal sparring match, I can't deny that it feels kind of … good. I don't have to worry about making him hate me, because he never liked me in the first place. And by now, I know nothing is going to change his mind. Arguing with him is easy because there are absolutely no stakes. A tiny part of me likes holding his attention, too. Whatever that means.

And of course, there's the fact that he seems to enjoy it as much as I do.

Chapter 7

Spending more time with Parker goes as well as I expect. It's been several days since Tabitha metaphorically chained us together, and so far, she's the only one happy about it. On the other hand, Parker and I have barely exchanged more than a few words, despite being practically on top of each other for chunks of the day. He gets so far under my skin that I hardly have time to dwell on how spectacularly my life has fallen apart, like a Jenga tower that will topple completely with one more wrong move. I have to stay on my toes, prepared to meet him snark for snark so as not to let him one-up me. It's distracting, but it also means I haven't had a chance to figure out how to ask Tabitha if I can extend my stay—or tell her why I need to. Not that I'm upset about that second part. I feel a little more guilty every day that I don't tell her, but at least it's time that Tabitha and I can just be ... *us.*

"Hey! Watch it," I snap at Parker, jumping sideways on my way back to the barn and narrowly avoiding a mud puddle when he comes barreling out the door with a wheelbarrow. "These are my good shoes and I'd like to keep them that way."

He shakes his head but doesn't stop what he's doing. If there's anything I've learned about him in the past few days, he stops for nothing.

"You're the one saying good shoes and barn in the same sentence, so that's on you, Princess."

"I *have* barn clothes, but my crappy shoes are in my other suitcase." According to the grumpy lady at the bus company I spoke to last night, it is on its way back from Denver and won't arrive for another day or two. The suitcase I managed to get off the bus contains mostly pajamas and toiletries.

I glare at him as he tips his wheelbarrow on the muck pile and steers it back to the barn, pausing beside me. "Crappy shoes," he repeats slowly. "As opposed to...?"

"As opposed to these, which I'd like to be able to wear in public again."

He shuts up, a smile working its way onto his lips.

"What?" I demand.

"Nothing. Nothing at all."

That turns out to be a bald-faced lie. That afternoon, after lunch, my toes squished against something soft. I pull my foot out and tip the shoe, stunned as three mushy brown balls roll out. Smelly ones.

I storm towards the barn in nothing but my socks, ready to blow a gasket. I'm halfway to the barn when the large door slides open and Parker steps out.

"You put manure in my shoes?!" I shout, holding up the evidence.

He doesn't slow down, continuing to his truck with the worst poker face I've ever seen.

"You said you wanted crappy shoes." He lifts a hand towards my sneakers, still held aloft. "Your wish is my command, Princess."

"What is your problem with me?" I demand.

"You mean other than the fact that you're trying to get me fired?" he asks as he reaches his truck.

"I never said that!"

"You did, actually. You've also been watching me like a hawk. Do you think I don't know that you're looking for something to report back to Tibby?"

In one smooth motion, he hauls a large bag of feed from the back of his truck onto his shoulder in some sort of farmer's/firefighter-carry and walks smoothly towards the barn without a backward glance. It should not look that easy, and yet it does, which makes it even worse.

"*If* I've been watching you—and I'm not saying I have—it's because you insist on redoing almost everything I touch," I say to the back of his head, trailing after him in the afternoon sunshine.

"Do it properly and I won't have to." He drops the bag at the door and returns to his truck for another.

I wish I could protest, but a tiny kernel of doubt roots itself deep in my brain and I can't help but wonder ...

"Am ... am I actually doing things wrong?" I ask. "You're not just messing with me?"

He slows to a stop, the bag of feed resting on his shoulder. His surprise is clear enough by how he answers, like he doesn't relish telling me this. "You miss a few spots in the stalls. And ... there's a quick-release knot that's safer to tie the hay bags with than the way you do it."

"Oh." I cross my arms, averting my gaze. Great. I *have* been making more work for him. So much for this being the one place I have my shit together.

"Are you cry—"

"No," I lie, all but sprinting to the house.

I'm sprawled on the patchwork quilt in my room, clutching my phone while Lyla's sympathetic, yet stern, face stares down at me from my phone screen. After hosing off my ruined sneakers, I came straight here to FaceTime her after nearly breaking down in front of Parker, and as soon as she picked up, the dam burst. I promptly spilled everything: how I haven't been able to motivate myself to do a lick of work, haven't returned any calls from my parents, and, of course, that I still haven't had *the talk* with Tabitha.

"Lyla, what am I doing here?"

"You've far exceeded your five-minute wallow and now you're spiraling, that's what."

I sniff, trying to be quiet so Tabitha doesn't come looking for me. "I shouldn't have come here. I'm just ignoring my problems, and worse, I'm infecting my favorite place in the world with my presence."

"That's not true," she says firmly. "You're just scared because you haven't told her."

"Of course I'm scared!" I whisper-hiss. "Tabitha's always felt more like an older sister than an aunt, and now I'm about to tell her we're not related at all? Oh, and by the way—I want to stay here for the next few months. Hope that's cool."

"Look, you don't know how she's going to react until you tell her. We need to put on our big girl pants and own up to how we feel."

"We?" I hiccup, sitting up. "Wait ... are you keeping something from Adam?"

"No, right—you. That's what I meant," she says quickly, her hand flapping in front of the camera. "This isn't about me. You wanted to go to Salem Stables to tell Tabitha the news in person. It might feel like you're escaping your problems, but you haven't. Now the only question is, what's stopping you from telling her?"

I let out a long exhale, wiping the tears from my cheeks. "The moment I got here, this sense of relief washed over me. It felt like when I came here for that whole summer in high school."

"When your parents almost split up?"

I nod. "Back then, it was like nothing outside the farm even existed. I'd forgotten what it felt like to be so ... content. All I want is to feel that way again, but no matter what I do or where I go, every move I make is the wrong one."

Lyla sighs, and I can feel her shifting into big sister mode. "There's nothing you can do about the things that are outside your control. But you *can* start making the right moves if you really want to. All you have to do is focus on the things within your control. Talk to Tabitha."

My lip trembles, and I bite it, willing myself to pull it together because I am so sick of crying. "Is it even worth it? I don't know if it's just because of what I know, or if it's because Parker's here, but ... it just feels like I'm getting in the way."

Tabitha's been busier than ever with the farmer's market and hasn't spent nearly enough time in the studio working because she's spending the rest of her time with me. Parker sure as hell doesn't want me here, underfoot. No matter the angle I look at it from, I'm the odd person out in this equation.

"Do you want to go home?"

"No." My answer is so automatic that I know being here—even if it's challenging—is the best thing for me.

"Then maybe you need to talk to him, too."

That finally gets a laugh out of me. Talking to Parker seems about as likely as teaching Zeke to tap dance, but at least one of her suggestions seems possible. If it means me staying, and possibly getting back to feeling like myself again, it's worth at least trying. So, after saying goodbye, I take a deep breath and head downstairs searching for Tabitha.

Going back to the barn at this point might be the textbook definition of masochism, but after finally sitting down with Tabitha and getting her enthusiastic permission to stay as long as I need to, the only thing left standing in my way of reaping the full benefits of Salem Stables is Parker. That, and the burning need I have to prove him wrong. He's already called me lazy and criticized my work. They say practice makes perfect, so I start showing up even earlier in the mornings for the next two days. By the time he shows up to feed, I'm finished doing every stall twice to ensure I haven't left so much as a single dirty shaving behind.

At least when it comes to ignoring each other, Parker and I seem to be on the same page. There are no more blowups between us; it's just me quietly going about making him eat his words as I continue to show up for manual labor. The arrangement was working just fine until day three, by which time the blisters I've developed make it difficult not to yell out in pain every time I lift the pitchfork, the slightest contact resulting in searing pain. I grit my way through it. They'll heal eventually, and not letting Parker make a fool out of me is surprisingly strong motivation.

With the stalls clean, I start filling each one with fresh water, unclipping the bucket hanging from the wall and carrying it down the concrete aisle to dump outside. Parker, annoyingly, can take two at once. I'm barely managing one, trading it back and forth between my hands as I shuffle awkwardly towards the door. I make it a few steps before I have to set it down, flapping my hands.

"Come with me."

Crap. I've conjured him.

"Where did you come from?" I demand. "I didn't spin around and say your name three times in front of a mirror in the dark."

Parker leans against the barn door, plaid-covered arms folded. It's a mirror image of the other day when he scared me two-thirds to death. (Yes, I was more than halfway there. No, I'm not being dramatic. That one hand on my shoulder took years off my life.) His bedhead is flattened under a dark baseball hat that makes his ears poke out, ever so slightly, and he looks like ... he's dressed in the same clothes as yesterday. He ignores my question, telling me once more to follow him.

I decide to give him a taste of his own medicine. Giving him my best impression of his stony look, I grab the bucket handle and try not to wince as I lift it.

"Would you just come with me, already?" He huffs.

"No thanks. I'm good," I answer with a satisfied smirk as I step around him. Granted, it would be more convincing if I didn't choose this moment to hiss in pain and hinge forward, setting the bucket down again.

"You're not winning any Oscars. Leave the bucket and let's go."

The heels of his boots echo slightly off the floor in the otherwise silent building as I grudgingly trail after him. "Don't you have anything better to do than check up on me?"

He disappears into the office at the front of the building. The large barn door beside it is pushed open, sunlight pouring in, the gentle fall breeze drifting through to break the stillness. Loose bits of hay and dust scatter along the concrete floor. When he doesn't emerge or answer, I follow him into the small office.

"Did you hear what I said?" I ask.

"No."

He doesn't ask me to repeat myself or even bother looking up.

"I *said*, don't you have anything better to do than spy on me?"

"I've gone from checking to spying? That escalated fast."

I raise an eyebrow. "I thought you weren't listening?"

He ignores the question again and I give up, watching as he rifles through the drawers of a desk overlooking the driveway from a large, dust-covered window, nearly obscured by the mess of file boxes stacked beneath it. The wall beside the door is lined with low shelves, holding rows of scuffed and dirty rental helmets and equipment from when Tabitha offered trail riding once upon a time.

"I get paid to make sure things get done around here. Technically, I'd say that gives me the green light to check in once in a while. Sit." He gestures to the desk.

The metal chair is pushed aside. I'd have to reach past him to get it, so I perch on the edge of the desk instead.

"Hands," he says gruffly.

I rest them on my lap, palms up. Without hesitation, he touches the fingers of my left hand, straightening them. He winces when he sees the blisters, and I feel myself soften at this show of concern. But then he's shaking his head like this is all a big inconvenience, and my annoyance comes back in an instant.

"You wouldn't have to check in if you didn't keep pulling me away from my chores," I say.

He shushes me and pops the lid off a small tube of something with his left hand. "I had to pull you away," he replies, eyes focused on his task. "It was obvious you weren't going to stop."

"Of course not. All the waters still need to be changed."

"Not a chance. You're not doing anything with hands that look like that."

My hand jerks back at a sharp pain, followed by cool, sweet relief. Whatever balm he's dabbing onto my blisters feels like heaven. It's distraction enough for it to take a few extra seconds for his words to sink in. "Wait, what? No. No way! You don't get to walk in here and decide—"

"Don't worry about it. I can finish the rest for today."

"I told Tabitha I'm staying," I blurt. I swallow when his eyes meet mine. Up close, I notice for the first time a green starburst in the brown of his irises and study the way his nose turns up slightly at the end. "I mean, I asked ... she said I could. I just thought you'd want to know that I'm going to be here for a while. Sorry."

He clears his throat, looking away. "Why are you apologizing? Is this your way of telling me I'm fired?"

I roll my eyes. "For the last time, I won't get you fired. Besides, you're annoyingly good at your job."

It's true. I've been watching Parker closely all week, and not only did he redo my work, but he also never cut a single corner. Lyla will get a kick out of me telling her I received first aid from the hot resident farmhand.

Whoa. Hot? Where did *that* come from?

I chalk the slip up to my defensive mind in overactive imagination mode. The better to serve up witty comebacks with. Rationally, I know he's good-looking. He has a normal-sized head, proportioned features, and no strange horns or other growths protruding from his forehead. But he also strikes me as the kind of guy who must know precisely how good-looking he is, and I don't doubt that at some point in his life, he's used that to his advantage. Points deducted.

Wait, no! I am not keeping score.

We've both fallen quiet. I could pick up the argument again, but don't, choosing to watch as he plasters my hands with carefully criss-crossed band-aids.

"You're not usually here this early," I point out, fascinated by his movements. "And you're wearing the same clothes as yesterday." I look up, shocked. "Wait—are you doing a walk of shame?!"

He laughs, and I can hardly believe I'm the one who made that sound come out of him.

"No," he says firmly, shaking his head. "My dad lives in town. I went over there last night and ended up staying. He ... needs a lot of help sometimes."

Lyla's voice is in the back of my mind. *Maybe you need to talk to him, too.*

I chew my lip, remembering how he clammed up when Tabitha asked about his dad at dinner. I don't want to pry, but maybe he's bringing it up because he wants to discuss it.

"Is he ... sick?" I ask as gently as I can.

His eyes go distant, and he disappears for a few beats into his head before he answers. “Not in the way you’re probably thinking. He’s just never been very good at … taking care of himself.”

“What about your mom?” I venture.

This earns me a quick shake of his head. “She’s long gone.” Whatever his feelings towards her, they’re much less complicated than his relationship with his dad. He switches to my other hand; eyes focused on his task.

From the sounds of it, it’s just him and his dad, who doesn’t seem like he can work. No wonder Parker was so worried about losing his job.

“You don’t have to pity me,” he grumbles.

“I wasn’t.”

He scoffs. “I know what people think of me when they hear the story. Guy from a broken home on the wrong side of the tracks. You’re doing an inventory of all the valuables in the house right now, aren’t you?”

“Actually, no. I was thinking it sounds like your dad is lucky that you’re the one taking care of him. Even if your first aid skills could use a little work. I look like a papier mâché squid.”

My attempt at lightening the mood works. His mouth quirks up in a tiny concession, and I notice the hint of a dimple in his right cheek.

“You make it work,” he says softly, his voice a low rumble in his chest.

He chooses that moment to look up at me from under his thick, dark lashes. A strange energy crackles between us, sending a tingle darting up my spine. His eyes drop and catch on my lips, his Adam’s apple bobbing with a hard swallow.

He pushes back and stands, clearing away the first aid kit with swift, steady movements. “You’re done for the day.”

Before I can even open my mouth to thank him, he's out the door. I stand stock still as I listen to his retreating footsteps down the barn, wondering what the hell just happened. I don't like it, but I may have to accept that Parker might not be as bad as I thought.

Chapter 8

The afternoon sun streams through the open windows as I drive along the mostly quiet country road, taking advantage of the warm fall day before the cold snap the weather app calls for. After he bandaged me up this morning and we shared that weird moment in the barn, I hightailed it back to the house, desperate for *something* to do to take my mind off it. Tabitha took mercy and gave me a shopping list and the keys to her Jeep. It didn't take long, but the trip to the hardware and feed stores was the most exciting thing on my schedule this week. It made me realize how much I miss the structure of working every day, with deadlines and projects. Even though I'm not excited about the products, it's time I stop neglecting my social media clients. I'll give myself the rest of today, and tomorrow I'll open my inbox and see what's waiting for me.

I make a left onto the two-lane highway that heads straight to Salem Stables, my karaoke sing-along interrupted by the sudden jerk of the Jeep.

I clench the wheel tighter, but after that sharp pull to the left, all I feel is resistance. What the hell is going on? I didn't hit anything. I take my foot off the gas, quickly scanning the dashboard for flashing lights

—something to tell me what is wrong with the vehicle —but everything looks normal. A car behind me honks, then veers past me.

"Shit," I mutter.

There's no way I can make it back to the farm like this. I need to pull over, but the steering wheel feels locked. With both hands, I crank the wheel as hard as I can, easing to the right until I slowly stop on the gravel shoulder, surrounded by farmers' fields. I punch on the hazards and kill the engine, slumping back in the seat. I've passed the outskirts of town, too far to try and push through the rest of the way home and far enough away from town that I'm surrounded by nothing.

A frustrated growl rips through me and I repeatedly tilt my head against the headrest. *Thud. Thud. Thud.*

"Of course, this is happening to me." *Just call me the luckiest girl alive.*

I call Tabitha, who agrees to come and get me as soon as she can get out of her meeting. Grabbing my purse, I leave the reusable shopping bag with the rest of my goods on the seat, lock the car and start my journey to town on foot along the deserted country road, surrounded by nothing except fields that look as barren as my future. I walk for about twenty minutes before signs of civilization pop up around me and I spot the small diner on the corner where I told Tabitha I'd wait. It's the last unit in a small business plaza with a bakery, a health food store, and a bar at the opposite end that looks closed. Too bad. Despite the early hour, I could use a drink.

Soft bells jingle overhead as I enter the diner. The scent of French fry grease greets me instantly. I find a seat, and the cracked vinyl squeaks under my jean-clad thighs. I peer through the menu, not because I'm hungry but because it's what you're supposed to do.

The server pops over, her round face open and friendly. "What can I get you?" She looks a few years younger than me, with a smattering of freckles across the bridge of her nose and a few strands of light hair coming loose from her bun.

"Onion rings, and the number for a psychic if you have one. I think I'm cursed."

She tucks her notepad into her apron without bothering to write down my order. "No problem and check the bulletin board on your way out for the number."

My eyebrows shoot up. "Seriously?"

She chuckles, nodding. "Entertainment is scarce around here. We get desperate. I'll get your order in."

Before she walks away, I ask for a couple of kid menus and a spare black marker, which she delivers a few minutes later with no comment. While I wait for my food, I flip the first menu over to the back and stare at the blank page. I haven't done any calligraphy since the business fell through, and even though I miss it, I've been afraid to return to it in case it makes things worse.

Finally, I begin to doodle. Over and over, I draw my name in calligraphy-style letters, some round and bubbly, others narrow and pointed. Slightly hindered by my bandaged hands, it's not as good as my usual work, but I manage, the familiar strokes soothing my frazzled nerves.

"Most people want them for the word search," the server says when she returns, examining the now-filled menu over my shoulder. I push the placemats out of the way to make room for the plate she puts down in front of me. "That's pretty neat. Did you teach yourself to do that?"

"It's not as hard as it looks." I hold up my heavily bandaged hand as proof. "Anyone can do it. Trust me, I've run workshops for people without a creative bone in their body."

"You teach this?"

I nod. "Lots of birthdays, girls' nights—"

"Bachelorette parties?"

"Exactly! Here." I gesture for her to sit and push my plate out of the way, pulling the placemats back into place. "What's your name?"

"Veronica. *Not* with a 'k.'"

I draw her name on a blank spot on the menu, then hand her the marker to try. She follows my instructions on when to put more pressure on the tip, brows knit together in concentration.

"See? You're a natural."

"Oh my gosh, that's so fun!" Veronica says excitedly. "I would totally do this with my friends."

I grin, feeling the same rush of possibility after giving an elevator pitch that goes exceptionally well. But I know she's right—tons of people would want to do this, which is precisely why Lyla and I thought it would be worth investing in. I still can't believe we're leaving the opportunity untapped.

"This is like, totally fate or whatever that you're here," Veronica says. "My best friend is getting married in a couple of weeks and her sister is the maid of honor—which I like, totally don't mind, because they're family, you know? —only she dropped the ball big time on planning the bachelorette party, so now we're scrambling to find something, and this—well, this sounds perfect!"

"Oh. Well..."

I'm stunned speechless as I think it over. I thought getting back into calligraphy might be too much of a reminder of what I'd lost, but that's not something I'm going to forget easily, regardless. Maybe letting myself have it in my life, even in the small, side-hustle way it was before, would be enough to soften the blow. Hosting one event might even offer the closure I need to let go of that dream and move on. In the last five minutes here with Veronica, my stress levels have dropped. I might not have been looking for this, but—unless the universe is playing tricks on me—this could be the best thing to happen to me lately.

"Sorry, forget I said anything," Veronica says, standing, her cheeks slightly pink as she forces a laugh. "I've been told I have a habit of inserting myself uninvited."

"I'll do it."

"Wait—seriously? Because you would be literally saving us, you have no idea."

She looks up as the bell jingles above the door.

"You called for a chauffeur?"

My spine stiffens at the gruff, familiar voice behind me. I spin around to find Parker hovering in the doorway, hands shoved into his coat pockets, face painted with a scowl. "What are you doing here?"

"Driving Miss Daisy, apparently."

Impatiently, I wave Parker over to the table, since he has no concerns about having this conversation loudly enough to disturb the other diners. I scribble my number on a blank corner of the menu and tear it off for Veronica. "Here's my number. Call me with the details, and we'll figure something out."

Veronica slips away as Parker reaches the table.

"What was that all about?"

"Where's Tabitha?" I ask when he reaches me, ignoring his question.

"She was working when you called, so she asked me to come and save your ass. You're welcome."

Thanks, Tabitha. It is as if Parker needs more ammunition to believe I'm a helpless princess.

Veronica chooses that moment to swing by with the check, leaving it on the table with a smile that she dials up a notch when aimed at Parker.

"Thanks," I say quickly, trying to cover the unexpected edge in my voice with my own smile. I reach into my purse for my wallet, my heart dropping with a plunk to my shoes as I come up empty. *Crap.* Did it fall out on the side of the road on my walk here? Getting more frantic, I dig through my jacket pockets before realizing what I've done. *Oh no.* My wallet isn't on the side of the road. It's in the shopping bag on the passenger seat of the Jeep. I look up wide-eyed at Parker, who's watching me knowingly with a quirked brow. My cheeks redden. "I swear I didn't plan this."

With an eye roll and a sigh, he drags the bill towards him with a blunt fingertip, reaching for his wallet in the back pocket of his faded jeans, and dropping some cash on the table. "Let's go, your highness," he says brusquely before I can thank him, brushing past me.

Oh, how I love to be rescued.

He props the door open with his forearm for me to pass under.

"I'll pay you back."

He ignores me, whipping his head to scan the parking lot. "Where's the Jeep?"

"I thought Tabitha filled you in?"

"She said you had car trouble and that you were here."

"Yeah, her Jeep broke down."

"What?" he snaps. "Where?" I point down the dusty country highway. "Shit. Are you okay?"

"Um ... yes?"

He lifts his eyebrows, probing. "I thought your car wouldn't start, or you ran out of gas, or something." He ignores the unimpressed look I give him for that one. "You weren't in an accident?"

Is that worry I detect? "No," I say slowly. "I think something is wrong with the steering. I pulled over because I didn't think it was safe to drive home and I didn't want to make anything worse."

He nods, then jerks his head, signaling me to get into the truck. As I climb in, I can't take my eyes off the hard line of his stubble-covered jaw as he settles in behind the wheel opposite me. He shoves the keys in the ignition, pausing before turning it on. He doesn't meet my eye when he speaks, but his voice is much softer now. "Tell me again what's wrong with the car?"

For a second, I wonder if this is a test and brace myself to get mansplained all the way home. But there's something different in his expression than when he first walked into the diner, maybe even since I met the guy.

"Beats me. All I know is that in one minute, everything was fine, but then the wheel jerked, and I could barely move it enough to pull over."

"That's ... unlucky."

I let out a long sigh. "Nope," I mutter quietly. "Just my life."

Although maybe not forever, I remind myself as I think about my chat with Veronica inside.

Reaching past me, he pops the glove box open and pulls out a cell phone that looks functional, if a little old and a lot beat up—kind of like his truck.

"I don't know much about cars, but my buddy Sam's a mechanic. I'm gonna call him and see if he can help."

When someone picks up on the other end, Parker quickly explains the situation. As he tells him where to find us, I marvel at the realization that this might be the longest conversation we've had without a hint of sarcasm. There's a pause on the other end before the muffled voice begins again, and a flush creeps over the collar of Parker's corduroy jacket. "No one. Can you help or not?"

He jerks the phone away from his face, hangs up while the voice is still talking, tosses the phone back in the glove box and fires up the engine.

"He'll meet us there."

Chapter 9

The silence is stifling on the ride back down the quiet country road until Parker stops at the abandoned Jeep, parking us nose to nose. When we get there, I climb out of the truck and head over to pop the hood of the Jeep, then rifle through the reusable shopping bag on the passenger seat to find my wallet. Gravel crunches under my shoes as I march back to where Parker is leaning against the Jeep's front bumper.

"Here," I say, shoving some money into his hand. I ignore how warm and strong his fingers feel when they briefly make contact.

"What's this?" he asks, not taking it from me.

"For the food," I explain. "You covered my bill at the restaurant, remember?" I'm sure he does, but he could be playing dumb now so he can hold it over me later.

"I don't want your money, Sloan."

He crosses his arms, and after a few seconds, I drop my hand, tucking the money back into my purse.

"Really? No argument? You're in a better mood than I expected," Parker notes. "Especially considering you broke down on the side of the road," he points out, turning so he's facing the road as well, his shoulder inches away from mine.

I want to be irritated, but after meeting Veronica, I'm finding it difficult to stay angry. Much as I hate to admit it, if I hadn't broken down, I never would have been in that diner in the first place. With a grin, I mirror his pose and together we stare out at the empty field ahead, wide-open and sun-soaked. Until now, the fight in me has been shriveling like a paperback novel left out in the rain. Finally, the sun is starting to dry my pages.

"I'm starting to think things might be turning around for me."

I look up to find his loaded gaze on me, the two of us standing closer than I realized. He goes to say something, but the jovial beep-beep of a horn cuts him off.

A weathered white and blue tow truck drives past us and does a sloppy three-point turn before stopping behind my car. The hazard lights flick on and a shorter guy with a mop of shaggy blond hair hops out. He pushes it back from his face by sliding on a red baseball hat backward and strolls towards us.

"Hey buddy! How's it hangin'?" The newcomer slaps Parker's hand, who, to my *enormous* surprise, doesn't fight the enthusiastic hug his friend gives him. When the stranger spots the Jeep's popped hood, his face falls.

"Uh oh. You didn't try to fix anything, did you?"

Parker holds up his hands. "I wouldn't dare."

"Sweet." The mechanic gives me a nod, that easy grin showing his white teeth. "If he had, I would have said that's your problem. Poor guy is mechanically challenged." He backhands Parker in the gut, shooting me a conspiratorial wink.

"Sloan, this is Sam. His dad owns the garage in River Glen."

Sam's blue eyes dart back and forth between us, his knowing grin widening. He raises his eyebrows knowingly at Parker, and I clear my throat pointedly to stop their silent communication.

"I'm so sorry we dragged you out here."

Sam waves me off, and I realize he's hardly stopped moving since he arrived. He looks like he's in his late twenties, maybe a couple of years younger than me. I wonder how he knows Parker, but they seem close enough. He's a full head shorter than Parker, about my height. The biggest difference is that Sam is instantly likable.

"No worries," he says with a grin, pointing at Parker. "I owed this guy a favor. Let me get a look at this puppy." His head is buried in the hood for all of three minutes before he spots the problem. "Looks like some faulty spark plugs. Not super common, just bad luck."

I raise my eyebrows pointedly at Parker.

"Good news is, it's not expensive." Sam lets the hood fall shut and brushes his hands off. "Bad news is, I'll have to take it in to get it fixed. That cool with you?"

I nod.

"Thanks again, man," Parker says when he's finished hooking the Jeep up to the tow truck.

"I should be thanking you for not doing any more damage to it. He's just like his old man, he'll break an engine by lookin' at it," he says to me, jerking a thumb at Parker. He hands me a business card with the shop's address and contact info.

"You know Parker's dad?" I'd assumed Parker's wasn't from here. If his friend knows him, maybe he's more permanent than I gave him credit for.

"Yeah, he—"

"When will the car be ready?" Parker cuts him off before he can say any more. Sam rolls with it, completely unfazed by the interruption or the bite in Parker's tone.

"Could be a few days if we need the parts, but I'll give you a call when it's ready."

"Thanks," I say, my mood improving with the knowledge of Parker's particular brand of kryptonite.

"You're still down for The Cabin tonight, right, buddy?"

Parker's eyes dart to me briefly before he gives Sam a curt nod. His friend's blue eyes light up as he turns to me.

"You should come! It'll be fun. It's nothing wild, but if you like pool and—*oof!*" Sam doubles over as Parker smacks him in the gut.

I gesture at a scowling Parker. "I'm sure it'll be a barrel of laughs if this one's going, but I have to work. Thanks anyway."

Sam chuckles, then casts Parker another knowing look before he waves goodbye and drives off. For the first time in what feels like a lifetime, I'm looking forward to spending an evening buried in work, and I can't keep the smile off my face as I climb into Parker's truck.

"Sam seems nice," I say when the silence becomes too much. It's a poor attempt at conversation, even for me.

Parker grunts.

"So, is he a family friend, or ...?"

"No."

My fingers drum against the dark blue denim covering my knees. "Are you allergic to human conversation, or what?"

One of his big hands tightens on the wheel, and he drops the other to the gear shaft between us, flexing his fingers. "Jesus Christ, you don't give up, do you? My dad worked at the shop for Sam's dad, that's how I met him."

"See, that wasn't so hard." Beyond the windows, one farmer's field after another rolls past as we bump along the uneven road, and I wish there were something more to look at.

"What does he do now?"

Parker's eyes dart to me briefly, then back to the road. "Who?"

"Your dad. You said he worked there, past tense."

"Nothing, he ... nothing."

We reach the driveway and roll down beneath the leafy canopy of trees.

"Didn't like being a mechanic then?"

The gravel crunches as he stops abruptly in front of the house.

"Next time you need rescuing, don't expect me to come running."

The thanks I was about to offer dies in my throat when I look over at him. His eyes may as well be laser cutters, the way he's trying to burn a hole in the windshield. Glowering right back at him, I slam the truck door as hard as possible.

He pulls away in a cloud of dust. I'm guessing there's a zero percent chance of this being something we'll laugh about later.

Chapter 10

"I can't believe you did that!" I call out to Tabitha as soon as I'm in the door, toeing off my shoes and teasing her as I head down the hallway on the main floor to her studio. "Unless I need to brush up on my Morse code, I am fairly certain that I requested *you* be the one to rescue me, not the grumpy man who hates—"

I jerk to a stop as I step through the French door. Tabitha is hunched over an empty table beside her pottery wheel, hands braced, head hanging low.

She knows.

Did Dad tell her? I still haven't stopped dodging his calls; maybe he got sick of waiting for me and just told her the truth.

I swallow hard, pulse pounding in my temples. "What's wrong?"

I know she knows, but I still can't bring myself to say it now. The following words on the tip of my tongue are *I'm sorry*—but then she lifts her head.

"Oh, hun, I'm so sorry I didn't come get you myself. I've been working on this *stupid* vase all day and the damn thing decided to collapse on me *again* right before you called. I asked Parker to borrow his truck, but he insisted I stay to keep working. Not that it made much difference." She gestures at the table where she usually keeps her ceramics before they're fired in the kiln. It's empty.

The relief I feel is instant, but short-lived. "Can you try making something else?" I suggest. "Sometimes when I'm stuck on something, switching projects helps to get the creative juices flowing again."

She sighs. "I wish I could, but this is a custom order. The commissions are piling up, which is a good problem to have, but I can't seem to deliver anything."

Tabitha slumps down on the stool before her pottery wheel, staring at an unformed lump of clay. The walls in this room are beige and natural light pours in through the large windows behind her onto the hardwood floor and the shelves lining the walls with her pottery—no two pieces are the same. The ceramics offer splashes of color, but most of the shelves are empty too, and I realize this problem goes far beyond one bad day.

"Is this why you haven't been sleeping?"

She gives a resigned nod. "The holidays are right around the corner, and at this rate, I'll have nothing to sell."

"But I mean ... you've had slow years before, right?" That's the life of an artist, she advised me when I first told her about the business Lyla and I wanted to open. Fulfilling, but unpredictable.

"Yes, but it's different now with Parker here. The people I hire tend to come and go, so I've never had to pay a consistent salary to someone. When they left, I managed the farm just fine on my own. At this rate, I'm not sure I will be able to afford him past next spring."

I swallow, surprised at feeling mildly guilty about Parker possibly losing his job here. It's odd, considering a few days ago I was convinced he'd be gone soon anyway. It's different, though, imagining it caused by factors outside his control. I'm too familiar with that to take any pleasure in the possibility of it happening to him.

Tabitha pushes to her feet. "Okay, enough self-pity. I promised you we'd go for a trail ride this afternoon."

Immediately, I lift my hands to stop her in her tracks. "Not a chance. You need time to work."

"I've had nothing *but* time for months!" she protests. "Ever since Parker started working for me, I have way more time on my hands because he has the horses under control all alone. It's why I let my friends talk me into joining the farmer's market committee—I needed something to do that wasn't staring at nothing in here."

Moving closer, I place my hands on her shoulders and guide her back to her seat. "Creative blocks are no joke. I can't give you any tips on pottery, but I can tell you that sometimes when you're staring at a wall, the worst thing to do is back away from it."

That's what I've been doing for the past two weeks, and it's gotten me nowhere. Today, I looked at what I'd been avoiding in the face, and I finally felt like I could do something about it. I had to figure that out for myself, the hard way. The stakes are higher for Tabitha, and it's not just about her—this affects Parker, too. Maybe I can help Tabitha find her way quicker than I did.

"Are you sure?" Tabitha looks up at me, guilty, but her fingers are already inching towards the clay on the stationary wheel before her. "We haven't gone riding since you got here."

I nod, moving to the door. "Positive. I'll be fine on my own, and by the time I get back, you will have something beautiful to show me."

She scoffs. "Let's not push it."

"Fine, how about you'll have *something* to show me. Keep it simple at first."

She shakes her head at me, but at least she's smiling again. "For you, Sloan, I will do my best. And take Bailey."

I pause in the doorway. "Not Zeke?"

"He was lame again last week. I want to make sure he gets enough rest before we put any extra strain again, and Bailey could use the exercise."

"Is she ..."

"Don't worry, you can handle her and she's great on solo rides," she says, sensing my hesitation. I have some experience riding, but it's been almost a year. Tabitha knows her animals better than she knows herself though, and she also knows me. Her confidence in me erases my worries immediately, and as I head to the barn, my first ride of the season has excitement and adrenaline buzzing under my skin.

Beyond the barn sit two large pastures with a dozen horses between them, grazing behind a white fence. Next to the closest one is a large outdoor riding ring with ancient trees providing shade over one side. Interrupting Bailey's lazy afternoon, I take the gentle horse into the barn and saddle her up as quickly as possible. Parker doesn't even acknowledge me whenever he wanders by, except to scrutinize my every move with his silent glare. I hardly notice, too distracted by thoughts of Tabitha. I'm combing through every one of our conversations since I arrived, wondering if I missed how stressed she was because I was too caught up in my drama. Plus, now I'm sure that telling her about my dad could cause even more stress, worsening her creative block. This is her livelihood on the line—not to mention Parker's—telling her now would be selfish.

Deep in my thoughts, I pull my copper waves into a low ponytail. I shove on a helmet and then lead Bailey outside to the mounting block.

The steady palomino stops short when we get close, backing up a few paces. I cluck my tongue and try pulling her forward. She tosses her nose up. I rest my palm on her forehead to steady her and try a third time; she spins around it, but not close enough for me to climb up.

"You'll be there all day if you keep trying that."

Startled, I whip around to find Parker watching me from the barn door. How long has he been standing there? Focusing my attention back on Bailey, I gently pat her and try again.

Grumbling something incomprehensible, he marches over and takes the reins out of my hands. With the mounting block a safe distance away, Bailey stands perfectly still for him, unbothered.

"Here." His hand is outstretched to give me a boost, palm facing up.

I drag my disbelieving eyes back to his face. Will I ever understand this man? His mood swings are giving me whiplash. Honestly, if he decided to hate me, this would be so much easier.

Slowly, because I don't know what else to do, I grip both sides of the saddle and bend my left knee. His hand closes around my shin and lifts in one swift movement, hoisting me into the saddle like it's nothing. Slightly winded, I clear my throat, looking down at him for the first time after I get comfortable.

"Um ... thanks."

He gives a curt nod. Heat radiates through my thigh where his hand is now sitting. And he's making no moves to back away. When did it even get there? He slides his hand down to my jean-covered calf and swings my leg back. Bailey protests when he cinches the girth tighter, adjusting her stance under me. I reach forward to soothe her with a pat on the neck.

"You don't have to—" I stop when I realize how much he can tighten the saddle. "I thought I tightened that," I say with a frown, annoyed at myself for leaving anything for him to fix.

"She's a sneaky one with that," he says, gripping my foot by the ankle and tucking it securely into the stirrup. "Likes to bloat. Could happen to anyone. You know what you're doing?"

Well, isn't that the million-dollar question? I haven't got a clue what I'm doing. But he's not asking about my life. He's asking if I know what I'm doing *up here*.

"Do you honestly think I'm dumb enough to climb on the back of a twelve-hundred-pound animal without knowing where the brakes are?"

I glance down, expecting him to fire back some snarky comeback, but his eyes have no evil smirk or mischief. He looks ... invested in the answer, somehow. The same way he was outside the diner earlier when he found out I'd broken down on the side of the road and had to walk into town.

When he asked if I was *safe*.

Holy crap. He's concerned. About ... me?

There *is* a heart somewhere in this beautiful Frankenstein monster. Maybe his attitude is some form of hazing I'm not aware of.

As the thought spreads roots in the back of my mind, I register that his palm is still resting on my leg. It's flat, warm, and solid ... and not going anywhere.

Kind of like the errant thought that wants me to imagine that hand in other places.

"Don't worry, I know my way around a horse," I assure him.

Parker seems taken aback by the gentleness in my tone. He clears his throat, pulling his eyes away to check the length of my stirrups one last time, and I instantly miss the warmth of his hand on my thigh. "Good. You have a phone with you, just in case?"

Nodding, I pat the pocket of my puffy red vest to double-check.

"Can I come with you later to the Tractor Trailer?" I blurt out.

He tips his face up to mine, squinting in the afternoon sunlight. "You mean The Cabin?"

"Yeah, whatever," I say. "If the invitation still stands, I'd like to come."

"Technically, I'm not the one who invited you. Whether or not it still stands depends largely on whether Sam has found another lady to set his sights on since we saw him ..." he pretends to check an invisible watch on his wrist, "forty minutes ago." He lifts his eyes to mine. "The odds of that are higher than you'd think."

I give him the flattest look I can muster. "I'll take my chances."

"Why do you want to come? I thought the one thing you and I agreed on was that we spend far too much time together as it is. Plus, who will do the night feed if you and I are both gone?"

"I think Tabitha needs to spend some time in the barn. She hasn't needed to since you started working here, and—" His eyes harden immediately, but I cut him off to explain before he blows a gasket. "Calm down, it's a compliment. She told me that ever since she hired you, she's been able to leave the horses to you completely. She's never been able to trust anyone to that extent, but with you, she doesn't have to keep an eye on things."

"That's what she pays me for. If she has to check on things, I'm not doing my job."

"Right, but she *likes* being in the barn. I think getting back into some of her old routines might help her with her art. It's counterintuitive, but sometimes it's easier to do more creative work when you have less time to do it."

He lifts his left hand to block the sun from his eyes. It's a fight to keep my gaze from drifting to his hand on my jean-clad thigh, but I do in case acknowledging it spooks him. I chew my lip, waiting for his response. This is the actual test to see if he cares about Tabitha more than he hates me. You'd think by now I'd be used to rejection, but relief courses through me when he finally nods.

Before he can change his mind, I gather the reins and nudge Bailey into motion with my heels and a tongue click, heading for the break in the yellow, orange, and red trees across the expansive lawn.

"Hey, Sloan," he calls after me.

I glance back over my shoulder as Bailey's hooves clip-clop on the gravel driveway towards the trailhead. I expect him to rescind his offer at worst, at best to offer another quip about my skills, or a promise to send a search party if I'm not back by tomorrow.

"Be careful," he says instead. With a lingering look, he backs away and disappears inside the barn.

Oh boy. This is dangerous.

Because now that I know there's a heart in there, I'm determined to find out exactly what makes it beat.

Chapter 11

Tabitha eyes me from her cross-legged position on my bed while I get ready after dinner. "Tell me again, but slower this time."

I meet her eyes in the mirror above the old wood dresser—the one she insisted we paint yellow one day, the summer I turned seventeen, because I mentioned it was my new favorite color. It seemed ridiculous, but she insisted she wanted me to feel like this room was my own space. Looking back, I feel like it was more than a little bit motivated by what was happening between my parents that summer, but every time I visit and find the dresser still yellow, it makes me happy.

"I'm ignoring you now."

"You're really going out with *Parker?*" she asks.

"No, I am not *going out* with Parker. We're just going out. See? No inflection. *With* his friend, by the way. This is not a date," I insist for the fifth time while I twist a piece of hair around my curling wand. My reassurance does nothing to convince her.

"Blink twice if you're being kidnapped and need me to intervene."

"Where was this concern earlier today when I literally called you for help?" I tease.

She leans back on the pillows, a grin forming. "I thought you and Parker spending a little quality time together couldn't hurt. Guess I was right, wasn't I?" She waggles her eyebrows, dodging the lip gloss I send sailing at her.

"You call it quality time, I call it forced confinement."

"To-may-to, to-mah-to. I don't know if you've noticed, but you're awfully dressed up for this so-called punishment."

She's not wrong, but the outfit is purely for me, not for anyone who might see me in it. After deciding to help Veronica, my brain immediately kicked back into work mode for the first time since the business hit a brick wall. I feel energized and eager to jump into planning, and it's been a relief to finally feel like myself again, even if there are certain things I'm still figuring out. So, I decided to chase that feeling and dress how I normally would for a night out. Like Lyla said, baby steps. I wear a soft black turtleneck with sleeves that end at my elbows, a black patterned skirt that sits high on my waist and flares out at my mid-thighs, and black boots with a chunky heel. Once I add my cropped, light-wash jean jacket, the outfit will look more casual.

"This is my chance to celebrate a good thing finally happening to me, and I'm taking it. That's all. You owe me after today—and for sending Parker to pick me up from the bus station. I'm collecting by taking the night off and using your porch to have a bunch of strangers over next weekend."

After my ride this afternoon, I got a bunch of texts from Veronica with details about the party and told Tabitha about the emergency bachelorette party I've agreed to host. She didn't even blink when I asked if I could have it here at Salem Stables, and we agreed on the front porch. It's picturesque with a great sunset view, and we can dress it up with string lights—nothing special, as they're coming for the activity, not the ambiance.

Tabitha pushes up from the bed and comes to stand behind me. "You missed a spot." Taking the curling iron from me, she fixes the loose waves I've been putting into my otherwise straight hair. "I still feel like I've met the bride-to-be. I *know* I've heard that name before. Maybe I'll recognize her when I see her."

With free hands, I grab my phone. If she's under thirty, it's a solid bet she's on social media. Most couples also have a wedding website nowadays, and it's a good shortcut for getting a sense of the bride's style. I use the keywords Lucy + Cooper + Wedding and... bingo.

Except, what I find isn't a social media profile or a wedding website like I expected. It's so, *so* much worse.

"Oh shit," I blurt.

Tabitha's hands go still. "Okay, you know I don't have a problem with the language because I have a bigger potty mouth than you, but that's unusual enough for me to be fairly alarmed."

I click on the first link, which takes me to a blog called *The Country Bumpkin*. And not one of those blogs that look like a side-hobby created in the early aughts, either. A *nice* one. I swear I've seen that logo before, the cute white lettering outlined with the silhouette of a pumpkin. I must be in the wrong spot. I'm about to close out of it when I notice the post pinned at the top of the page, titled: *We're getting married!* A professional black-and-white engagement photo fills the screen when I click on it, and I scroll down with a few quick thumb brushes.

This can't be the same Lucy Cooper that Veronica is friends with. I scroll back through the (highly professional-looking) posts, and sure enough, it doesn't take long to see the wedding-related ones that make my stomach drop.

"Sloan, what is it?" Tabitha pushes.

"Just the universe's sick sense of humor," I say miserably.

"Why, do you know her or something?"

"No, but I think everybody else does." With a trembling thumb I click over to her Instagram page—and nearly drop my phone. "Oh god ... she has over *a hundred thousand* followers!" I break out into a cold sweat. "This is ..."

"Great?" Tabitha offers.

"A nightmare!" I jump up from the chair, coming dangerously close to being branded, but luckily Tabitha pulls the curling iron away in the nick of time. Honestly, though, the pain might have been a nice distraction. Without it, I'm forced to face the fact that I've made another impulsive decision that has turned out to be a *huge* mistake.

"Sloan, don't panic. This is not as big of a deal as you're about to make it."

"Not a big deal?!" I repeat, eyes wide. "On the pressure scale, this event has just gone from zero to a hundred!"

In theory, Tabitha is right. I should be over the moon about this. If Lyla and I had opened the shop and landed an influencer of this magnitude as one of our first clients, we would be popping the champagne to celebrate. But there's one crucial difference—Lyla's not here. I'm going to have to do this alone. Sure, a good review from this client could lead to incredible things. But I have to *earn* a good review first. I'm not set up to host an event worthy of being shared with a hundred thousand loyal followers. With Lyla, I wouldn't have hesitated for a second. The risk would have been a thrill. But ... I've never had to do this on my own before. I can't shake the feeling that I might not have what it takes. And if things go sideways, my failure will be immortalized on the internet as a permanent blemish on my resumé. What if I ruin the chance for Lyla and me to start our business together someday?

Out front, a horn blares, snapping me from my inner turmoil.

"Your chariot awaits," Tabitha teases.

"At least he didn't leave without me," I grumble.

"What are you waiting for?" she asks when I don't move. She grabs a claw clip off the yellow dresser and twists my hair into a half-up, half-down style.

I hold up my phone. "I'm not in the mood to celebrate anymore."

Honk! Honk!

She *tsks*, grabbing my jean jacket off the bed and holding it open for me to slip my arms through. "Don't celebrate then. Just go out, have fun for no reason. *Be young.*" She steps in front of me, grabbing my head and pressing her forehead to mine. "I promise, it'll do you some good to get out of that wonderfully tangled up head of yours."

I hold onto her wrists, searching her hazel eyes. "How do you know—"

Tabitha smiles. "Because you get it from me."

She doesn't notice the way my eyes instantly go teary. Or maybe she did and doesn't realize they're not happy tears. Why would she? I still haven't told her the truth.

Hoooooooooonk!

Laughing, she turns me by the shoulders and pushes me to the door. "You better go before he really does leave without you."

Dropping my lip gloss into my small black purse, I sling it over my shoulder, then quickly kiss her on the cheek and hurry downstairs. She's right. This crisis is just going to have to wait.

Parker's impatient eyes meet mine when I emerge from the house, closing the door behind me. Despite his apparent hurry, I take my time to prove a point, waggling my fingers at him in an obnoxious wave as I cross the gravel driveway.

HOOOOOOOOONK! HONK! HONK! HONK!

I slow my step even more, and he drops his head back against the headrest in defeat.

"Sorry, I didn't know you were here," I chirp as I climb into his truck. "You should have honked or something."

I buckle my seatbelt, pausing when I find him staring at me. No, not me ... my legs. I resist the urge to tug my skirt over my bare knees, noticing it's crept a few inches higher.

"What?" I say, managing to sound normal.

He wrenches his gaze away and throws the truck into gear. "I have to make a couple of stops on the way. That okay?"

I shrug. I'm already spending an entire night with the guy. What's a few errands along the way?

Except I didn't plan to sit in a freezing cold truck for longer than the fifteen-minute drive to town, and with the sun long gone, the temperature has dropped considerably. I'm realizing I may not have picked the smartest outfit. I cross one knee over the other in the meantime, trying to warm my legs in the chilly truck. Parker's eyes track the movement, but he quickly looks away, adjusting his grip on the wheel.

"Would you mind turning the heat on?" I ask, rubbing my arms. "It's freezing."

"It's broken. Sorry," he adds as an afterthought.

I sigh. Of course. "You could get that fixed."

"You could wear more clothes."

He pulls into the gas station at the edge of town, bright lights illuminating the pavement. Parker opens the center console between us and pulls out his wallet and a Salem Stables pay stub before telling me he'll be back in a minute and heads to the ATM beside the ice cooler and bags of chopped wood.

I lean back against the seat and remember what Parker managed to distract me from as soon as I laid eyes on him tonight—I'm screwed.

Unless I was wrong, Veronica's friend is the same Lucy Cooper who has a popular lifestyle blog and 100,000 Instagram followers, but I didn't search very far. What if I was wrong? Hope flutters in my chest as I fumble for my phone to do a more thorough search, only to realize my battery is running low—I must have forgotten to plug it in while I was getting ready. Remembering that Parker keeps his cell in the glove box, I pop it open, hoping to find a charger so I have enough juice to call Tabitha in case Parker decides to leave me stranded later.

I realize my mistake as soon as I lay eyes on an envelope full of cash.

That definitely wasn't in here earlier.

I stare at it for a few long moments, wondering if I'm seeing things, before I spot movement through the windshield. Slamming the glove compartment shut, I lean back in my seat as far away from the money as possible.

The driver's side door opens, and Parker climbs back in, turning the engine on and pulling back onto the road, driving us to a part of town I've never been to before. When we pull into a small residential area a few minutes later, I can't take the silence anymore.

"Where are we going?" I ask, the truck rumbling beneath us.

"Uh, I have to drop something off for my dad." My neck jerks sharply to the left, and he chuckles at my reaction. "Don't worry, you can wait in the truck."

"Oh." I'm not sure where my disappointment is coming from. "Not gonna lie, I wouldn't mind seeing you next to Parker Senior. Do you look alike?"

His expression fades a little, and he gives a slight shake of his head. His expression becomes unreadable in the shadows that keeps flicking us into darkness between streetlamps. "Same hair color, but that's about it. No, my inheritance consists mostly of every bad decision he's ever made."

I want to ask him to elaborate, but he stops along the curb in front of a fifties-era house with a small yard surrounded by chain-link fencing. The screen door is slightly crooked, and even in the near dark—a single bare bulb illuminates the porch—it looks pretty run down. Is this where Parker grew up? No wonder he calls me a princess.

"Stay in the truck, okay? I'll only be a minute."

I watch him reach across me for the second time today to open the glove box, but instead of grabbing his phone, he takes the envelope and hops out of the truck. He stuffs a few more bills inside as he walks up the overgrown yard, then knocks on the door before letting himself inside.

He's in and out in less than a minute, coming back to the truck empty-handed and looking like he just went through hell. The smell of cigarette smoke now clings faintly to his clothes.

"Are you okay?" I ask carefully.

"I'm fine." He shoves the keys in the ignition but doesn't turn it on, gripping the wheel with both hands.

"Is your dad okay? Because I'm not in a rush, you know. If you need to stay—"

"I don't," he says firmly, then winces at how harsh his words sounded. "Sorry. It's just that I know my dad. When he's been drinking, he gets agitated if I hover too much, and I don't feel like starting our night by getting yelled at for how much I look like my piece of shit mom."

Whoa. That was a lot.

"Parker," I start, not knowing what to say.

"Sorry," he says again, deflating. He presses his eyes shut, leaning his head back. His hands are still on the wheel, like he's anchoring himself. "That wasn't directed at you."

"It's okay if it was," I say after a beat. "If it makes you feel better, you can tell me how much you hate my outfit again."

A soft breath escapes him that sounds dangerously close to laughter. "That comment wasn't about you, either. You look ... nice."

My eyebrows shoot up. "I'm sorry, was that an *actual* compliment?"

This gets a real laugh out of him, and for some reason, I feel relieved. Unbuckling my seatbelt, I open the passenger door and hop down, rounding to his side of the truck. I open the door and gesture for him to get out.

"What are you doing?"

"I'm driving. Come on, out you get. It's your turn to be the passenger princess."

He stares for a beat, making me wonder how often people go out of their way to help him. After a pause, he wordlessly changes places with me, quietly letting me orient myself until I start driving. Thanks to his directions and gentle prompts about his truck's quirks, he navigates us to the bar without issue.

The bar is full when we get there, with a group on the dance floor and most of the tables already spoken for, where groups of people are chatting and laughing over drinks. Sam is waving across the room at the end of the long bar. To my surprise, Parker doesn't jet off without me. I guess by now he's accepted his fate and resigned himself to spending one torturous evening with me. He holds out his arm, gesturing for me to go first. As I step in front of him, his hand rests on my back for a second. I'm too shocked to say anything. It happens again as we squeeze our way through a group of people, and this time the electric current from his palm on the lower curve of my spine is impossible to ignore. I'm hyper-aware of his body behind me as we reach Sam. I hope it's not bright enough in here to see the flush on my cheeks.

"Hey, you made it!" Sam grins widely as he stands, pulling me in for a friendly hug before he gives Parker a one-armed hug and back slap combo. "I'm so glad he talked you into joining us. Here, sit, sit!"

I climb carefully onto the offered barstool he was sitting on, noting Parker's eyes flick to my legs before darting away.

"Sorry if we kept you waiting," I say to Sam.

"Nah, don't worry about it," he says easily, drumming the bar's edge while he talks. "A bunch of the guys I work with are here too, so I had someone to talk to while I waited for the main event." He flashes me a wide, easy smile.

Parker frowns at his friend. "Down, boy."

"What? I can't compliment the lady?"

"I don't mind," I say, cocking one shoulder in a playful shrug.

Sam grins. "See? She doesn't mind."

"I do." Parker levels me with a gaze and my stomach flips. I ignore it, because the irritation in his eyes has to be a trick of the light. Leaning towards Sam like I'm about to tell a secret, I say, "He minds you calling me a lady, that's all."

Sam laughs loudly as Parker lifts his eyes to the ceiling and takes a breath. "Is this how it's going to be tonight? The two of you ganging up on me? Awesome."

His friend claps him on the shoulder. "Nah, man. Tonight is gonna be epic. You guys hungry? It's not a big menu, but they have good wings here."

"Sloan's vegetarian," Parker says.

My head whips to Parker, who stares intently at the drink menu like he didn't just toss out that statement about me like a well-worn fact. Tabitha only mentioned it once, on my first night here, but he remembered.

"I already ate," I manage.

"Wasting no time getting to the epic part of the night, then, I love it," Sam carries on, oblivious to the uncomfortable somersaults my insides are currently doing. "First round is on me."

"You don't have to do that," Parker says.

"No, no, no. I insist!"

Parker reluctantly stays put, and over his shoulder, Sam gives me an enthusiastic thumbs up and a wink as he backs away, mouthing "*Epic!*"

A laugh bubbles out of me as I watch his mop of tangled blond hair navigate to the bar.

"You know he's a total ladies' man?" Parker tells me with a scowl.

"I'm shocked," I say flatly. "Next thing I know, you're going to tell me he's blond and has two legs, too."

He shakes his head, though his shoulders relax a little. "I'm just saying. He was already checking you out, so don't let your guard down with him if that's not, you know...what you're looking for."

I shrug. "I like him. He seems nice."

"He is. Makes it hard to hate the guy," he admits, a hint of fondness creeping into his voice.

"In that case ... when exactly was he checking me out?"

"I said hard, not impossible." There's a bite to his words, but he's watching me with a slight tilt to his lips. Is he ... *teasing* me?

"Why would you care if anything happened between Sam and me? You hate me, remember?"

His expression flickers, like he's surprised I'm being so direct about it. "I wouldn't call it *hate*."

"No?" I arch a brow. "What would you call it?"

He tips his head back and forth, considering. "You tell me. How should I feel about someone actively trying to get me fired?"

An impatient noise escapes my throat, but the arguing back and forth feels more good-natured than it usually does, and I find myself relieved to see the weight he seemed to carry out of his dad's house is mostly gone. "I'm *not* trying to get you fired."

"You sure about that? Because I've been working for Tibby for six months, and suddenly you show up and she thinks I need help."

I laugh. "You have trust issues. She doesn't think you need help; she wants us to spend time *together*, you bozo. Hence, her very transparent plan to send you to my rescue today."

A tall guy from a group behind me bumps me with his elbow and Parker shifts so he's standing closer. He stretches an arm behind me and rests it on the bar to keep them from getting in my space again, leaving a few inches between his arm and my back. I resist the pull to lean back into it.

"Why would she want us to spend time together?" He wrinkles his nose as he says it, like she's suggested we do something disgusting, like a spit handshake or chew a piece of gum from the underside of the bar.

The stool I'm sitting on is tall, but I still have to look up to meet his eye. This close, I can see the dark stubble lining his jaw and upper lip. There are bare patches on either side of his mouth, probably why he doesn't grow it out completely. But I find it oddly ... endearing.

"Because she knows I never like the people she hires, and ... for whatever reason, she thinks you're different."

He's looking at me closely, frowning like he's trying to figure something out. "Why don't you like the people she hires?"

"Historically speaking? They haven't been the nicest people. Look, Tabitha is like my favorite person in the whole world. She's kind, generous, and will give you the benefit of the doubt even when you've done nothing to deserve it. I don't like seeing people take advantage of her big heart. So, there's a slight chance that—based on years of well-earned prejudice—I *may* have expected you to be as bad as all the others. But ..." I admit, grudgingly, "You seem like you care about the farm. And you have stuck around longer than anyone else, which says a lot about you. My guess is, she thinks that if we spend more time together, I'll see you're a decent person."

He studies me closely while I speak, though it's impossible to guess his thoughts. "How likely would you say that is?"

"I don't know. Thirty is kind of young to have a stroke, but I'm sure it happens."

He ducks his head as he laughs, trying to hide it.

Damn Tabitha and whatever voodoo she used to make this happen.

Before I can suss out what this means, Sam is back and the three of us fall into easy conversation. Parker lets us do most of the talking, but I can tell he's comfortable around Sam. There's an ease between us that wasn't there before. His posture is relaxed, and he's smiling more tonight than he has the whole time I've known him. He hasn't moved away from me either, distracting me by standing a few inches to my right and nursing a beer as Sam entertains us with stories about his college buddies.

"So, beautiful, what brings you to our humble town?" Sam asks, rolling the base of his beer bottle in a circle on the bar to his right.

Parker glares at his friend for the compliment, which rolls off Sam's tongue like he's said it a million times before. I don't mind, but it doesn't send heat pooling in my core, not like the mere nearness of Parker's arm, which hasn't touched me in over an hour.

"A string of record-breaking bad luck," I deadpan, draining the last of my amaretto sour. "Where should we start? The failed business, or getting dumped?"

This piques their interest, and I find myself explaining the whole story—everything except the DNA kit part. That feels too personal to share, not to mention I'm not even sure how to describe it. I'm looking at Sam, but paying close attention to Parker in my periphery, though he doesn't seem to react. He's back to frowning, his factory default.

"And there was some family stuff too ... but that's the gist of it," I finish vaguely, lifting the glass to my lips again before I realize it's already empty. I lower it to my lap. "Tabitha's letting me crash for a while until I decide what's next."

Sam holds his hand up. "Hold up. You're telling me your boyfriend bailed on you *while* you were having the worst day of your life?" He exchanges a look with Parker, who looks equally murderous. "Where the hell did you find that chump?"

"We met on New Year's Eve last year. Caleb was a club promoter, and I was doing a marketing campaign for a new line of flavored Vodka." My eyes widen at the memory. Despite hating the product, I put so much time and energy into that campaign—one of the many things I poured my creativity into that I never cared about. How did I ever consider that success? And yet, that's what's waiting for me as soon as I can bring myself to get back to it. I take a swig of my drink, choosing to drown the knowledge in alcohol for now.

Sam props his elbows on the table. "I know I just met you, but I feel like it's my job to tell you that you deserve better than that absolute tool. Right, Parker?"

"Caleb wasn't a bad guy," I say, replying so Parker isn't forced to answer the question. "We fit into each other's lives when we met, and then when everything happened with my business falling through and finding out my dad—" I stop myself short. That was *dangerously* close to revealing TMI, and based on the curious looks I'm getting from both the guys, they know it too. I set my drink on the table, figuring I should slow down unless I want them to know all my deepest, darkest secrets before the night is through. "Let's just say I had some personal stuff going on.

"Anyway, I didn't fit into his life anymore and it turned out he wasn't willing to rearrange his stuff to *make* me fit. Which is fine, you know? I don't want someone to force me into their life. That wouldn't be fair to either one of us. Honestly, with everything else going on, I've hardly thought about him. I'm not sad about the breakup, which makes me think I didn't make room for him in my life, either."

My cheeks go warm as I feel their gazes focus on me.

"Yeah, well, I think you're better off," Sam tells me, glancing at Parker. "Having someone around who doesn't want to be there isn't worth it. I'd rather be let down once by someone leaving than let down over and over again. People can be around and still never show up, you know?"

Parker avoids his friend's gaze, instead holding his hand out for my empty glass. "Can I get you another?" he asks.

I wait for him to follow it with an insult about me being a pampered Princess, but it never comes. "Um ... sure. Thank you."

He holds my gaze for a beat, then nods and slips away, leaving the space beside me drafty and empty.

After finally having an honest conversation with Parker tonight, something in how he looks at me has shifted. It's almost like I have more to offer than he thought ... like he's finally giving me the benefit of the doubt.

I watch him leave, the two of us standing quietly for more than what would be considered a natural pause, when I realize it's not for lack of things to talk about—Sam's watching me with a knowing look on his face that makes me instantly uncomfortable.

I direct the focus back to him. "So, have you always worked for your dad?"

His expression changes quickly. It's a flicker, but for a brief moment, his happy expression since I met him falters to something more serious than I thought he was capable of. Sam edges closer, one hand in his pocket, the other clutching a nearly empty beer bottle. "Uh, no. That was always the plan when my dad opened the garage, but I wanted to do something *important*." He shakes his head, like he's annoyed with himself for the thought. "Turns out working for a big organization isn't as meaningful as I thought, so I went back. I like doing something that makes a difference. Help people, you know?"

I nod. "Your dad must be happy to have you back."

He chuckles, looking more than a little uncomfortable. "Not so much. He, uh ... thinks it's only a matter of time before I end up leaving again. I'm hoping to convince him eventually that I'm sticking around, but ... well. Our relationship is complicated."

I place my hand on his arm. "I'm sorry. I know what that's like, and it sucks."

Sam's gaze drifts down to where my hand is on his arm. "Look, I'm sorry about earlier ... if I came on a little strong? It's just ... I couldn't tell if anything was going on between you two and if there was—Parker sometimes needs a little push to go after things that he wants."

I snatch my hand away, nearly choking on my drink. "Oh—no, there's definitely nothing going on," I say quickly.

He arches an eyebrow at me and grins. "I beg to differ. I know Parker—about as well as anyone can, anyway—and the fact that you're here right now, in his world ... well. It's big."

There's an uncomfortable fluttering in my chest, and I rush to correct him. "Honestly, before tonight, we could barely stand to be in the same room. I mean it—this is what us tolerating each other looks like."

He chuckles. "Well, in that case, hopefully I can find someone who will *tolerate* me like you tolerate him. I'm happy for him. I know he seems like he's got a tough shell, but underneath that, he's a good guy." Something else flickers across his face briefly, and when he speaks again, the playful edge is gone. "Just be gentle with him, will you? He's been let down a fair bit. I'd hate to see him get hurt."

His concern is sweet and seems genuine. Who knew Parker was the bromance type?

"I think you're giving 'the talk' to the wrong girl," I say after a moment, pointing a finger towards the bar.

Sam follows my sightline to where Parker's standing, deep in conversation with a bartender with raven hair running straight down her back. I caught sight of her earlier tonight, and it felt like she was sizing me up. Now I think I have a better idea why, though I'm no closer to understanding the sick feeling swirling in my belly. Maybe the acid reflux is just a side-effect of the drink I downed far more quickly than I intended.

"Oh, that's Cass. She's his brother's girl. Or ... ex-girl, I guess ... He—"

"It's none of my business," I say quickly. Now that the ice between Parker and me seems to be broken (or at least, thawing), finally, something about playing his friend for personal information about him feels wrong. So, I ignore my curiosity, at least for now—about as hard as I'm ignoring the beautiful woman he's leaning over the bar to talk to. Their conversation doesn't look flirtatious, but it does look intimate. I tamp my pesky curiosity into a box and cram it deep into the *don't care* section of my brain.

Turning my focus back to Sam, I tell myself to do what I set out to do tonight and have a good damn time, with or without Parker.

Chapter 12

This is the most important decision of my life.

I stare into the glass case, a hand braced on either side of the full-sized jukebox—a freaking jukebox!—in the far corner of the bar, my face awash in the neon lights framing it as I try to pick the next song. It's not hard to tune out the din of the crowd and the music, which is a nice and reasonable volume—unlike the clubs Caleb used to drag me to constantly. Instead of dark, loud, and impersonal, this place is bright and welcoming, the vibe more like a large house party than anything, where most people seem to know each other and will say hello even if they don't.

"Get lost on your way to the restroom, Princess?" Parker's deep, rumbling voice rolls down my spine. Somewhere along the line, that nickname stopped being an insult, and the box of pesky thoughts I was ignoring must have inched its way back to the front of my brain, because I'm acutely aware of what it's doing to me. Or maybe it's the alcohol talking. That third drink packed one hell of a punch.

I flip my hair over my shoulder and focus on my task. "Shush. I need silence to make this decision."

I *had* gone to the restroom, though, where by force of habit, I'd opened Instagram while waiting in line only to be greeted by a photo of Caleb, looking cozy with two beautiful girls draped over his lap at a fancy-looking club, with the caption: *Massive thanks to these lovelies for taking care of me this weekend @oppulenthouse_club and reminding me that it's fun to be single! #overit #findyourbliss*

I meant what I said earlier that Caleb and I were *not* meant to be. I couldn't care less about him being with someone else. But can you blame me for trying to numb myself from remembering that a few weeks ago, I was trying to move in with that asshat? As it turns out, Long Island iced tea makes that truth go down a little easier. It's also doing a pretty damn good job of letting me forget that I have to call Veronica in the morning and cancel on her, since there's no way I can pull off an impressive enough event for her Instagram-famous BFF. But none of that is important right now.

"I've got it narrowed down to three options," I tell Parker, nodding toward the juke box. I focus on the machine instead of Parker, definitely *not* noticing how he props an elbow on top to lean against the side of it, or what the move does to remind me of his height. "S Club Seven, 'Bring It All Back', Miley Cyrus' 'Party in the USA' and 'Take Me Home, Country Roads.'"

"I say this with all due respect, but back away from the jukebox."

I gasp loudly. "How dare you. I'll have you know, I have excellent taste in music."

"Not to this crowd, you don't."

I frown, instantly annoyed. I don't need the reminder that I'm the outsider here. "Stop calling me that."

He frowns. "Calling you ... what? I didn't call you anything."

I wave my hand in front of my face, annoyed that he can't keep up with my logic. "No, before. Princess. I'm not a princess. You need to stop calling me that."

He grabs the finger I'm pointing at his face and lowers it. "You're right. Sorry." A beat goes by, and all I do is blink at him. "What?"

"You agreed with me. You never agree with me."

He tucks a hand in his pocket, brown eyes zeroing in on mine. "Yeah, well. I didn't know about your bad luck streak or the whole business thing until tonight. I assumed ..."

"That I was some spoiled rich girl flitting around, content to let someone else take care of her?" I finish for him.

He drops his gaze briefly before looking at me again. "Something like that."

I fold my arms, cocking my hip as I stubbornly wait for him to elaborate.

He rolls his eyes but continues, nonetheless. "Tabitha has a big heart and probably a lot of family money. I wanted to make sure you weren't only here because you were using her."

I'm about to let loose a hailstorm of insults when I register what he said. He was worried about Tabitha? Huh. That's ... amazing. And not at all what I was expecting. But then my thoughts catch on something else.

"Wait ... how do you know she has family money?"

He shrugs. "Horses are expensive, and she's an artist. She runs the barn with all those animals and somehow pays me, too, so I logically assumed she inherited money along with the farm when her parents died. Your grandparents, I guess."

"Yeah." My eyes go glassy as I think about them. I used to think I shared my grandmother's blue eyes, something I know now to be impossible. An unfamiliar numbness starts in my fingertips, creeping up to snake around my entire body.

"Sloan? Are you okay?"

Parker's voice sounds further away than it did a minute ago. He takes half a step closer, his hand resting on my elbow. The concern in his eyes is too much, making the sudden tightness in my throat worse and I have to look away.

"Um ... yeah, I ..."

I don't need to dump this odd and confusing bit of personal trivia on him, especially not when I'm buzzed. We might have gotten past the initial threshold that's had us at each other's throats, but we're not quite at the secret sharing point in our relationship yet. Nor do I think we ever will be. I catch sight of a familiar mop of shaggy blond hair and latch onto the opportunity for distraction, calling Sam over. If my sudden shift in demeanor throws Parker, he doesn't say anything.

"What's up, party people?" Sam says, bouncing up to us.

"There's a jukebox," I say, reaching behind to place a hand on the glowing machine. "A *real* jukebox."

Sam grins. "Cool, right? You should pick a song."

Parker groans. "Don't encourage her."

I half turn to see him closer than I remember, and an idea pops into my head. "We should take a picture!" I exclaim. This is the perfect opportunity to give Caleb a taste of his own medicine. And the only thing better than a photo with one guy? A photo with two. I reach for the little black purse at my hip, hunching over it as I try to fish my phone out.

I let out a breathy exclamation when I manage to find it, straightening triumphantly.

As Sam leans in, I scooch sideways, press my back into Parker's chest, and stretch my arm out to take the photo. I feel more than hear his sharp intake of breath, and his hand comes around to rest on my hip, almost as if to catch me. But I didn't stumble; the move was intentional. I pretend to fumble for a few seconds before I take the picture because, for whatever reason, I don't want his hand to move. I like it there, the warm, steady weight on my body, sending a pleasant heat through my core.

But I'm not *that* drunk, so after a few fake fumbles, I take the picture of the three of us with the jukebox in the background and lower my hand, putting a tiny bit of distance between me and Parker as I pretend to examine the photo. I can already imagine the look on Caleb's face when he sees this on Instagram, his only news source.

"Hey, do you mind if I ...?" a bearded guy in unironic plaid points at the jukebox.

"Actually, I was about to—"

"It's all yours." Parker catches me by the elbow, pulling me a few steps away. Someone else calls Sam's name and he disappears behind more plaid.

"But I was almost ready to pick!" I complain.

"No, you weren't. You were going to be there all night."

I peek at the time on my phone and realize how late it is already. I've been having such a good time that I didn't bother to wonder if Parker might want to leave. He was supposed to be meeting Sam here for one drink. He finished his one drink an hour ago and has been nursing an empty bottle since then.

"Sorry. We should go. You have an early morning."

"I do, but I'm not ready to leave yet. Besides, you're supposed to be celebrating."

I wince. In addition to sharing my plan with him to get Tabitha back in the barn more, I may have also bragged to him earlier about the event I thought I would be hosting.

"Turns out I may have been a bit pre-emptive about that."

His amusement shifts to concern. "How come?" he asks, and I could throw my arms around his neck and hug him for taking me seriously right now.

I manage to refrain, explaining in as few words as possible that the bride-to-be isn't a regular bride, but an uber-famous blogger whose expectations would be impossible to meet, let alone exceed.

"So, what ... you're just not doing it?"

I shrug. "There's no way I can pull it off. The whole point of doing it was to get some closure for the business that—let's face it, I probably won't ever open." I've come to accept that if Lyla and I can't make it work now with no kids or other responsibilities getting in the way, it will never happen. "I've already failed to launch the business; I don't need the only event I host to be an epic failure too."

"Why are you assuming you'll fail? Sloan, you're the most stubborn person I've ever met. If you want to crush this event, you'll find a way to make it happen."

I grab his shoulders, feeling much too drunk to convey the severity of this situation. "Parker, you don't understand. She's not a regular bride! She has like *a million* followers. A bad review from her would forever tarnish my reputation. Forget ever starting my business, my side hustle would be history, too."

He mirrors my pose, his hands settling on my shoulders. "Isn't every bride-to-be supposed to feel like the most important person in the world?" he asks.

"Well ... yes."

He lifts a brow. "Then why would someone famous be any different?"

I let my eyes travel across his features, the alcohol coursing through my veins, meaning I don't bother to worry about the fact that he's watching me do it.

"Why do you care?" I ask, the music and chatter of people around us falling into the background.

He shakes his head. "Because it's important to you. I think people should do the things that matter to them."

The music changes, and our eyes widen at the same time.

"You've gotta be shitting me."

I hop up and down, clapping my hands excitedly as the crowd around us sings along, the place suddenly louder than it's been all night. "I *told* you it would be the perfect song!"

At the chorus of *Country Roads*, he leans in closer than he has to for me to hear him.

"Okay, okay. I guess you were right."

I draw back so I can see his eyes, glinting with amusement.

"Wow, admitting I was right twice in one night? Careful, Parker. You're making it hard to remember that you hate me."

He dips his chin so his gaze falls to the floor. Again, he doesn't meet my eyes, but he leans close to answer. His voice is warm in my ear, my entire body tingling. "I thought I made it pretty clear that I don't hate you at all."

My legs wobble. Without thinking, I place a palm on his chest to steady myself. One arm curls around my waist, his nose grazing the shell of my ear. He dips his head, the sharp stubble of his cheek rubbing against mine as he pulls me closer. Bodies surround us, everyone singing along as the song crescendos—everyone except us. I can feel the heat of his chest radiating through the fabric of his button-down shirt, and all I can think about is how badly I want to sink into him and let him swallow me up. Then someone jostles me roughly from behind.

We stumble, the fragile spell that had fallen over us breaking. I take a step back. I need to get my head on straight before I do something stupid. Something I'll regret tomorrow. The touching, the sexy things he's saying—it's all in my head. I'm spinning his words, his touch, into something it isn't, and it will get us both into trouble. With the tension coiled tightly inside my stomach right now, gathering between my legs, being alone with Parker is the last place I should be. So, when the song ends and he asks if I'm ready to call it a night, I do what any sane woman would do in my position.

I order another drink.

"Whoa, Sloan, hold up," Parker calls after me when we finally leave the bar an hour later, but I hardly register it as I peel left and march down the sidewalk to the thing that's beckoning me.

"Hey! Where do you think you're going? The truck is that way!"

"Need. Pancakes." I half-slur, half-shout over my shoulder as I power-walk down the empty sidewalk, the yellow glow of streetlights lighting my way.

Sam laughs and wishes him luck, and I glance back to make sure the quickened steps behind me are Parker before I continue forward.

"Goodnight, beautiful!" Sam calls after me.

I wave over my shoulder without looking back. I'm mad at him right now. It's his fault I feel like this; the fog thickened into a permanent fixture in my brain. It took me two more shots with Sam to finally decide it was safe to be alone with Parker without the risk of climbing him like a tree. Once I'd walked away from him on the dance floor, I'd been careful to keep a healthy distance between us. It was enough to clear my brain of the unwanted lust he'd somehow inflicted on me—the bastard.

At this point, I'm sure I'm only feeling this way because of sheer biology. It has little—to nothing—to do with me being attracted to Parker, specifically. Let's face it, my sex life with Caleb hadn't exactly been anything to write to *Cosmo* about at the best of times. At the worst of times, as lately, it was almost non-existent. Which was mostly my fault. I was busy working long days and late nights that I was asleep before I hit the pillow by the time I went to bed. And everything has been bottling up.

A girl's got needs. Just not ones that should be addressed by her aunt's sexy farm hand, who, until three hours ago, couldn't even stand to be around me.

"For the last time, you won't find pancakes at midnight."

I frown, but I'm a woman on a mission, and several paces ahead of Parker, so it's less than effective. I power forward until I reach the diner, ignoring that all the lights are off as I reach for the door, which doesn't budge. I try again.

"How's that working out for you?"

I turn and glare at Parker with his cocky grin. The cold night air and fog in my head leave no room for the pleasant thoughts I was starting to have about him earlier. Good. I give the door one last tug before cupping my hands against the glass and peering inside.

"This is tragic," I declare.

"My god, you're dramatic. It's late. I told you everything closes by nine."

"*Ughhhh.*" I slide my back down the glass door until I'm in a sitting position, my legs stretched out on the cold concrete. My bare skin immediately pebbles with goosebumps as a shiver runs through me.

Parker crouches in front of me, his eyes filled with worry. "Whoa, Sloan. Are you okay? Why are you sitting on the ground?"

"Because I can't get pancakes."

His pretty mouth flickers. "And ... what? You're going to wait here until they open in the morning?"

I shake my head firmly, then dig my phone out of my purse again and tap the screen to set a timer. "I'm having a five-minute wallow."

"I'm sorry ... what?"

I hold up my phone for him to see. "It's my rule. When something goes wrong, I let myself have five minutes to acknowledge that whatever is happening is shitty. Five minutes, and five minutes only. Then I pick myself up and move on."

"You make it sound like this is rock bottom. Trust me, you didn't see the guy who barely reached the bathroom after doing a tray of tequila shots. *That's* rock bottom."

"I know. And when the timer goes off, I'll remember that. But until then, I will let myself be dramatic and feel like not getting a pancake is the worst thing that could happen to me right now. After that, I'll focus on all the reasons it's not."

I say this all firmly, without a hint of apology. Not that I need to explain myself, least of all to Parker. But he questions me so much that I want to. Even though I don't care what he thinks about me, I want him to know that there's a valid reason behind my actions.

Parker frowns at me. "Five minutes, huh? In that case, take this." He shrugs his jacket off and gestures for me to move so he can set it on the pavement. Too stunned to say anything, I settle back onto it, my bare legs now protected from the cold concrete below me, if not from the night air, but it makes enough of a difference. He shifts, lowering himself beside me with his back against the wall, feet outstretched like mine. A few inches separate us, but I'm too drunk to feel the chill in the space between my arm and his.

He chuckles. "You are ..."

"Obnoxious? Unbelievable? A hot mess?"

"I was going to say ... not what I was expecting."

I swivel my neck to stick him with my best attempt at a hard look. "Why? What were you expecting?"

He thinks about this briefly, tilting his head to one side. "When Tabitha would tell me about you—which was a lot, by the way—she always used the word 'sweet.'"

I laugh, dropping my eyes. How many times have I heard that in my life? Sweet, nice, quiet, helpful. I'm pretty sure they'll all end up on my tombstone.

"I'm not convinced it's true," he says. "No offense, but I still haven't seen that side of you."

I grin at him. "What can I say? I like to defy expectations." My smile fades, and I drop my gaze to my lap. "No, that's a lie. Usually, I like to be exactly what people expect. No ruffling feathers, no rocking the boat, no ... I can't think of another metaphor."

He chuckles softly beside me. "Usually," he repeats. "But not with me." It isn't a question.

His eyes are on me again, soft and probing. I have to tilt my chin slightly to meet them, so my gaze drifts first over his mouth and the stubble that's a little more pronounced than it is during the day, even in the shadowy light of the darkened street.

"No. Not with you."

His lips twitch. "Keeps my days interesting, at least. Between you and me, sweet is overrated."

I'll give him that. Life has been more interesting since I've abandoned my mission to people-please regarding Parker. Somehow, in such a short time, it's become the part of my day I look forward to the most. He challenges me. Instead of shoving the big feelings down when I'm around him, letting out only a fraction of what I'm thinking, it's freeing to say whatever's on my mind. Though after a few drinks, it seems my filter is gone entirely.

"You'd be much easier to hate if you weren't so pretty."

His eyes snap to mine, eyebrows raised high on his forehead.

"I mean it," I continue, scrutinizing his face. "Why couldn't you have had ... an eye patch, or a big scar, or something?"

Amusement dances in his brown eyes. "What you're describing is a pirate, Sloan."

I click my tongue impatiently, looking straight ahead as I bristle with annoyance. "Whatever. Knowing you, a scar would probably make you *better* looking, anyway. Dick."

He laughs again. I peek at him from the corner of my eye, and his smile is contagious.

Shifting, he angles his shoulders so he's facing me a bit better. "So, to be clear—because I don't mind saying you are a mystery to me at the best of times—you don't hate me?"

"No, Parker insert-last-name-here. I don't hate you."

"Ryan."

"I wish I did, though." I frown. "Who's Ryan?"

"It's my last name, genius. Why do you wish you hated me?"

"That's a first name. Parker is a last name. Your names are backward, did you know that?"

He ignores me. "Why do you wish you hated me?"

My eyes get trapped in his as he waits for my answer. I sigh, a deep, long, heavy breath that forces all the air from my lungs. *Because you're not part of the plan. Because you make things messy and complicated, and I came here to get away from messy and complicated.*

Between us on the ground, my phone trills, breaking the moment.

"Time's up," I say, turning it off. I prepare to push up from the ground, but he stops me.

"I never thanked you for earlier," he says quietly, and it doesn't take a genius—or a sober person—to realize it took a lot for him to say that out loud.

I could brush it off with a *don't mention it*, but I know him well enough by now. He wouldn't bring it up if he didn't want to talk about it, and it sounds like Parker is used to taking care of everyone around him.

He has people in his life, but I don't know if he can talk to them about the more complicated things, the messy, grey area thoughts you're still working through, that can feel like a burden to put on someone else. It's why I keep telling Lyla I'm fine, that nothing has changed. Except ... I think I have. But having no one to talk to about it makes going through this not only scary but lonely, too.

Knowing what I do now about Parker, I wonder if he's in a similar boat. So I ask the question he probably hasn't been asked before.

"Do you give your dad money often?"

His head snaps to mine, but I'm still too drunk to be self-conscious.

"Sorry," I say. "I saw it in your glove compartment. I wasn't snooping, I swear, I was looking for a phone charger and it was right there."

He sighs. "It's okay. If I didn't want you to know, I probably shouldn't have brought you with me to deliver it."

We're quiet for a beat, neither moving to get up.

"I think it's really big of you to help your dad out," I say, choosing my words carefully. "You shouldn't feel like you have to hide that."

"I don't." He lets out a breath. "Or maybe I do. I don't know. I don't have the best relationship with my dad. Certain people have told me I should do myself a favor and cut him off for good, let him figure out how to fend for himself. Otherwise, he never will."

I remember the bartender he was talking to, the woman Sam said was his brother's ex.

"Cass?"

He nods. "Sam's mentioned it once or twice, too. They know he doesn't always use the money super responsibly. I guess I got in the habit of hiding it without even realizing it." His head tips back, letting it rest against the glass door, looking tired for reasons that have nothing to do with being up past his bedtime.

"But you won't," I supply, knowing the answer.

"Maybe there's part of me that likes knowing he needs me. Whether he likes it or not. It means he can't disappear. Not for longer than a few days, at least."

I remember what he told me that day in the barn about his mom. *Long gone*, he'd said.

Reaching out, I place my hand on his arm. "I'm sure he appreciates it, even if he doesn't know how to show it," I say gently. I'm not sure I believe that, but if it makes Parker feel better, I don't mind the lie.

He scoffs, the air escaping his nose as he drops his chin. He picks at a fraying seam on his jeans, shaking his head. "It's penance. He says I owe it to him for trying to leave with my mom."

I frown, my mind racing as I try to imagine the circumstances. In the distance, noise from the bar continues to drift out into the otherwise deserted area, the music swelling every time the door opens.

"When you told me she left, I assumed you chose to stay here."

He doesn't meet my eyes. "Yeah, well. Most people don't assume that a mom would refuse their fifteen-year-old kid begging her to take them with her because she wanted a clean break."

"She said that?" My question comes out breathy with disbelief.

He nods. "Said I looked too much like my dad when she met him. She couldn't stand looking at me, waiting to see me turn into the man he did."

"Parker," I whisper, my heart breaking for him.

"People make mistakes," he says, stoic as usual. "I know I do. I try to be a good person and keep mine to a minimum. That's why I like working at Salem Stables for Tibby. I can keep to myself, keep my head down, and still be close enough to keep an eye on my dad and Cass. Tibby's the only person who has ever judged me for me—not the mistakes my dad has made." He turns his head to catch my eye. "Well, and now you, too, I guess. Thanks for that."

A laugh bursts out of me. "We've been at each other's throats since I got here and you're thanking me?"

He shrugs. "Yes. There's no question when it comes to you, Sloan—if you're pissed at me, it's about *me*. I can own that. And when I say if, I mean when."

Everything about him makes so much sense now. In one night, my entire perception of Parker has changed. I came in having judged him before I met him based on the actions of Tabitha's past employers—people he'd never worked with, or even met. Of course, that was going to rub him the wrong way. Salem Stables isn't just *my* happy place anymore—it's his, too. And I threatened to take it away from him when I got here.

"I held you accountable for other people's actions when I met you, which was wrong of me. I hated you for making assumptions about who I was, but I was doing the same thing. Can you forgive me?"

"What, like ... start over?" he asks hesitantly.

"Yeah, but let's not do that cringey thing where we re-introduce ourselves and pretend we're meeting for the first time, because *blech.*" Beside me, he laughs, the sound travelling through my arm where it connects with his and pooling in my belly. I beam, grateful that he seems a bit lighter than before. "Besides, you have done plenty for me to hold you personally accountable, and I don't plan to let you off the hook, mister."

The grin in his voice is audible. "Is that so?"

"Mhmm." I hold up my fingers and start ticking things off. "There was the horse poop you put in my good running shoes." He snorts, and I pretend to scowl at him. "Hiding the pitchforks so I couldn't do any work, and don't think I've forgiven you for letting me think I was losing them myself."

His laughter is full-on now, and I cross my arms, pretending to be annoyed. "You're on thin ice, my friend. *Very* thin ice."

As his laughter fades, I turn my face to his. His eyes drop to my lips for a second. "Guess I'll have to find a way to make it up to you."

There's a weight to his words that wasn't there a moment ago, and my smile fades as I peer up at him, meeting his intense gaze.

Oh boy. I am definitely in trouble.

Chapter 13

When we arrive at the farmer's market the next morning, the parking lot of the local baseball diamond is already full with vendors setting up tents, tables, and unloading their goods for the day. Joining Tabitha was my idea, but in my defense, it seemed like a much better one last night when I was looking for ways to avoid a certain someone. Shivering next to the trunk in the brisk fall air, my eyes barely open in the early dawn haze, I want nothing more than to crawl back into the warmth of my cozy bed—the one I had to vacate before five a.m. to make sure Tabitha didn't leave me behind.

"Put some pep in your step, girl. We're going to be late." Tabitha passes me a tote bin, propping another on her hip before she shuts the trunk of Parker's truck, which he let her borrow until the part comes in for her Jeep.

"Nobody in their right mind should be vertical this early. It's inhuman."

"Don't you mean inhumane?" she asks, ushering me along the outfield where dozens of pop-up tents are set up in neat rows and locating our table amidst the other vendors setting up shop.

"Same difference," I mutter, struggling to keep up. "Seriously, how do this many people collectively agree to social activities this early in the morning?" My frown deepens at her chuckle. "I'm so glad you're enjoying this."

"May I remind you that you're the one who insisted on coming with me, even though you didn't stumble through the door until after midnight?"

I pull my jacket tighter around me and grunt. "I didn't *stumble*."

She laughs, not bothering to lower her voice as people wander by. "You ping ponged your way down the hall to your room. Not to mention, you nearly threw yourself down the stairs this morning to catch me before I left."

True, but that was by necessity, not choice. My other option was facing Parker at the barn. How was I supposed to do that after revealing as much as I did last night? I practically admitted I'm attracted to him. What scares me more than that is that those feelings didn't seem entirely one-sided. Do I really need to let myself get pulled into something that will make my life even more complicated than it already is? What's the point when it will blow up in my face like everything else?

He probably woke up just as baffled by last night as I am. The one good thing that came from last night is that we no longer actively hate each other, so there's a chance that once we let whatever happened ... fizzle a little ... we might actually be friends.

I won't lie; my pounding headache is helping me forget about any warm and fuzzy feelings brewing last night in the darkened bar.

"Buckle up, missy," Tabitha says, insisting on speaking at a higher-than-usual volume this morning. "Everyone you'll meet here has been up for hours. And you're a new face, so they're all going to want to talk to you."

"Great," I mumble. *Just great.*

Within thirty minutes, I've met Gretchen the jam-maker, Denise at the booth next door who sells free-range eggs, and Barb, who sells hand-knit Christmas ornaments year-round. All three ask if I'm married and have kids.

"Sorry about that," Tabitha says after waving off the last of them. "They're nosy but harmless."

"I can't wait for the day when the billboard above my head comes down."

"Billboard?" she asks with a frown.

I take a last sip of coffee and set the empty travel mug under the table. "The one that says, 'Ask me about my personal life.' I figure it'll happen at thirty-five."

"Oh, honey," Tabitha says, draping an arm over my shoulders. The easy gesture makes my heart swell. "I hate to break it to you. The questions? They never stop."

"Seriously? Even for you?"

She nods, straightening the products displayed on the long folding table under our tent. "I'm a single woman in my fifties. What do you think? You're shiny and new, so they were distracted today, but wait until next week. You'll see."

"If they were better friends, they'd have set you up with a hot piece of man candy by now."

She makes a face and smacks my arm gently before rearranging the table. "Believe me, they try every week. I swear they have a rotation schedule of who's trying to set me up—lately they've been inviting someone new to cards every week." She rolls her eyes.

"And?"

She laughs. "And nothing. I'm like an old dog, set in my ways. I love the farm and my studio. There was a time when I could have been whisked away from it, but that time is long gone. I like my life, my routines. Things are perfect just as they are. I don't need somebody coming in and shaking things up now."

I feel a sharp dig in my ribs, reminded that I'm keeping something from her that is bound to *shake things up*, but swallow it down.

"You're telling me you *never* think about getting back out there? Like, romantically?" I waggle my eyebrows playfully, suddenly feeling very invested in getting her on board with this.

She places her hands on my shoulders. "You're sweet to worry about me, like all my meddlesome friends, but I'm not a hermit. I'm on the farmer's market committee, and I play cards with my friends every Wednesday. I'm quite content."

"Then it means absolutely nothing to you that a handsome man in a trucker hat is headed this way?"

She jumps and whips around. The man, dressed casually in jeans, work boots, and a puffy black vest over a green Henley, falters slightly, like he wasn't expecting her to turn around so sharply. Hesitantly, he lifts his hand in a wave, smiling as he continues towards us.

"Oh, that's just Jim," Tabitha says, laughing me off. There's a flush in her cheeks that has nothing to do with the brisk morning air.

"*Just* Jim, huh?" I tease. "Well, 'Just Jim' managed to turn your face awfully pink."

"That's—the wind," she says nervously before he reaches us. "Jim, hi!"

I have to cover my smile with my hand at the loudness of her greeting, suppressing it quickly as he looks over at me. Tabitha, suddenly flustered, introduces me.

"It's great to meet you finally," he says. "Tabitha's told me a lot about you."

I shake his hand, smiling at Tabitha as I do. "Has she now?" I ask slowly. "So, you two know each other well, then?"

"Oh, you know," Tabitha says casually, her voice still pitched at a higher-than-normal register. "It's a small town."

"It helps that we sit on the farmer's market committee together," Jim adds, giving me a soft, self-assured smile. He's tall, with thick brown hair graying at the temples under a trucker hat. He gives off that wholesome, farmer vibe—and based on the way he keeps glancing at Tabitha, who is needlessly rearranging things on the table again, I'd guess he's also single.

"Listen, not to pull you away from your lovely niece, but I wondered if you had time to discuss ideas for the last market?" He turns to me to explain. "It's been a slower-than-normal year, so we want to do something special for the last day to end with a bang and get people excited for next year. We need to get creative to generate some interest, but so far, we're stumped."

Looking around the sparsely attended market, I see his point. I'm not at this time of year, but Tabitha's had a booth at the farmer's market for years—every Thursday all summer and fall, like clockwork. Second to the Christmas bazaars in December during the holiday season, it's where she makes a decent chunk of her income every year. But we've been standing here for an hour already, and although we had a few people stop to look, she hasn't sold a single piece today.

"Sure, I suppose I can spare a few minutes," Tabitha says, regaining her composure. "You don't mind holding down the fort for a few minutes, do you, Sloan?"

Normally, I would agree in a heartbeat, but an idea tickles the back of my brain, and I pause. Tabitha's already starting to move away, so sure that I'm going to tell her I've got it covered.

"This sounds like a bigger conversation than a few minutes, don't you think?" I say, surprising them both. "I mean, you want to ensure you're setting next year's market up for the kind of success these vendors depend on. This is their livelihood, after all." Tabitha looks at me warily, and I rush on, pretending to be struck with a brilliant idea. "I know! Why don't you talk about it over dinner?"

"*Dinner?!*" Tabitha echoes, her head snapping between Jim and me.

"Tonight," I say, careful not to make it sound like a question.

With his hands in his pockets, Jim dips his chin to hide his amusement. At least one of them is clueing in. "Sounds good to me," he says, playing his part perfectly. "Is seven okay?"

Smooth. Tabitha, however, looks quite the opposite and has gone back to being completely and utterly flustered. "Oh—uh—I—"

"Seven is *great*," I answer for her, grasping her arm and snapping her close to my side to steady her. The poor thing looks like she's about to fall over. "You have the address to Salem Stables?"

He nods, his eyes twinkling—actually *twinkling*—with amusement. I'm pretty sure this guy walked straight out of a Hallmark movie. "Yes, ma'am. I'm up the road myself. We're practically neighbors."

"She'll see you then!" I say firmly.

He nods, his eyes on Tabitha. "I'll be looking forward to it. Nice to finally meet you, Sloan." He tips the brim of his trucker hat at me and gives Tabitha one last charming smile.

"I can't believe you," Tabitha mutters as he strolls away. "Who are you, and what have you done to my niece?"

Frazzled, she busies herself with straightening up the already tidy booth. I can't lie, I'm feeling smug—until I realize that Tabitha is going out tonight, which means I'll be home alone without a buffer if a certain farmhand decides to stop in.

A woman has needs and having a whole house to myself for the first time in months, there's only one thing on my mind. The mood is set; lights low, a glass of wine left over from the other night, doors locked (of course).

And a *Scream* marathon is about to start on TV.

The microwave beeps, and I hurry into the kitchen to dump a fresh bag of popcorn into a giant plastic bowl. I step over to the sink to wash the butter off my fingers—and find a face staring at me through the window.

The shriek I let out rattles the windowpane.

Popcorn goes flying.

And then I realize who's standing there.

"Jesus, would you stop doing that?" Parker yells from the enclosed porch.

With a hand on my heart, I unlock the back door and fling it open, stepping aside to let him in the rest of the way.

"Stop sneaking up on me and I won't have to. That's it. I'm buying you a bell."

"Or you could just leave the door unlocked."

I've listened to far too many podcasts ever to do that again. "Yeah, that's not happening. So ... what's up?"

"Oh, uh ... the plumbing in the cabin is acting up again. Tabitha said I could shower here ... didn't she tell you?" He crouches down to help me gather the spilled popcorn from the tiles, and that's when I notice the towel he's holding.

"She must have forgotten," I say, knowing she one hundred percent did this on purpose as payback. But then I look up and realize how close Parker's face is to mine, and my brain goes offline for a beat.

"So ... is that okay?" he asks, lifting his eyebrows. Oh god, how long have I been staring at him?

"Oh, right. Of course," I sputter, going for casual and missing it by a mile. *Smooth, Sloan.* "Obviously, you're welcome to use the shower."

He gives me a strange look like he's trying to figure out if I'm serious, and eventually, I wonder what he's waiting for.

"I'm not a bridge troll; I'm not going to make you answer a riddle first or anything."

He shakes his head, looking more baffled than annoyed. "There it is again."

"There's what?" I ask, his brown eyes holding mine hostage.

"Every time I think I have you figured out, you go and say something like that."

The air in the kitchen feels thick, a hyper-awareness zinging through me from head to toe. Dropping the last handful of popcorn back in the bowl, he pushes to his feet, leaving me crouched, frozen on the floor until the bathroom door upstairs clicks shut. Somewhere in the ten minutes it takes him to shower—during which I am *not* thinking about him upstairs—I pull myself together and relocate to the couch before the water shuts off.

"I'm coming down, don't freak out," Parker calls from the top of the stairs a few minutes later.

I hit the mute button. "I've got a firm grip on my popcorn this time, just in case."

He pokes his head around the wall, the corner of his lip edging up. "Thanks for the shower. I won't smell like horses for at least ten hours, now." He nods in the direction of the TV. "I guess this explains your greeting. Sorry I made you miss the beginning."

"Don't worry, I've seen it at least twenty times. Here, I'll walk you out to lock the door behind you." I'm halfway to standing when I pause, and the next thing that pops into my head is off my lips before I can think it through. "Unless you want to stay and watch?"

He seems as surprised by my question as I am, but after a beat of indecision, he nods and sits on the opposite end of the couch, literally as far away from me as he can get.

"Beer?" I offer.

He nods.

I bring him one from the kitchen and trade it for the wet towel and toiletries kit on his lap, which I set down on the coffee table for him. He looked unsure of what to do with them, and I don't want to watch him awkwardly hold them for the whole movie as he tries to decide whether he's allowed to put them down. Unmuting the TV, I settle in again on my side of the couch, studying him from the corner of my eye. He doesn't seem as comfortable in this part of the house as in the kitchen. Mentally, I file 'respecting boundaries' away as another item in the pro column for Parker, an area where Tabitha's other staff have been sorely lacking.

He opens the beer (good, it was a twist-off—unless he's just that freakishly strong) and asks what he missed.

"I can't believe you've never seen *Scream*," I say after explaining the first half hour of the plot.

He takes a handful of fresh popcorn when I offer him the bowl and shoves it all in his mouth, talking through it. "I can't believe someone as jumpy as you watches horror movies voluntarily."

The truth is, I know exactly why I watch scary movies and listen to true crime podcasts. I've never told anyone—not Lyla, my parents, or even Tabitha. Somehow, Parker is different. Whether he's being his usual, infuriatingly grumpy self or uncharacteristically gentle, something freeing about him lets me open up and tap into the parts of myself that I always keep locked away because I'm trying to be reasonable. Likable.

I certainly haven't tried to hide any part of myself to get Parker's affection. Yet, here he is, watching a movie with me.

"It's like a test," I say finally, the movie forgotten in the background. "I'm not brave. I've never been a risk-taker. But I'd like to think that if it ever came down to it, I would be when it counted. I guess it's my way of holding my finger over the flame."

He's quiet for a minute, letting my confession settle between us. "You mean your hand."

"My hand what?"

"The saying. It's holding your *hand* over the flame, not your finger."

I kick out my right foot that's tucked under me and drive my big toe into his side. It catches him off guard, causing him to double over, and my god, the smile that splits his face as a peel of uninhibited laughter bursts out of him is a thing of beauty. I want to take a picture to freeze this moment and capture it forever —this precious smile I somehow get for free.

No, not for free. I've *earned* this smile.

After a weeks-long battle that I still don't know the rules to, the constant needling, holding my ground when he wanted to push me away, I thought I was still trying to figure him out. But maybe ... I already have?

That truth settles as deep as the blood in my veins as his hand closes around my ankle and stills my foot. My world narrows to the sound of my heart hammering in my eardrums and the feel of the soft pad of his thumb on my exposed ankle.

Can ankles even be an erogenous zone? It's never been one for me, but Parker is making me feel all the things I never have before. No wonder women used to have to keep them covered up. For the first time, I get what all the fuss was about.

It's a night of firsts. This is the first time I've seen him relax since I got here. The first time he's let his guard down. His hair, still wet from the shower, curls slightly above his ears, his clean, forest green T-shirt clinging to his still-damp skin. It's also the first time we've had any prolonged physical contact. The movie keeps playing and we stay like this, my foot propped in his lap. Eventually, his thumb begins to move. Tiny, gentle brushstrokes over my skin, giving me a reassuring squeeze when I tense up at the scary parts, even though I know they're coming.

During one of the last commercial breaks, an ad for Scream 2 pops up, starting next.

"There's another one?"

"Yeah, a bunch, actually. You chicken?" I hold my breath, waiting. If he takes the out, it's possible he's still touching my foot because I haven't removed it from his lap. In which case, I'll have to schedule a lobotomy first thing Monday morning.

"Sure. I'm in." He leans forward, reaching for his beer on the coffee table, holding my foot in place as he drains it.

No longer (as) afraid to pop this bubble we're in, I stretch my other leg out when he leans back, resting it on his lap. His hand hovers for a second, then two, before it settles back into place.

"So ... what did you decide about the event?" he asks as the commercials continue to play.

His voice is a low rumble I can feel through my leg. Heat pools in my core, and I do my best to ignore it.

"I haven't canceled. Yet." Last night, Parker's words had bolstered my confidence, but the cold light of day has brought back all the doubts that had me twisted up in the first place. "I want to do it, but I'm not sure I could handle it alone. My friend, Lyla, she—"

"Bailed on you. Yeah. I remember."

"'Pressed pause' is how she worded it," I correct, though the last few times we've talked, she's changed the subject almost immediately whenever I ask her if she wants to start planning for a new launch date. "I'm great at coming up with ideas, but I've never been the decider, you know? Lyla always knows which idea will work, even when it's half-finished and looks like we've made a horrible mistake."

"But I mean, you could. Right?" he presses.

I sigh. Suppose I was a bolder person, yes. But to be bold, one must be confident. That's an area I have always lacked. "I've always been part of a team. It's safer that way." My words are small when they make their way out. "Because if I fail, it's not just my fault. Not because I want someone else to blame, it's just that ..."

The words catch in my throat. On screen, blood splatters against the glass of the AV room as Courtney Cox screams from the other side for her boyfriend. But neither of us is watching TV anymore.

"You don't want to let anyone down."

How about that? Without me even trying, he seems to have figured me out. I nod.

"Listen, Sloan. About what you said before ..." He swallows hard, staring at my feet. "I think you're braver than you give yourself credit for."

His chin lifts as he turns to face me, his brown eyes meeting mine.

"I know we said we were starting over, but can you at least pretend to hate me?" I say, my voice shaking slightly.

The air thickens, my blood pumping faster as I sit trapped under the intensity of his gaze.

I jump up. "Let me grab you another beer." I would have preferred amputating both feet to removing them from his grasp, but I'm short on time.

In the kitchen, I don't bother turning on the light. The yellow glow from the fridge is all I need to find another beer buried at the back, and I stay there several seconds longer than I need to, letting the cool air lower my body temperature. It might be October, but I am on fire.

Closing the fridge, I let out a strangled yelp when I find I'm not alone. Parker takes one step closer, then another, backing me up against the fridge door, moving every time he goes to say something and can't find the words.

And boy, do I hope he never speaks again. My skin is electrified from how he's looking at me right now, the way our thighs brush when he closes the gap between us completely, his chest bumping mine.

"I don't hate you," he chokes out. His big arms frame either side of my head against the stainless steel. "Far from it."

His eyes dart to my parted lips and he leans closer. My back arches, but he stops me. As his left hand drops to my cheek, his forearm rests against my shoulder, blocking me from getting any closer. But not like he's pushing me away, more like he's trying to keep his distance. He strokes his thumb over my jawline, eyes dipping to my lips.

"Sloan, I ... need this job. I can't do anything to risk it."

I hear the fear in his voice, but the words don't match the burning look he pins me with next. Heat licks my skin from head to toe, my mind racing as I imagine what he'll do next. Imagining his hands lifting me against him, wrapping my legs around his waist, his hips pressing hard into mine. My hips rock of their own accord, the pressure doing little to ease the growing ache between my thighs. A curse falls out of him, and I witness his resolve break in real time as he leans closer, our mouths a breath apart.

The slam of a car door has us jolting apart, and we both blink as laughter rings out on the porch. In the same instant, my brain registers it's Tabitha coming home, he's moving away from me and into the living room. I'm still propped up against the fridge, grappling with his words, when he passes me again with his belongings. He meets my eyes for one last lingering look, his own full of something I don't recognize, before he slips out the back door, leaving me stunned in the cow-filled kitchen.

What the hell almost just happened?

Chapter 14

The problem with avoiding someone you basically live with is that it's virtually impossible, especially when you have a meddlesome, revenge-seeking aunt with an ax to grind.

"Tabitha, *please* don't do this!" I beg as I chase her across the sun-soaked yard to the barn, fallen leaves crunching underfoot.

"What was that? I can't hear you over all the dates you're setting me up on," she replies coolly, undeterred from her mission.

"It was *one* dinner! And I thought it was a *business* meeting; you're the one calling it a date. But you know what? I'm not going to read into that, because we have a relationship based on mutual respect. *Right?*" I ask pointedly.

Tabitha doesn't miss a beat. "Nuh-uh, I don't think so. Besides, fair is fair. You meddle in my love life, I meddle in yours."

My cheeks are on fire, and it has nothing to do with the above-seasonal average temperature today, one of those random fall days that feels more like the end of August than October. I'm noticing the change in seasons, which is a stark reminder of how long I've been here already. It's been almost a month, and I still haven't told Tabitha about our new family dynamic. I haven't had a real conversation with my parents about the situation or discussed with Lyla what happens next. But it hasn't been a complete waste of time. Parker and I have come a long way in the last few weeks—from hostile enemies to grudging adversaries to ... what exactly *are* we now? Friends? More than that?

Friends generally don't push each other up against kitchen appliances and look at each other like they want to rip each other's clothes off. But Parker was honest last night about his concerns—even though he didn't say much, I heard him loud and clear. And whatever we are, we're not enemies anymore, so I plan to respect his wishes. Granted, sending his boss storming into the barn to demand an act of chivalry typically relegated to a boyfriend is not a great way of showing him that.

"*Shhh!*" I hiss desperately, grabbing her elbow. "Please, for the love of god—*Tapioca!*"

It's a last-ditch attempt, my Hail Mary.

And it works.

Tabitha stops dead in her tracks, facing me with an all-knowing grin. "Well, well, well," she says smugly. "This is gonna be good."

My eyes fall shut. I've raised a red flag, but even if I have to suffer the humiliation of explaining myself to Tabitha, at least I can spare Parker. *Tapioca* is the code word we came up with years ago, and we use it any time we need to share something that must, under all circumstances, stay just between us. It's our version of going off the record. No matter what it is, we have to respect it.

I close the distance between us, lowering my voice as much as possible in case Parker is nearby on the other side of the barn door. "Okay, *fine*. There *may* have been a moment between Parker and me last night. And at the bar."

Her eyes widen like she's just heard the best news of her life, so I continue quickly before she can start weaving any fantasies in her mind.

"But it won't lead to anything because we both agreed it wasn't a good idea." Not true, strictly speaking, since I had a very small role in last night's conversation in the kitchen, but I'm trying hard to hold onto what little dignity I have left. "We agreed to stay friends, and I'm trying to give him space, so you can see how you marching in there expecting him to drive me around would be a little awkward," I finish, throwing my arm toward the barn.

She frowns. "You two were never friends."

"Well, we're going to be."

I know I've made a mistake before she says, "Perfect! He won't mind doing his new *friend* a favor then. Oh, *Par*-ker!"

I groan as she sings her way into the bright barn, afternoon sunlight pouring in from the windows above the concrete walls of every stall. I never should have gone with Parker to the bar the other night. Tabitha likes to stir things up, but at least she's been in a better mood since she started to make progress with her commissions.

Something rustles directly above our heads. I tilt my chin—and push Tabitha out of the way as a bale of hay careens toward us.

"Are you trying to kill us?!" I shout.

Parker's confused face peers over the edge of a hole in the ceiling, a few seconds later. "Shit, sorry. Thought the barn was empty. You okay?"

"I ... yes. We're fine."

"Almost done?" Tabitha asks, completely unbothered by the near squashing.

"Give me a second, I'll be right down. Stand back, I'm sending a few more down."

"That was close," Tabitha says, steering us to stand against an empty stall—all of the horses are outside enjoying the weather—and we watch three more hay bales drop from the ceiling in succession to bounce on top of each other before rolling onto the concrete floor—the previously *spotless* floor, which I just finished sweeping an hour ago.

"That was karma," I mutter as the trapdoor slides shut, scowling when Tabitha laughs at me. Heavy footsteps clunk down the wooden staircase to the hayloft.

"What's up?" Parker asks when he comes into sight, his eyes locking squarely on Tabitha. He's wearing a T-shirt that shows off the muscles of his arms, which I force myself not to look at. I wait for him to look at me, but he doesn't.

"We're in a bind," Tabitha tells him, looping an arm around my shoulder. "Sloan needs to gather supplies for the event this weekend, but I won't have my Jeep back until tomorrow. You don't mind driving her into town, do you?"

Finally, his eyes cut to mine, the panic evident. I try to communicate a silent apology, but he looks away.

"I've still got a lot to do today."

Well, that was ... blunt.

He bends, grabbing a bale by the strings, hauling it in front of him, and depositing it at the side for the evening feeding. Tabitha slides me a look, as if she thought that was going to be an easy yes before trying again.

"Oh, come on, surely you have time to take a break to go for a drive?"

"Not really."

"What if—"

I widen my eyes, pleading with her to stop.

"You know what?" she says, taking mercy on me, "You're both grown adults, I'll just leave you two to figure it out."

She breezes back into the daylight, humming a tune that's a little off-key and a lot snarky.

Parker says nothing.

"Sorry about that," I say. "Obviously, I'm not expecting you to drive me around."

He frowns, not looking at me, and I half expect him to say no. "I need the truck back by seven, but you can have it until then."

"Oh," I say, surprised. "Thank you."

I stand there, waiting for the keys and awkwardly watching as he returns to work, hauling the hay bales into a neat stack against the wall for the night feed later. Why does he have to make all manual labor look so damn easy? Distracting myself, I grab a broom propped against the wall and sweep the loose hay.

After stacking the last one, he turns to me and wordlessly fishes his keys out of his pocket, tossing them at me. I fumble but manage to catch them.

"Do you need any help?" I ask. He still won't look at me, and an uneasy feeling uncoils in my stomach.

"With what?" he asks.

I shrug. "Anything. You said you had a lot to do today."

"I'll manage."

He disappears into the feed room. I follow, leaning against the doorframe as I watch him bounce around the room doing one thing after another, anything to keep his hands busy, to keep him from having to look at me.

"Is everything okay?" I ask.

"Why?"

"You don't seem like yourself." Not like him from the past few days, anyway.

"What makes you think you know me?"

I freeze mid-sweep, looking up because I'm *sure* I heard him wrong. Except when I see his face, I know I haven't. This isn't the Parker who opened up to me in his truck outside his dad's house or sat with me outside a closed diner and told me I can do anything I put my mind to. This is the Parker I met at the bus stop, the guy who wrote me off before we even met—closed, distant, unyielding.

The fridge—last night's crime scene—may as well be wedged between us. He's redrawing the line we almost obliterated, but I'm okay with it. He doesn't want to risk his job? Fine. I've been down this road with Caleb, and business and pleasure do not mix. It looks like we're going right back to square one, as if last night never happened. In that case, I'll do the same. Nothing more than a fever dream. I stuff the laughing, supportive, sexual-tension-laden version of Parker from last night as deep into the recesses of my mind as I can manage, along with the most gruesome murder stories that gave me nightmares, in exchange for the pitchfork-hiding, shoe-ruining, insult-throwing version next to me. He wants to go back to fighting? Well, sir, consider my gloves off.

The broom clatters against the nearest stall as I shove it away from me, about to head out the door and away from him, when I finally register the stack of hay and stop in my tracks. That feeling in my chest condenses into a bowling ball of dread as I thunder up the narrow stairs to the hay loft and lay eyes on the space, only to find it worse than I expected. Way worse.

Fuck.

Chapter 15

When Tabitha suggested I use the hayloft, I had imagined an ample, airy space with high ceilings and exposed beams, ready to be strung with lights after a bit of sweeping and light cobweb removal. She mentioned it would need a cleanup, but I figured it was nothing I couldn't tackle in an afternoon with my elbow grease and a few podcasts to keep me company. I turn in a slow circle, taking it in little by little. I'm afraid to look at everything at once. I might panic and run for the hills, never to return, because the space that I'm supposed to be hosting a chic bachelorette party in this weekend is currently set up for the most traditional use of a hay loft.

In that it's *full of hay*.

It's the calm before the storm. I am ten seconds away from a mental breakdown.

"Sloan? Sloan. You look like you're going to pass out," Parker says. "Or puke."

"Yup," I croak, taking in the visual before me, blinking to make sure I'm seeing this right.

"Which is it?" Parker demands. "I'd prefer to be prepared, if that's alright with you."

"I'll be honest, either one seems entirely possible."

"If you're worried about floor space, we can push the hay to the sides."

The hay is piled high, but it's not filling the room to the brim. Half, maybe. But that's the least of my worries.

"What if one of them is allergic to hay?!"

"Well, then they're morons for organizing a party in a *barn*," Parker shoots back.

I take a deep breath. If I'm going to do this, I can't be getting emotional at every turn. I don't have time for a five-minute wallow, not with this behemoth of a problem on my hands. "You don't understand. Aesthetics are everything. These women don't want a barn. They want rustic chic."

"Rustic *what*?"

With another sigh, trying to check my brimming impatience, I tug my phone from the back pocket of my jeans and pull up Instagram. With one quick search, I've found what I'm looking for. I hand him the phone, moving so I can see the screen too, as he scrolls through. The feed is one photo after another of barns turned into wedding venues, twinkle lights wrapping around exposed beams in the rafters, antique shovels painted in pastels, artfully arranged in corners, and—most importantly—not a single piece of hay.

"None of these places look like they've seen a live animal in years."

"Exactly."

He looks at me like I'm insane, then squints at the screen again, forehead creased. It's the same expression Caleb had when I told him about mine and Lyla's business—doubt. I pluck my phone from his fingers and shove it in my pocket, doing the same with the emotions threatening to swell and spill over.

"Sloan—"

"I can't deal with this right now," I say, my voice unsteady. *Focus on what you can control.* "I have to get to the stores before they close. Thank you for your truck; I'll have it back by seven, like you said."

"What about the hayloft?" he calls after me.

I don't look back as I start descending the stairs, at the years of cobwebs caking every nook and cranny, or at him. "I'll figure it out tomorrow."

What other choice do I have? Lyla's not here. I'll either succeed or fail at this, but one thing is suddenly crystal clear to me.

No matter what the outcome is, I'm in this alone.

Not long after I abruptly left Parker in the barn, I realized how badly I was spiraling. I threw myself into the shopping trip with singular focus, methodically working my way through my list, compartmentalizing like the best of them—and that's when I realized: I *can* do this.

Caleb doubted me because of his own fears of inadequacy, and somewhere along the way, I absorbed that doubt like it was my own. My jump without a parachute, as he so lovingly called it. I wish he wasn't, but Caleb's been in my head since I posted that stupid picture on Instagram to get back at him for his post. He thought I needed to focus more on building my brand before we opened our doors, and I think that fueled my doubt that we were moving too quickly. But Lyla had been hesitating too, and if I hadn't urged us forward, we never would have taken the leap from talking about it to *doing* it. I realize now that it wasn't about me, at least not entirely. Caleb is pragmatic to the point of pessimistic; he wasn't holding me back on purpose —he was scared for me, the same way he is scared to start his podcast. If he isn't, he would have done it already—and if his Instagram profile is anything to go by, which it is—he hasn't.

I don't want to be like that. Not anymore. Being so pessimistic lately, I hardly recognized myself. Until I started planning for this event, I didn't even realize how *un*like myself I've been feeling. Not until Parker reminded me that I'm more in control of things than I thought. Getting into organizing mode has been the closest to me (pre-disaster me, that is) that I've felt, and although spiraling in self-pity would be the easy thing to do, it's not going to help me accomplish anything.

So, instead, I'm pulling up my socks, doubling down. I might be doing this alone now, but maybe I have to get used to that. I'm not as connected to my family as I once thought, my best friend has other priorities, and Tabitha may start to pull back after I tell her the truth. Instead of relying on others to help me, maybe it's time for me to start leaning on myself, which is why I'm taking Parker's advice and going for it. I spend the afternoon at the big craft store in the next town over, picking out all the supplies I'll need, then make a trip to the hardware store for some more essentials like folding tables and chairs, some string lights, and anything else I can find to jazz up the hayloft.

There's just one thing I wish I didn't have to do: return Parker's car keys. After the way he treated me earlier, I'm not in a hurry to see him again, but I told him he'd have his truck back by seven.

I've stalled for as long as possible since returning to Salem Stables, taking over the living room with the art supplies littering every surface.

"Looks like everything's coming together," Tabitha says, stepping into the room. "Ready for a break? We have plenty of leftovers for dinner if you're hungry. I'm starved."

My aching back pops when I stand. I groan and stretch side to side to work out the kinks from sitting on the hard floor. "Let me wash up first. If Parker comes in, I left his keys on the kitchen counter." My voice doesn't squeak at all when mentioning his name. Not one bit.

She peers through the window towards the barn. "It looks like he's still at it. He won't quit, either. Not until he's done. He can never leave anything half finished, that one."

"Still at what?"

"Emptying the hayloft."

"He's *what?!*"

Tabitha jumps, then slides out of the way as I barrel towards the window. Sure enough, in the dimming light, one hay bale after another comes tumbling out of the hayloft onto the driveway below.

Toss, *thump.*

Toss, *thump.*

Toss, *thump.*

The same guy who bit my head off earlier because he had *'things to do'* dropped everything to help me, without my even knowing. I scramble away from the window. Kicking myself for putting off facing him, I call over my shoulder as I pound upstairs for Tabitha to eat without me. I've been home for almost an hour, and instead of helping him fix my problem, I've been hiding out in the house. I need to get out there and help.

There's just one thing I have to do first.

Chapter 16

I only chicken out twice before climbing the stairs up to the hayloft, sandwich in hand. I'm not sure how Parker will react to my being here, but there's something deeply curious inside me that wants to know. He may dismiss me again. But something inside me tells me he won't.

From the top of the stairs, I catch sight of his rippling, capable muscles as he lifts a hay bale easily and tosses it outside, sweat leaving a sheen on his forehead—*down girl.*

"I'm not sure this is union-approved overtime."

His step stutters, and his eyes lock on mine. My stomach drops half an inch. I've never seen him smile like that. His greetings typically consist of a nod, at least when it comes to me.

He passes by, carrying a heavy-looking bale by its twine and tosses it out the square door onto the driveway below before turning back to me slowly, dragging an arm over his damp forehead as we stare each other down. His T-shirt is darkened with sweat, and it takes me a solid half minute to remember what I came here to say, because the sight I'm taking in is so distracting. He's certainly made a dent, but there's still a lot of hay left in the loft.

"Thanks for your truck." I toss his keys, arcing them through the air.

He catches them against his chest, then reacts quickly when I toss the wrapped sandwich at him, too.

"What's this?"

"Food."

He eyes it, suspicious. "Is it poisoned?"

I fight a smile. "No, it's a thank you. For this," I add, tipping my chin towards the hay. I take a breath. "Why are you doing it?"

He frowns at the sandwich in his gloved hand, struggling with something. He lowers his head and drags a hand over his thick brown hair. "Because I'm sorry." His eyes flash to me quickly, then drop again. "I was a dick earlier. I'm not used to being ... friendly. I'm still trying to figure it out."

His eyes finally meet mine, and I nod, clasping my now-empty hands in front of me. "Okay."

I cross the wooden floor, covered in a layer of loose hay, and sit in the loading door, letting my legs dangle outside. "Well, if you're going to work all night because of me, the least you can do is eat the sandwich I brought you."

"You didn't have to do this," he says quietly, pulling off his work gloves as he sits beside me on the floor, mimicking my position.

"Get ready to experience the culinary mastery of Sloan Sanders. Fair warning, it's not real bacon."

He examines it to figure out what he's in for, then pauses, arching an eyebrow at me. "You gonna watch me eat the whole thing?"

"Just the first bite."

I lean back on my hands, pretending to settle in for it. He takes an enormous bite, letting his eyes roll back and moaning like it's the best thing he's ever tasted. A bubble of laughter escapes me, but there's no denying what that sound does to my insides. I adjust myself so I'm no longer facing him. We sit shoulder to shoulder, about a foot of space between us, and look out over the house, bathed in golden hour light.

"Are you wearing what I think you're wearing?" he asks, a mouthful of sandwich tucked in his cheek.

I grin because he noticed, like I hoped he would. "I know how much you love this tracksuit." I peek at him from the corner of my eye, my smile widening when I see him grinning back at me.

"I get it, you know," I say gently. "I'm not saying it was okay, but I understand why you put your walls up."

His throat works in a hard swallow. "Yeah. I think that's why I—"

"Freaked out?"

He breathes a laugh through his nose, shaking his head at himself. "That's fair. I'm not used to ... sharing. Even Tibby doesn't know most of that stuff I told you about my parents."

"I won't say anything, I promise."

He shakes his head. "That's not it—I know you wouldn't spread something like that around. But *that's* what freaked me out so much, I think. I'm not used to trusting people. My family—the people I consider family—is small. I didn't think I'd be adding anyone to it, but ..." Our eyes meet, and I can't help but hold my breath as I wait for what's coming next. "Somehow, I trust you."

His words land on me like a weighted blanket, warm, heavy, and comforting. He trusts me. And not just by default because I was friendly and likeable—this trust feels like I've earned it. It makes me want to give something back to him, and the truth about my own family is suddenly on the tip of my tongue. I swallow it down, because it feels wrong to share it with Parker before Tabitha, but I offer him something else—a piece of the truth.

"When I was seventeen, my parents sent me up here for the whole summer," I say, speaking into the setting sun. "The first thing I said to Tabitha when I got here was that they were getting divorced." His eyes land on me, but I keep my profile turned to him. "They hadn't told me, but they'd been fighting for months, it felt like. Always behind closed doors, trying to keep it hidden from everyone, even me. Whenever I asked what was wrong, they lied and hid the truth behind fake smiles." Fighting, I know now, because I was about to turn eighteen and they couldn't agree on whether to tell me the truth about my father, whether to keep lying to me about who I am. "At first, I was able to smooth things over when things would get tense between them, but eventually, nothing worked. The cracks in the surface were too deep to gloss over, and I knew they'd sent me away so I wouldn't watch their marriage end. Salem Stables was always my happy place, but it became a refuge that summer. Somewhere the outside world couldn't hurt me."

Beside me, Parker shifts. "The way Tibby talks about your parents ... I thought they were still together."

"They are. When I went back in the fall and everything was back to normal, it was almost worse. Like they work as a unit when I'm not around. Then I left for college, and they stayed solid." Until I moved back in with them a few months ago, which made everything worse again. "It's never felt like home again, though. This, Salem Stables, is the only place that's never stopped feeling like home. So, I get why you want to protect it. It's as important to you as it is to me." I meet his eyes. "That's what I want this place to feel like for Lucy and her friends this weekend. I want them to feel like they've been here before, like they belong, like—"

"Like they never have to leave?"

A slow smile spreads over my face, and I nod.

"You never explained what the tracksuit was for," he points out.

"Consider it an olive branch," I explain with a shrug. "You felt weird about opening up to me, not once but twice, and pulling back was some form of self-preservation. So, this is me giving you ammunition to level the playing field. I can't be morally superior with the word *Juicy* stamped on my ass."

"Jesus," he mutters, though his scruffy mouth tips up in amusement. "It's kind of scary how well you know me."

We fall into comfortable silence while Parker polishes off the last of his sandwich, our shoulders almost touching. I stare out at the sun, a bright, glaring orange ball in the distance as it sets over the ridge of trees that line the property. It's stunning. I fish my phone out of my pocket to snap a few pictures, leaning to get the perfect angle.

"Feeling a burning need for everyone to know exactly what you're doing right at this moment?" he says through a mouthful of sandwich.

I narrow my eyes at him, and he twirls his hand.

"Don't let me stop you. Go ahead, tweet whatever you're Snapchatting. I don't mind."

"How refreshing, a guy who hates social media," I grumble, my voice dripping with sarcasm. "But no, this is just for me." I feel his eyes on me again, watching me closely.

"Can I ask you something?" he says several moments later, polishing off his sandwich. "If it's way too personal, you can tell me to go to hell."

I chew the inside of my lip for a second before giving him a nod of encouragement.

"Why are you doing all this? You don't know the girl who's getting married or her friend. And it doesn't seem like you enjoy the chaos of event planning. Why go to all this trouble? Why not just say no? I mean, Tabitha mentioned you do pretty well for yourself. She made it sound like you can pick and choose the jobs you want to take."

"Were you asking about me?" I can't help but tease.

His lips twitch, and he seems dangerously close to letting a smile slip. "It came up in passing. I don't remember the details."

"Mhmm, sure." I don't answer his question right away, listening to the buzz of the crickets as I mull over my answer. I don't have to explain, but I do it anyway because it's him. Because it's safe.

"Veronica's best friend is getting married. She's worried that they won't be as close anymore and wants to do something before then to remind her friend how much she loves her before everything changes." I feel his eyes land on me again. Parker is quiet, and so am I as I let the words sink in, understanding the thoughts I didn't even know I had. "I know what it's like to be sidelined as the backup person."

I think about how Lyla and I used to be inseparable and practically telekinetic and how we are now. How her marriage was the beginning of a slow series of cracks in the foundation of our friendship and what that will eventually mean for us—a slow, painful unraveling.

"What if it's not enough? What if things are still different between them, after all this?"

I look over at Parker, a sad determination in my smile. "Then at least I'll have helped her give her friend a beautiful send-off."

As he studies me, I notice the color in his eyes again. Not just boring brown. Not boring at all, actually. Rich, warm brown with a green starburst ringing his pupils. One of a kind. Just like him. Rising to his feet, he reaches down and offers his hand to help me up.

"Sounds like I should get back to work, then."

The contact of his skin on mine warms my hand and then some.

"Let me help you," I say, my voice coming out strangely husky as I back up, peel off my sweater, tossing it aside, and reach for the nearest bale.

"What are you doing?" he snaps, voice gruff.

"Helping," I say, grabbing the strings of the nearest bale and hoisting. *God,* that's heavy. I half-carry, half-shuffle it across the floor to where we were sitting.

"Sloan, stop."

"I can help. Do I yell 'bombs away' and throw it down from here?"

"Let me do the throwing. And the rest of it too, while you're at it."

"No way, I just managed to convince you I'm not a princess." I use my foot to shove the hay-wrapped cement over the edge, where it lands with a satisfying thud on the driveway below.

"Sloan."

"I know I can't go as fast as you, but—"

"*Sloan.*" He stops me reaching for another bale with a hand, tight around my wrist.

He's in my space, standing close enough that I can still smell the lingering hints of his shampoo, his grip warm and firm and sending shocks up my arm and straight through my core. "When I said I'll work faster on my own, I meant I won't get any work done at all with you here looking like that."

My chin dips to follow his gaze to my white cotton V-neck T-shirt, the fabric loose but low over my chest. No stains, no embarrassing bra showing. What's his problem? The intensity of his eyes answers my question.

"You're saying I'm a distraction?"

He swallows hard. And when he answers, it comes out as a rasp. "Yes."

I'd ask him to draw me a map of where exactly he redrew these lines between us if I had any faith he knew where the hell they were, himself. He's asking me to leave, but he doesn't want me to this time. Not really. Based on the silent battle of wills between my legs and my brain right now, I know I don't want to either.

My thoughts race and stumble. What am I doing? Sabotaging the one person I need to pull this party off, that's what. I know myself well enough not to think this could end any other way than badly.

But just because there are plenty of reasons why we shouldn't cross this line, doesn't mean we can't go right up to it and peek over the edge, just for fun ... right?

I don't lean forward into his space. With his fingers still closed around my flaming wrist, I turn my palm until it's pressed flat against his chest, until I can feel the thump of his heart through his shirt, a thrill coursing through me. He swallows again, his Adam's apple jerking. He's struggling to steady his breathing, and I can tell from how he twitches at the contact that he's coiled, holding back. Based on the breath coming rapidly through his nose, he's holding on tight.

Being this wanted zings my whole body back to life, waking the part of me that had been hibernating until last night. A playful smile toys at my lips, and instead of grabbing a fistful of his shirt to pull him close, like I want to, I push him gently away.

"You know, Parker, sometimes distractions are a part of life, and you just have to deal with them."

His dimple appears as a grin tugs at the corner of his mouth, and he reluctantly concedes to my help. I may not know much about him, but I know one thing for certain. I most certainly have not seen *that* smile before.

Chapter 17

All around me, pages and pages of cardstock are scattered, each filled with large, elegant calligraphy. While I've made progress, I'm nowhere near where I should be. A whole whack of castoffs is at my feet, crumpled and tossed aside for one stupid mistake after another. The wooden chair creaks as I slump back and stretch my aching arms behind my head, exhaling. It shouldn't be taking me so long. And it shouldn't be such an effort. I used to be able to do this in my sleep. That I can't even count on my one area of expertise is beyond frustrating. Then again, being creative has always been an easy way to zone out and silence the world around me. But I've never had so much distraction to contend with, either.

Part of me wants to blame this on Lyla, but deep down, the most insecure part of me wonders if it's the pressure of the event tomorrow. I've never had an issue with deadlines before, but I've also never had so much at stake. Because if the party doesn't go well, I won't have a business partner beside me to shoulder some of the responsibility of that; I'll have no one to blame but myself.

I'm running out of time, so I can't waste what's left of it worrying. Leaning forward with my elbows on the table, fingers steepled under my chin, I scan the finished phrases, trying to find motivation from what I've already produced.

All you need is love.

Home is where the heart is.

Forever starts now.

Gag me.

This is pretty much the same content I create regularly through my online store. I know I resolved to shake the pessimistic cloud hanging over me for the last month, but while I used to think these sayings were cute, they seem fake now. A glossy, TV screen portrayal of life. None of it has an ounce of truth, and my stomach twists in disgust at the thought of feeding into the bullshit. Something pops into my head, and I grab a blank piece of card stock, pop the cap off a brush pen, and begin to sweep across the page with practiced strokes. The movement flows better than it has all morning.

Tying the knot, time for a shot.

I tilt my head to the side, considering it. I like it. I set it with the others and do another.

I might be bad with directions, but at least I can find my way to my G-spot.

I snort. Now that's more like it. I would never have dreamed of posting anything like this, but I'm pretty sure I can get away with it at a bachelorette party. My mind is quick to remind me that if I put this up in the loft, Parker will see it. Would he notice? Would he blush? I can't help the devilish grin on my lips, my neck warming at the thought.

I gather what I need and hurry to the barn, finding Parker in the feed room scrubbing water buckets. He smiles easily when he sees me, and this time I don't suppress the backflip my stomach does.

"You done already?" he asks. "I thought I wouldn't see you until dinner."

"Not done yet, I just needed a break. My back is killing me."

"Sore from yesterday? I told you to take it easy, but you didn't want to listen."

If I thought the first bale of hay I picked up was heavy, it was nothing compared to the fiftieth. But eventually, we'd managed to empty the last of the bales—except for a few I decided to leave there for décor.

"Yeah, well. Not to be dramatic, but I think I might be dying," I say wryly.

Parker chuckles softly, holding my gaze a little longer than usual.

"I'm gonna head upstairs to clean up. Why take a break when you can do more work, I always say."

"No! Sloan, wait!" He dives in front of me, blocking the stairs. "The thing is, I didn't think you'd see it again until later."

My mind immediately jumps to the worst-case scenarios: I dreamt it all and we didn't empty the loft last night; Parker found a nest of angry, territorial possums; he slept-walked and put all the hay back where he found it or filled the loft with something equally difficult to clear out, like feathers or cotton candy.

Eyes wide, I duck under Parker's arm and thunder up the stairs to find out what exactly I'm dealing with. By the time I reach the top of the staircase, I'm already planning my apology call to Veronica. The room opens up in front of me and I gasp. I stop so suddenly that Parker crashes into me from behind, knocking me forward a step.

"It's not as bad as it looks," he says, breathing hard. "It's a work in progress, that's all."

The loose hay on the floor has been swept into piles, and the Edison string lights we bought are draped overhead, crisscrossing between the beams. One end is dangling loose, but even though it's not finished, I can tell they'll look amazing.

"When did you do all this?" I breathe.

He rubs the back of his neck self-consciously. "I couldn't sleep, so I got up early this morning and thought I'd get a head start. I hoped to be done by the time you saw it, but you snuck up on me."

I can't even express how beautiful he is right now.

"So ... you're not upset?" he asks, his eyes darting back and forth between mine, trying to read me.

I try not to cringe at how much of a control freak he must think I am to be so concerned. "There are no possums, so it's perfect."

"Uh ... possums?"

"Never mind."

Once he realizes I'm not upset, he visibly relaxes and describes the possible layout options. "I wasn't sure exactly how you want to set up, but there are six tables, right? You could space them out so there's a couple at each table, or line them up to make one long table and we'll string the lights right above it, and then I thought food and drinks and whatever can go against the wall over here."

His words hit me like a slap, forcing the wind from my lungs. "Oh god."

He pauses mid-step, his hand falling to his side, limp, face crestfallen. "You hate it."

"No. That's not it at all. It's perfect. More perfect than my plans, which somehow failed to account for food."

I lift my hands to my cheeks as I pace. There was so much else to deal with, and then with the barn, such an unexpected disaster, the thing I'd bumped to the bottom of my list had been forgotten entirely. I take a deep breath, jumping into problem-solving mode. Parker watches me, quietly waiting for me to decide what to do next.

"I'll call Lyla," I say after a minute, doing the mental math. There's enough time for her to get here, and I can pick up the supplies to start baking as soon as she arrives. It'll be a whirlwind, but it's possible—and having her do this with me feels right.

Parker leaves me alone in the loft while I call her, seated on one of the lone bales in the open space. It rings and rings, and Lyla finally picks up before I expect it to go to her voicemail. A rush of relieved air escapes me, but after a quick catch-up, I don't waste any time filling her in on the situation.

"So, what do you think?" I ask. "Can you come for the weekend? I am prepared to grovel endlessly for your culinary services, and I'll cover your bus ticket and everything!"

Lyla laughs on the other end of the line, but it sounds ... odd. There's a long pause before she finally speaks.

"I wish I could, but there's so much going on here right now. Adam has a second job interview next week, and if it goes well, the position starts pretty soon."

"That's great news! Wish him luck for me."

"I will. It's just ... the position isn't exactly local."

"Oh," I say, trying to hide my surprise and the immediate sinking feeling in my stomach. I tug a piece of hay from the bale I'm seated on, bending it absently between my fingers. "How not local are we talking?"

"It's ... in New York."

Oh. Now I understand why she sounds so hesitant to tell me; New York City is two hours away from where we live and where we planned to open the shop. They'd have to move closer for Adam's sake, and even if they found somewhere halfway between the two places, that's way too long of a commute for one of them, if not both.

"Do you think there's somewhere with that main street vibe we're going for, somewhere near there? Not in the city, because there's no way we could afford the rent for a storefront downtown."

"Oh ... I dunno ... I haven't had time to give it much thought, honestly."

Somewhere above me in the rafters, a bird takes flight—at least I hope it's a bird—sending dust cascading through the gloom. Anxiety builds in my chest as I sense her reluctance, and I decide to drop it for now. I don't want to push it when she already has so much on her mind with Adam, and I can't worry about that with the party just two days away.

"Never mind, you don't need to worry about that right now," I say, forcing a false brightness into my voice while my gaze snags on the cobwebs caked so thick on the walls that I wonder if I'm going to need a pressure washer to get them off. "Focus on getting Adam that job, and we'll figure the rest out later."

"Right. Obviously, this is all hypothetical for now. I probably shouldn't even be talking about it yet—I don't want to jinx it," she adds, a nervous laugh rolling out of her. "Sorry, I can't help with the party. How is it coming together?"

"Really good," I say truthfully, filling her in on everything. "It feels good to get back to it. I didn't realize how much I missed it until I picked it up again—why am I telling you this? You probably know exactly what I mean."

"Honestly? I haven't baked a thing in a month, and ... I have to say, I'm kind of loving the break."

"Wait ... seriously? But you love baking. You used to give away cupcakes every day in college so that you could make more. You even figured out a way to make them in the crappy toaster oven in the dorm kitchen."

"I guess when you start doing your hobby as a job, it's inevitable that at some point it becomes work."

I rub my arm with my free hand, warding off the air that suddenly feels chillier than it did a moment ago. "Look, I should probably get going. I've still got a lot of stuff to prepare for this weekend. And learn to bake." I mean it as a joke, but it falls flat when I can't follow it with even a fake laugh.

We say goodbye, and I head downstairs. Parker finishes the turn-in, leading a horse in each hand to their stalls and latching them securely and methodically, one by one.

"Lyla can't do it, so it's on to plan B," I explain in a rush. "Problem being that I don't have a plan B, and I'm running out of time. The party is the day after tomorrow, so I may have to stock up on grocery store desserts and hope they don't notice. Do they still make those cute mini cupcakes? Everyone loves those, right?"

I'm doing my best to remain calm this time, to keep my voice from sounding as crazed as I feel. Even if it's not ideal, there is a solution right in front of me. It might not be how I envisioned this, but Lyla's not here, and it's up to me to solve this problem. I have to do whatever it takes to make sure this party happens.

Parker raises a hand and runs it through his short brown hair. "I might know someone who can help."

My heart skips. This might be the answer I need.

A sharp, cold wind cuts through the open door at the barn's end, dust swirling around our feet. There's no logical reason for Parker to want to help me pull this off. And yet he's done so much already. I don't need his face to tell me if I can trust him. The proof is right in front of me.

Chapter 18

My thumb reaches my mouth, and I chew absently at the cuticle. When I glance at the clock on the dash of Parker's truck, I instantly wish I hadn't.

"Remind me again why we couldn't call this person?" My knee bobs up and down as I dwell on how much time we'll have wasted if this doesn't work.

"She doesn't keep her cell phone on her when she's working," Parker explains.

"Good thing we're just going to show up unannounced, then," I deadpan. "Much less disruptive."

"It's barely four o'clock. It'll be quiet at this time of day, I promise. And we won't be long."

The clock ticks forward another minute, mocking me.

"How do you know her, again?"

His eyes flick to the rearview mirror, then back to the road. "Old friend."

Oh-kay. Once we got in the car, Parker clammed up. I'm not sure if this is a sore subject or his way of boundary setting. Fair, I guess. How he knows this person is none of my business. But I can't ignore the feeling that I've been reprimanded for asking. Weren't Parker and I becoming friends? Judging by his tight grip on the wheel and his sudden, glaring silence, maybe I'm overreaching. Again.

Mercifully, we arrive at our destination. Parker guides the truck into a spot at the curb outside The Cabin, the same bar we came to with Sam the other night. In the middle of the day, we don't have to compete for a spot.

He throws the truck into park and climbs out, with me following his lead. He hesitates at the bar's door, a thick, solid wood with no window to peek through. A flicker of something like worry passes over his face, twitching his jaw beneath the faint smattering of brown stubble. Before I can ask him if everything's okay, he grips the handle and jerks it open, holding it for me to go ahead of him.

I duck under his arm, blinking as my eyes adjust from the bright October sunlight to the dim interior of the stuffy bar. Something sticky grabs at my shoes with every step on the dark, diamond-patterned floor, which I'm afraid to look too closely at in the light of day. A few day drinkers sit around the room, mostly alone. One of them lifts his glass at us, and Parker gives him a stiff nod of acknowledgment. Thankfully, he doesn't stop to chat. The man, with a long, thick beard and sallow skin, turns his glassy eyes on me next, and my step falters as he sizes me up with an unabashed leer.

Parker puts his hand on the small of my back and I let him tug me closer to his side and steer me forward. As we approach, the sharp eyes of a tall, striking brunette behind the bar lock on Parker from the other side of the bar. I recognize her instantly as the bartender from the other night, the one Parker seemed familiar with. Cass, I think Sam said her name was. She's wearing a buffalo plaid shirt unbuttoned over a tightly fitting black tank top, the bottom tied at her midriff. Her long, sleek hair trails down her back like she's freaking Rapunzel. I can't help my sinking feeling as I realize how Parker must know her. *Old friend?* My ass. As if any straight male would be *just* friends with a bombshell like her.

"Checking up on me again?" she asks as Parker approaches the bar. She sets a glass down and dries another.

Parker's hand drops from my back. At the loss of contact, I have the irrational urge to loop my arm through his to stake some claim—of which, of course, I have none.

"We both know you don't need checking up on," he answers stiffly. "I need a favor."

The woman's eyebrow quirks up over one of her heavily lined eyes. I stay back, one hand resting on my elbow as I wait for an introduction.

"A favor? That's a new one. You sure you want to be in my debt? I can think of a few ways you could repay me," she says with a wink.

Parker pulls the baseball hat off his head, runs a hand through his hair, and puts it back. He's uncomfortable, though, whether it's because of Cass's blatant flirting or because I'm standing right next to him while she does, I can't be sure.

"Uh ... not so much, but we're in a pinch."

She acknowledges me for the first time, her wary eyes grating over me with no reservations whatsoever. Suddenly, her smile doesn't seem so friendly.

"Hi, I'm Sloan," I say, stepping forward so I'm standing next to Parker on this side of the tall counter.

"Tibby's niece," Parker clarifies.

Huh. I try not to dwell on the fact that he hasn't included that we are also friends. Kind of. The way she's eyeing him, she clearly suspects he's leaving something out as well.

"Uh-*huh*. What do you need, trouble?"

Parker gives her the quick version of the situation before asking the question we came here for.

"You want me to make a birthday cake?" she asks.

Parker rubs the back of his neck and looks at me for help. As hard as he's trying, he still doesn't get exactly what I'm trying to accomplish. He's gotten us as far as he can, and now it's my turn to jump in.

"I was hoping for cupcakes. And it's for a bachelorette party?"

I'm not sure why I phrase it as a question. I cringe at how stupid it sounds. For a second, I'm back to doubting this whole thing. But then I remember what Lyla could do, and I know the word cupcake doesn't do it justice. Her decadent creations are unique and elaborate, they're more than desserts; they're a full experience. Shoving my doubt as far back in my mind as it will go, I shake my shoulders and lift my chin to reset my confidence.

"You can't make a cake from a box yourself?" Cass hasn't stopped working the whole time we've been here, and now starts deftly slicing limes into small wedges, filling a stainless-steel bucket in preparation for the evening rush.

I bristle at her implication. She seems to have a similar opinion of me to Parker's when we first met. But I'm no princess. And I'm suddenly more determined than ever to give Veronica the best damn party she's ever thrown. Even if that means taking shit from Parker's *'friend.'*

I bite back the correction I want to give her about wanting cupcakes instead of cake and instead address the most important issue, schooling my voice into something more confident.

"It's a little more involved than that. It's meant to be a classy, elevated experience. And it doesn't have to be cupcakes. Parker said you're an amazing cook. It could be an assortment of tarts, squares, that kind of thing. Whatever you can do. As long as it's not store-bought, I'll be happy," I try for a joke to find some way to connect with her.

Instead, her face closes off even more. "What's the pay?"

The bluntness of her question surprises me, but I've done this before and recover quickly, sharing what I think is a fair rate for the number of people I'm expecting. For the first time in weeks, I feel like I'm on firm ground. This is familiar. This is doable. I've been so focused on the parts of the business that I wouldn't be able to do without help that I'd glossed over everything Lyla used to lean on *me* for. A flicker of confidence and something like hope sparks inside me.

When Cass asks when the party is, though, I stumble.

Sensing my hesitation, Parker jumps in again. "That's where the favor comes in. It's on Saturday."

She scoffs. Towards me, she's been angry. When she turns her attention back to Parker though, there's worry on her features. "How did you get roped into calling in favors for this?" she asks, a reluctant softness creeping into her tone.

Parker lets out a long breath. "It's important to Tibby."

I drop my eyes to the sticky floor. Right. Tibby. Of course, he isn't doing any of this for me. I tell myself that doesn't bother me.

Cass shakes her head, going back to her task of slicing limes. "So, once again, a fire that has nothing to do with you is up to you to put out."

Parker rests the heel of his hand against the bar. "It's not like that, Cass. I'm just helping out a friend."

"It *is* like that, though, Parker." She sets down the knife, her hands braced on the counter as she fires a hard look at him. "When will you stop letting other people's problems drag you down?"

"That's not—look, I thought you could use the money. That's it. Okay?"

Her eyes cut to me, and I'm feeling like she'd rather I wasn't privy to this amount of detail about her personal life.

"I could," she answers. "But tomorrow's Friday; I'm working a double."

"Right, and tonight's Thursday. You never close on Thursdays."

She shoots him an annoyed look. "What am I supposed to do about Mason, huh? The sitter already bailed on me this afternoon, so it's not like that's even an option—"

"Wait, what?" he asks.

"I *said* the sitter canceled on me today. I missed three shifts this month when Mason was home sick with the flu, and I have rent to pay. I've got enough to deal with without taking on other people's problems."

"So, Mason is ..."

She waves her hand towards a door to what I presume is an office, maybe a kitchen. "He's in the back, coloring."

Parker's shoulders slump, and the look on his face is one I can only describe as tired. It screams *we've had this conversation a thousand times*. "Why didn't you call me?"

Her hands drop as she braces herself on the bar top to stare him down. "Because you have a job too, and it's not taking care of a six-year-old."

"Cass," he says, a small amount of pleading in his voice. "Hanging out with Mason isn't *work*. I'm happy to do it."

Cass's harsh exterior softens as her eyes lift to meet Parker's. "I know," she says. "And you have no idea how much that means to us. But ..." Her gaze cuts to me and I realize I'm leaning forward to hear her. I jerk back and look away, pretending I wasn't just listening intently to their—clearly very private—conversation. As I pretend to admire the ceiling, I see Cass's eyes roll from the corner of mine before she continues what she was saying to Parker. "But it's not fair to expect you to bail me out whenever I'm in a tight spot. Your dad is enough of a burden without adding my drama to the mix."

I might not know the woman standing on the other side of the bar, but my heart tugs at the guilt I hear behind the words, and admission disguised as an off-handed comment.

Parker's jaw twitches, his gaze darting to me and away so quickly that I almost don't catch the movement. "You and Mason don't even come *close* to being anything like my father," he says with enough force that there's no room to doubt it.

Behind them, the door swings open seemingly on its own, revealing a small child with round cheeks and a mop of curly brown hair, a piece of paper clutched in his hand—a child whose eyes reminded me of someone I'm starting to know pretty well.

Cass and Parker straighten hastily. When the kid I assume is Mason spots Parker, his little face lights up. He scurries around the bar, diving into Parker's open arms.

"Hey, buddy. What have you got there?" His tone turns light, and the slight waver in his normally steady baritone is the only hint that he's working hard to cover his emotions.

"A T-Rex, *raawr!*" Mason answers, proudly holding up his drawing of a bunch of green spikes.

"That's great, Mason." Parker studies the picture closely from his crouched position.

I haven't known him long, but I've never seen him genuinely light up like this. If I hadn't seen it with my own eyes, I wouldn't have believed it.

"How would you feel about showing me how to draw a T-Rex tonight? Maybe we could even watch *The Land Before Time* again?"

Mason cheers and babbles excitedly about his favorite movie parts, and I have to chuckle at his enthusiasm. Even Cass, who is standing with her arms crossed, softens.

"Why don't you go pack up your stuff?" Parker says, ruffling his hair.

Mason looks at Cass, and I hold my breath. When she finally gives in and nods, the little boy rushes to the back room as Parker stands.

Cass drops her arms and lets out a dramatic sigh. "Fine. I'll do it. But I want an extra hundred, to cover babysitting fees and the rush job."

It takes me a second to realize she's talking to me. I frown, trying to catch up. "But, Parker said he'd watch—"

"You wouldn't have known that if you weren't standing here listening to a private conversation, would you?" she snaps, but her words don't have the same bite to them they did before. "And I want to get paid upfront," she adds.

"I can do half up front, the other half for delivery on Saturday. *Before* the party starts," I clarify, avoiding any loopholes. "Four o'clock. Sharp."

I feel Parker's eyes drift my way, probably surprised by the firm, no-nonsense tone I've learned to use when discussing prices. Parker may vouch for Cass—and it's the only reason I'm agreeing to give her anything upfront—but I don't know her. I don't even know if she's ever cooked for money before in her life. Honestly, at this point, I'm afraid to ask. I'm too far down this rabbit hole to start checking references, and it's not worth fueling my doubt. Blind faith is the only thing that will get me through this event. Still, I'm not so naïve that I don't think there's a chance she could take the money and run.

Cass sizes me up for a few beats, then shrugs. "Fine."

"Great!" My face breaks out in a bright smile, and I step forward, hand outstretched over the bar. "Looking forward to doing business with you."

She rolls her eyes so hard it's a wonder she doesn't fall right over. Her handshake is limp, unenthusiastic at best. Parker grabs my elbow and drags me towards the exit. He shoves his keys into my hand, closing my fingers around them.

"What's this?"

"Your ride home. Take my truck."

"But ... how will you get Mason home?"

"We'll walk. They don't live far from here."

He can think I'm a princess, but I draw the line at letting him treat me like one. "I'm not making a little kid walk home, Parker," I say firmly. "Keep your truck; I'll find my way home. I'll call a cab or an Uber or something."

He gives me a look that mirrors my own doubt at finding something like that out here in the sticks. But I quickly realize that isn't the only thing bothering him when he glances back at the man from earlier. I follow his gaze to the bearded man licking foam from his mountain man mustache. Yup. Still leering. I try not to shudder visibly.

"Not a chance. This way, at least I'll know you got home safe."

Something flips in my stomach, warm and pleasant. There's something endearing about his sudden protectiveness, which he's doing his best to play off like it's nothing. Even though I don't need it—I lived alone in the city and have taken enough self-defense classes to feel confident that I could take on Mountain Man if needed—it's still nice to have someone looking out for me. A surprising thought needles me as I realize how nice it is to have *Parker* looking out for me.

"How will you get home?" I ask. Unless ... oh God. What if he's not planning to come home tonight at all? Did I just completely put my foot in my mouth?

I'm sure he's about to awkwardly say he'll spend the night with Cass and my cheeks start to flush, but then he shrugs, oblivious to my horrifying thoughts.

"I'll call Sam for a lift."

This makes me feel better, but only slightly.

I cast a glance back at Cass, who is crouched down helping Mason pack his things into a dinosaur backpack, and something Sam told me that night at the bar drifts back into my memory.

"That's Cass. She's his brother's girl. Or ... ex-girl, I guess."

Parker hasn't mentioned his brother, and I get the sense that wherever he is, he's no longer in the picture. But he certainly seems to know Mason. Is Mason his nephew?

Parker asks for the shopping list, which I dig out of my pocket and hand to him. He moves to take it, but I don't let go right away, holding onto it until he meets my eyes again.

"Parker, I ..." I trail off. " Thank you" doesn't seem like enough. He's saving my ass—and my party. A prickle of guilt works its way back into my mind as I remember what Cass said. I'm not taking advantage of him, am I?

With his gaze locked on mine, Parker's eyes soften, the urgency dulling around the edges. His rough fingertips brush my skin again as he curls my fingers closed over the keys and gently nudges my hand until I'm clutching them against my chest.

"Stop that."

My brows twitch into a frown. "Stop what?"

"Overthinking," he answers softly. "You do that a lot, you know."

I let out a laugh, tucking my hair behind my ear. "I'll work on that."

His hand drifts to my arm, settling there with a hesitant touch. I watch the motion with fascination, then glance back at Cass and Mason, unsure about leaving Parker without his truck. My lips part, but he cuts me off before I can protest again.

"You don't have time to argue. Take the truck and do what you need to do. I'll be back as soon as I can." With a gentle squeeze, he pulls his hand away and tugs open the door for me.

I let it close behind me before I reach up to touch the spot where his hand was a moment ago, my skin still tingling.

Chapter 19

The following two days pass in a blur. It's Saturday, and Veronica and her friends will be here tonight, so it's crunch time. There's so much going on that I don't even have time to dwell on the fact that Parker didn't come home last night until midnight, not long after I'd finished transforming the loft. Today, the only things that matter are the ones that have to do with the party. Everything else can wait.

Though I didn't ask her to, Tabitha has been sprucing up the yard to add to the aesthetic. I'd be mad if she was using it as an excuse to procrastinate, but her creative block seems to be well under control by now. I'm sure that her covering some of my chores this week—and the supposed uptick in meeting Jim to discuss the farmer's market—is doing the trick. Now that she's not singularly focused on her work and has gone back to the type of daily structure she's used to, rather than force herself to sit in the studio all day and stress, she's been able to get more done when she manages to find time to spend working in shorter spurts. Today, she arranged pumpkins from the patch beside the house to the front porch and stacked a few hay bales at the barn entrance with some pumpkins on top, which gives it a nice, welcoming aesthetic that I know will be great for photos.

Parker's been busy all day with his regular work, and he's spent two nights in a row watching Mason, not trusting the babysitter to show up. He took fifteen minutes to help me lug up the tables and get them roughly into place over the mishmash of area rugs I dragged up from the house this morning, but I've managed the rest independently. There hasn't been much time for anything else, let alone a conversation.

Miraculously, by late Saturday afternoon, I think I might be ready. Wiping my arm across my damp brow, I take it all in. The tables in the loft are set up, each seating identical with its supplies: pencils, markers, and brushes held in ceramic mugs from Tabitha's collection of unsold items, creating a common thread among the assortments. Each is similar in size and made from the same material, but is also unique in color and pattern. She hates making the same thing twice, which is exactly why her dishware has never sold well. But with the rustic-chic scheme of everything else, it adds charm to the décor. I finish hanging the last of my sample pieces on the walls and let the smile tug my lips free.

It's nothing like the chic vibe I pictured when Lyla and I talked about opening our own shop. But I might like it even better. Now I only have to hope Veronica and her guest of honor feel the same.

With a happy sigh, hardly believing that I'm ready, I go downstairs, at a loss for what to do with the next couple of hours. After running full tilt for days, sitting doesn't feel like an option. As I head towards the big door of the barn that opens onto the driveway, I pause at the chalkboard screwed to the wall outside the office. It's so dirty it almost blends into the wall, but a light flashes excitedly in my head and I rush to get a bucket and rag.

I snap a quick picture on my phone before I wipe away the feeding instructions and emergency numbers listed there, including my own, which I added the other day. With the board empty, I pick up a piece of white chalk and start. Halfway through the word *welcome*, Parker's deep voice sounds behind me.

"Finishing touches?" he asks, his tone breezy.

"Pretty much." Sparing him only a glance, I smile, but he doesn't move away.

His eyes are on the board, but I feel like they're on me. For a few seconds, I stare at the slope of his nose, the tilt of his focused brow.

In my T-shirt—it's a warm fall day and I worked up a decent sweat moving around all day—I can feel his breath on my arm and find myself fighting an involuntary rush of feelings.

I turn back to the board, finish the words, and fill the corners with embellishments, flowers, decorative leaves, and swirls. This part didn't come naturally to me when I was first learning, but I've worked hard at finding my unique style, and I'm pretty happy with how this turned out on the first try.

"I guess the artistic streak runs in your family."

A smile tugs at my lips. "I'm sure there's a special Ryan family trait you inherited. Though my guess is, it's the last thing people would expect. Like, you come from a family of trapeze artists or something. Please tell me I'm right, because the thought of you in a leotard ..." I trail off, realizing that instead of making him laugh, my comment seems to have done the opposite.

"Parker? Are you okay?"

"Fine," he says, but it's short and gruff.

I stand there awkwardly, wondering what I said to upset him, and what I can say to fix it.

"I'm sorry, by the way, that I haven't been able to help out much," he says. "I got a bit of a late start this morning. It was pretty late when I got back from watching Mason."

"I'll say." I cringe. I hadn't meant to let that slip out. It's not my place to have an opinion on how Parker spends his evenings.

Or who he spends them with.

But, since my foot is already well in my mouth, I'm in it now, regardless.

"What was that tone?" he asks, amused.

"Nothing, I just meant ... nothing."

I add a final flourish on the board, satisfied that my "Welcome Team Bride" sign is complete. I turn and head for the feed room, using the sink to wash the chalk from my hands. Note to self, sweat makes chalk dust extra clingy, just like Parker, who follows me into the small room.

"Hold up, what did you mean?"

I raise my voice to be heard over the running water. "I meant that you were gone a long time." I finish rinsing my hands and grab a towel hanging nearby to dry them, turning back to face him. When I'm finished, I ditch the towel and lean back, resting against the edge of the plastic wash basin.

"*So*," I go on when Parker stares at me. "I guess you and Cass must have had a good time."

His chin drops and he draws his arms in, folding them across his chest. I suck in a breath, bracing myself for him to tell me to butt out of his business.

Then he laughs. It's a low chuckle, and when he raises his eyes to mine again, they're soft. "Is that what you think?"

"Well ..." I did. Now I'm not so sure.

"Cass and me, it's not like that."

He must see the doubt across my face, because he keeps talking, taking a step closer. His hands drop to his sides.

"So Mason is ...?" I hold my breath, waiting for him to fill in the blank.

His eyes trace my face. "My nephew. They're family, Sloan."

"Is that how Cass sees it?" I ask, remembering how she looked at me yesterday, like a bull deciding whether or not to charge. "She didn't seem happy about you bringing me along the other day."

"Yeah, well. That's Cass. She doesn't like new people, so don't take it personally. She hasn't exactly had an easy life." His words hold a heaviness that has my mind churning out more questions about this woman and the past she and Parker share.

"You may know Cass, but I know women. That wasn't your average look of contempt. She practically turned green."

His face twitches into an adorable frown. "Like the Hulk?"

I laugh. "With envy, you idiot."

His eyebrows dart up. "You think she was jealous?"

With a subtle shift, he moves a little closer and the hairs on my arms prick to attention. I shrug, like it doesn't matter either way. The edge of his mouth quirks up.

"You know, you're looking a little green yourself."

My pulse quickens. "What?"

"You've got a little there, still." He steps forward, licking his thumb and moving towards my face as if he's going to brush away some dirt.

I swat his hand before he can touch my cheek, but I'm not quick enough to hide the smile on my face. I can tell from his smile that he knows I don't mind his teasing. And it's too late to deny it now, so there's no use pretending.

"Maybe I was jealous," I say, straightening up defiantly. "But only because I had to do all that work alone. And it's not even like she offered to pay you. I'm disappointed in your lack of loyalty, Parker."

"Oh, so one night alone with me in a dark, secluded barn wasn't enough?"

He steps closer now, a bold, obvious motion—no subtle shifting this time—and my breath hitches. With the sink behind me, I have nowhere to go, and from the sudden, thrilling darkening of his eyes, it's clear that he knows it too. Then his hand is on my hip, sending shivers up my body.

Okay, I'm not misreading signals.

His nose is inches from mine, his lips filling my field of vision. Sharing the same air, all I can think of is how desperately I want to feel them. My back arches and I sway closer, closing the distance between us. His fingertips tighten on my hip, pressing deliciously into my soft flesh.

"Still jealous?" His voice is a low rumble, thick with something that wasn't there a second ago.

I answer him by gliding both hands up his chest to his neck, my body alight with a thousand nerve endings, rapid-firing at once, all of them screaming at me to get closer. "Jealous of who?"

Those soft, straight lips twitch again, sending a blaze of anticipation through me. A thought tries faintly to cut through the sudden haze of my brain.

"Parker," I whisper, struggling to find words. "I thought ... you said you didn't want ..."

"I know," he rushes, his eyes dark and hooded with lust. "I don't care anymore."

This pulls my gaze from his lips to his eyes. I don't want to be an impulse decision he regrets later. His free hand comes up to cup my cheek, steadying me, anchoring me to him. Or him to me—I'm not exactly sure.

"No, Sloan, I ..." His lips press shut, and he frowns, searching for the words that I know can't be coming easily to him. "I care. About you. I've been trying not to, but I can't anymore. This isn't me *not* caring ... it's me choosing to let myself feel ... whatever is happening here." He swallows. "You feel it, too. Don't you?"

I let out a shaky breath.

And nod.

Because I do. I feel the magnetic pull of his body, the sensations he sends racing through me at the slightest touch, the briefest look. And I know how badly I don't want to walk away from him without knowing what he tastes like, what his body would feel like under my hands, over me, if we let ourselves give in to this. His other hand, the one on my hip, finds its way to the small of my back, finally pulling me closer—

"I could use a little help here!"

He jumps back at the abrupt screech, but not quickly enough. Cass pokes her head in before we can completely untangle ourselves, eyes narrowing.

"I'm glad you two are having so much fun while I've been busting my ass for you."

Parker doesn't bother explaining, but I can't help myself.

"We were just—"

"Save it. I have a trunk full of desserts that aren't going to carry themselves." She exits without asking for help, her boots clicking down the aisle.

Parker meets my eyes, his face twisting in a silent apology. With several feet between us, instead of mere inches, the haze clouding my thoughts has cleared.

Mostly.

I can't help but imagine what we'd be doing right this second had we not been interrupted. It's enough to make my cheeks bloom with heat.

He starts to apologize, but Cass's sing-song shout cuts off his words from the other end of the barn.

"They're *melt-ing*!"

I roll my eyes and hurry after her, knowing that she would let them melt to prove a point. I'm generally not one to jump to conclusions about people, but I'm beginning to dislike this woman.

At the same time, my first event will happen in a few short hours, and I absolutely need to focus. So maybe the bucket of cold water that Cass dropped on us wasn't such a bad thing.

I fly through the house after finally getting rid of Cass, who not only counted the money I paid her right in front of me, but also complained—again—about how inconvenient the whole experience was for her. I think she forgot I know precisely how much of the work she *didn't* do herself, like the shopping and unloading of her car, which I took care of on my own. For now, everything—which to my extreme relief, looks delicious—is safely in the fridge, precariously balanced in Tupperware and awaiting presentation.

As am I.

I jump in the shower, trying not to think about earlier. Parker's hands on my waist, his lips close to mine ...

Nope. Definitely not thinking about it.

Focusing on my outfit, I try to find the perfect balance between blending in and not disappearing from the group. I shouldn't get mistaken for one of them, so low-cut cleavage-revealing tops are out. That's not a problem since that style doesn't usually find its way into my wardrobe anyway. But after what happened back in the barn with Parker this afternoon, I'd be lying if I said I'm not factoring him in as I make my final wardrobe decision.

I settle on black leggings and a loose, white camisole with lace fringe at the top and bottom, paired with a loose denim button-up rolled up to my elbows. The material is soft and supple, practical for working, which, I remind myself, is what I'll be doing tonight.

Working. *Not* flirting.

I finish it off with a pair of black combat boots with a chunky heel, setting me a couple of inches taller than I normally am.

I've gone from dreading this whole thing to being excited for the guests to arrive. *My* guests. A quick time check reveals that I have enough time to do something with my hair, so I blow-dry it and run a curling wand through it. When I'm done, my copper hair falls in loose, beachy waves that brush my shoulders. I swipe some mascara over my lashes and dab on some pink lip gloss, thoughts of Parker once more crowding my head. After our near kiss earlier, my whole body is practically buzzing to know what his lips would feel like ... what he would taste like. My mind flashes forward to tonight's possibilities, after we send the girls off, the two of us finally alone again. With one last look in the mirror and a deep, calming breath to soothe my nerves, I give myself an encouraging nod and head to the barn.

The sun dips low over the horizon, casting everything in an orange glow. I'm about to pop up to the loft for one final check when a movement catches my eye at the far end of the barn. I squint in the dim light and see a figure standing by one of the stalls. My heart flips, but I only take a few steps before realizing it doesn't belong to Parker.

"Can I help you?"

The stranger turns towards me, strolling down the barn aisle. He's dressed head to toe in black, with scabbed knuckles poking out from the cuffs of his beat-up leather jacket. His greasy hair is pulled back from his forehead.

"Looking for someone. Maybe you can help me."

The hair on the back of my neck stands up. He stops six feet from me, and something tells me to hold my ground. For whatever reason, I don't want him to see that I'm afraid.

"Your hired hand around?"

Everything inside screams at me to lie. A flash of the money from Parker's cabin darts across my memory. What the hell kind of trouble has he gotten himself into? Because trouble is exactly what this man looks like.

"We don't have one."

A slow smile pulls at the man's thin lips, and I work hard to keep my face neutral.

"Sorry, this is a family farm. I think you have the wrong address."

He sucks his teeth, the sound echoing in the cold barn as he looks around, in no hurry to leave. The floor creaks above me, and my stomach drops. The stranger tilts his pock-marked face toward the sound.

"Look, I have guests arriving in a few minutes," I say, my voice slightly louder than before. "Sorry, I can't help, but I'm going to have to ask you to leave now."

"Come on now, there's no need to be rude," he drawls. "Besides, it sounds like you might already have company. And I have a sneaking suspicion whoever it is might be who I'm lookin' for."

Fear tickles up my spine. "I don't know what you're talking about. There's no one—"

"Sloan? That you?"

Shit.

Parker pops out from the stairwell to my left a moment later, and I jerk my head in a silent signal. One he ignores completely, stepping out into the aisle of the barn instead of keeping himself tucked away. His entire body tenses when he lays eyes on our visitor. He's in front of me in a flash, drawing himself to his full height. When I lean over to peek past him, his arm shoots back to hold me in place. The man's thin lips curl back over his teeth, and Parker stiffens before me.

"Well, well, well. Ryan Junior. You look just like your old man. Has anyone ever told you that? Like a goddamn carbon copy."

"What do you want?" Parker's voice is tight, barbed. He might not know this man personally, but that doesn't matter. He's only half-surprised to see him. Like he's been expecting something like this to happen.

I peer up at Parker, hoping for some sign of what to do, how to help, but his eyes are locked straight ahead.

"You know where he is?" the man asks, angling his head as he studies Parker.

"No. Looks like you made the drive for nothing." Parker's tone leaves no room for interpretation. He's telling him to leave.

But the stranger isn't listening. "Well, I wouldn't say it was completely fruitless," he says, leaning to get another good look at me. "I got to meet your lovely friend here, after all."

He sneers at me and Parker shifts, obstructing his view of me. I don't even recognize Parker's voice when he growls at him.

"Don't fucking talk to her."

The man's eyes turn black and sharp as he strides towards Parker until they're standing toe to toe, barely a foot of air between them.

"Listen, Junior. Your old man owes me two grand. Funny thing, he wasn't home when I went to collect."

"It's not my problem if you can't coordinate your playdates," Parker snaps.

The unfriendly smile drips off the man's face, replaced by a stone-cold sneer. "Last time your old man did this, it was six months before he paid up."

"So? What does any of this have to do with me?" Parker says through clenched teeth.

He shifts slightly, making sure I'm still behind him, as far out of view as possible. I don't know who this man is, but this still feels like the best place for me to be. My fingers reach blindly forward, and Parker's curl around mine, squeezing.

I flinch as the stranger lifts his hands to brush off Parker's shoulders, but Parker stays still as a statue even when the man's grip turns firm, a painful-looking hold. "Since Ryan Senior ain't at home, you're going to get a message to him."

"I'm not his errand boy," Parker growls.

"No, of course not." The man's face morphs into a grimace. "Not a bank, either. But I'm not waiting another six months to get *my* money back. So, you can tell your dear old daddy that Ray's looking for him. And if I don't find him in the next six *days*, I'm coming back here to get what's mine."

He pats Parker's shoulder and drops his hand, that greasy sneer of his shifting back into a smile that does nothing to fool me this time. His boot heels click across the concrete floor as he leaves. Neither of us moves until the gravel crunches under his tires as he peels away.

"Parker, what the hell was that?" I ask with a shaky breath.

He drags a hand over his face and sighs, a troubled, faraway look in his eyes. "You wanted to know what I got from my parents? That's what."

He strides forward, eyes on the car to make sure it's gone before he turns back to me. Exhaustion bleeds from his pores, and I want to wrap him in my arms. I close the distance between us, my hand drifting up to his stubbled cheek. Another silent conversation passes between us, like it did a minute ago when our hands were clasped behind his back. This time, staring into his eyes instead of his broad shoulders sends a different feeling coursing through me.

"What are you going to do?"

He shrugs and gives a quick shake of his head. The hopelessness on his face is unnerving. "Same thing I always do. Find a way to pay off my dad's debt before he gets himself killed."

"What? He won't—"

"Pay it himself?" He laughs bitterly, pulling away from me to pace in a tight circle. "He can't hold down a job to save his life. He's been out of work for months, which is why he risked borrowing money from someone like Ray to gamble with. He doesn't know how to take care of himself. I'm the one who's been keeping a roof over his head, food in the fridge. But I don't have enough for ..." he trails off, pacing in a small circle as he clasps both hands behind his head. "Two grand? Jesus Christ, Dad ..." he mutters.

I think of the money I saw in his glove compartment. He must have saved money to give to his dad to take care of him. I feel like a prize jackass for ever thinking badly of him for it.

"Can you call the police?"

"I'd only be ratting on my dad for illegal gambling. He barely speaks to me as it is. When I go over there once a week to drop off groceries and make sure he hasn't drunk himself to death, I'm lucky if I get a grunt of acknowledgement. But if I got the cops involved?" He shakes his head. "As much as I'd like him not to be my problem, he's still family, you know?"

"So, what are you going to do?" I ask weakly.

"I'll just have to come up with the money."

"How?"

"I don't know!" he snaps, then takes a breath.

When he speaks again, he's calmer, but I don't blame him for being worked up about this. I wish I knew how to help.

"I don't know," he repeats. "But I'll figure something out."

I'm worried for him. I hate that he's carrying this alone, this selfless man who would do anything to take care of the people around him. He might have been the one protecting me a few minutes ago, but I feel a surge of that same instinct to shield him coursing through me now.

That's when it hits me. I'm about to earn a decent amount of money tonight. I'd had it earmarked to pay for Lyla's half of the shop before someone else snatches it up, but I know there's a much better use for it. It's not two grand, but it'll help. And the rest, well ... we'll figure it out. We have a week to do that. But a weight lifts marginally off my chest, knowing it's at least a start. It's not uncommon for people who attend these types of workshops to tip, either, so giving them the best possible experience now is about so much more than a good review.

Parker's jaw hardens when I voice the idea, looking anything but relieved. He cuts a stern look at me through the dusty air. "Sloan, no. Not a chance."

"Why not?"

"Because I'm not your fucking charity case, that's why."

I flinch at the bite in his words, but it only takes a second before I step forward, spurred on by the determination roaring inside me. "Explain to me how this is charity when you've helped me with just about every aspect of tonight." My heart is pounding. "Exactly," I say when he fails to answer, stepping into his line of sight when he tries to turn away.

"I'm still not taking your money."

"You said you'd figure something out. Here it is. I'm not giving you an answer to all your problems, Parker, I'm just offering something to help."

"Why? Because you feel sorry for me? So you can hold it over my head?"

He wants me to balk, but I refuse, standing my ground. I could placate him, trying to convince him that my intentions are genuine. If he were anyone else, that's exactly what I'd be doing. However, his refusal to accept my help only fuels my anger. Not two hours ago, when we were about to get hot and heavy in the feed room, he told me he couldn't help the way he felt about me, and he knew I felt it too. Now suddenly he's denying that it means something?

"I'm not answering that. If you would let yourself see past your pride for a goddamn minute, you wouldn't even have asked me that in the first place."

Something like remorse flickers behind his eyes. "Sloan, I—"

"No." I hold up a hand to stop him from getting closer. "If you don't want my help, fine. That's your prerogative. But if you still don't think I'm being genuine with you about my intentions, that tells me everything I need to know."

I cross my arms, ignoring what the disappointment in his expression does to my insides. He already questioned me once; the first time we almost crossed this line. I thought I'd managed to convince him that he didn't need to, but what happened between us earlier was clearly nothing more than a moment of weakness. I'm not looking to fall into anything again without my eyes wide open. I learned the hard way with Caleb about what happens when I ignore the red flags right in front of my face. I'm not about to make the same mistakes again. Not when I've already wasted so much time.

Another vehicle pulls into the driveway, drawing our attention. We both stiffen, my heart instantly hammering in my chest, and rush to the door to see who it is. Instead of Ray coming back with more threats, it's a limo, which can only mean one thing. My guests have arrived.

Twenty minutes ago, I was about to break out in hives at the thought of doing this on my own. Now it doesn't even seem important.

"I'm gonna get out of your way," Parker says, his voice softer now, but his eyes still not meeting mine. "I won't be far. In case ..."

He doesn't say it, but I know what he's thinking. In case Ray comes back.

"Good luck tonight."

I nod, saying nothing. There's nothing more to say.

He disappears out the back door, and I turn to the limo as it comes to a stop in front of the barn. Eight young women in plaid pour out of it, giggling and wide-eyed.

This is it. I do my best to clear my head and focus on the event, shaking free all thoughts of Ray, Parker, and, most importantly, of Parker and me. Whatever I thought was building between us has already burned up faster than a barn full of hay, but I still have the thing I've been building on my own. Though I haven't been preparing for this party alone—Parker's been there every step of the way. As I step forward to greet my guests, I'm acutely aware that this is the first time I feel like I'm doing this with no one behind me. No one to catch me if I fail.

I quickly push all thoughts of Parker as far out of my head as possible. This is precisely why it was a bad idea to use him as a distraction in the first place. Sure, it might be fun in my downtime, but if I let it get in the way of what mattered, I'd never forgive myself for it. Tonight isn't about him, and so much is riding on this one event that I *have* to focus.

I swallow back the tiniest bit of vomit.

Alright, Sloan. Game face.

Chapter 20

"Ooh, that looks so good! Mine looks like a blob."

We've finished the demo portion of the evening, and now I'm roaming quietly while the women work on painting the signs they'll take home with them later. The Spice Girls' *If You Want to Be My Lover* plays in the background along with the sound of happy chatter and bouts of laughter.

"You can easily fix that," I say, moving in closer to the one I think is called Abby. She's sitting at the table nearest the desserts, working away under the warm glow of the string lights with a determined frown on her pixie-like face. Her expression, paired with the heavy club-ready makeup, is almost laughable, but—like the others—she seems to be enjoying herself.

"Widen the other letters a smidge to match, and you'll even that out. Easy."

"Maybe for you, you're like ... really good at this." Her blue eyes squint in concentration as she tries the technique I showed her. "Hey, it worked!"

I pat her on the shoulder. "Great work. I think you're going to love how that turns out." I check the time on my phone.

Only nine thirty. *Shit.* We got through the demo much faster than I'd planned. In part thanks to the bolstered confidence of my drunken pupils, who kept yelling, *Take the training wheels off!* I'm going around the room topping off champagne glasses as I chew my bottom lip, when there's a knock at the door. My heart skips when I see Parker stick his head through. We haven't spoken since the limo arrived. As much as I've tried to push him out of my head, I've been replaying our fight in my head the whole time. I wanted to trust my gut, to believe that I'd been right to call things off before we went any further. If he can't trust me to be real with him, then what hope is there that *anything* between us could be real? But I'd be lying if I said I hadn't felt the sting of disappointment as the implications of that settled in over my heart.

"Is that the stripper?" someone shouts. Parker turns red before waving me over and disappearing out the door.

"Hey," he says in a hushed voice when I follow him onto the landing, his eyes sliding over my face.

"Hey." I'm not trying to be cold or distant, but I don't want to send mixed signals, so I ignore the tailspin my stomach is in from his scent washing over me.

"Look, about earlier ... I'm sorry. You were trying to help, which is something I'm not used to. Clearly. I'm used to being the one to help, and I shouldn't have snapped at you." He rubs the back of his neck.

I cross my arms over my chest. This isn't a good time to have this conversation. I need to get back in there, but I can't tamp down my curiosity. "Why did you?"

"Before tonight, Tabitha's been the only person who's ever really helped me without expecting something in return. She's uh ... she's told me that I'm not very good at being on the receiving end of it." He pauses, pressing his lips into a thin line. His gaze drops briefly to his scuffed-up boots. "Guys like the one who came here earlier? That's my life, Sloan. I've accepted that dealing with this shit is my reality, but it doesn't have to be *yours*."

"It doesn't have to be yours either," I argue. "I don't understand why you won't take the money to get rid of him—"

"This has nothing to do with the money, Sloan." His eyes bore into me as he speaks, holding me captive. "Seeing you in the same room as that guy today made my blood run cold. My dad is really good at getting himself into trouble with the wrong people. Dangerous people. The idea of getting you involved any more than you already are ... I'm a grown man and I don't mind admitting that it scares the crap out of me, Sloan. I can't be responsible for you getting hurt."

I study the lines in his face, etched between his eyebrows and carved around the edges of his mouth, heavy with the weight of everything he carries for the people in his life who give him no choice but to bear it alone. But there's always a choice, even when it seems impossible, even when it's not the easy one. Sometimes you have to choose you.

"Parker, you're not stuck with it any more than I am." His eyes are deep, dark pools of emotion, and I want to plunge into them to extinguish the fire that's lit inside my chest. "Bad things happen. Even to people with perfect families, perfect jobs, and perfect marriages. Accepting it is easy because most people won't argue with you about it. A week ago, I was ready to give up on *everything* I've worked for, and if I had, none of these women would be in here having a great time," I say, jerking a thumb over my shoulder. "The only reason I'm doing this right now is because you and Tabitha were beside me the whole time."

He frowns. "We hardly did anything."

"But I wasn't alone, Parker."

We stand chest to chest, staring at each other as I wait, hoping that he'll agree to my silent plea. *Trust me. Let me go through this* with *you.*

"Okay," he says, his voice low, the word trembling in the air between us.

His shoulders relax in relief, and the vice grip around my heart finally loosens. He tilts his chin towards the door to the loft behind me.

"How's it going in there?" His nose wrinkles. "And *what* is that noise?"

I laugh, trying not to let my head go any foggier as he leans into my space to get a peek. "They brought their own playlist." Luckily, because I hadn't thought of music for tonight either. The list of things I'll do differently next time—if there is a next time—is growing. But I'm getting ahead of myself. "I think it's going kind of great. Just ... quicker than I expected. I need to fill their time so they get their money's worth. I don't know, I could have them make a second sign, but I'm worried they'll get bored. I think I understand why parents host their kids' birthdays at Chuck E. Cheese."

He grins, and I get lost for a second in his eyes. In my heeled boots, they're much closer to my level, and I take advantage of the guise that we're conspiring to stare directly into them.

"I was hoping you would say that. I have a surprise."

I perk up. "What is it?"

He winks. Like, actually winks. Who is this man, and what has he done with Parker?

"You'll see. Bring them down whenever you're ready."

"Parker, come on. What is it?" I demand, grabbing his arm.

He looks at me, all traces of teasing erased. The intensity of his stare sets my insides fluttering in a whole new way, and I can hear my heartbeat thrum in my ears.

"Trust me?" he asks, eyes still locked on mine.

I swallow, knowing this is crazy. Knowing if he asked me the same thing three days ago, I would have said no. But I'm choosing to take myself down a different path to see what's there.

So, with his warm hand on my arm, I nod.

***

Trust me.

As of recently, 'trust' is no longer a word I take lightly. Though he certainly hasn't steered me wrong yet. There's no reason I shouldn't—none except for the logical side of my brain that reminds me I barely know him. I don't even trust the people I've known my whole life, at this point. But here's the thing, I *want* to trust him. I want him to be in this with me.

With one final deep breath—I've now crossed over into expert territory in meditative breathing from today alone—I put myself in his hands. Again.

I freeze when we reach the bottom of the stairs and see Parker—

Wearing a freaking *cowboy hat*.

At least three different conversations screech to a halt. My first instinct is to burst out laughing. But damn if he doesn't somehow look incredibly sexy. I kind of wish he wore it all the time.

"Ladies," he greets us with a slight tip of his hat.

Hello, Sundance Kid.

"Stop it, there's a sexy farmhand and everything?" the bride, Lucy, says excitedly, clapping her hands together.

"Lucy! This isn't dinner theater; he can hear you," one of her friends says.

I watch the discomfort try to squirm its way out of Parker's body, one muscle at a time. But even with pink cheeks, he fumbles only slightly before he manages to keep the charade going.

"Uh, yeah so ... I understand this is a special occasion, and your host," he gestures at me, but I could probably strip naked and they wouldn't take their eyes off him, "has organized something extra special for you all. If you'll follow me?"

We trail after him like eager ducklings, and when we emerge from the barn, my gasp gets lost in the chorus of them that collectively rise up from the group.

The outdoor riding ring is illuminated with a soft, yellow glow. String lights, similar to the ones we put up in the loft, are draped around the wooden fence that surrounds the perimeter of the rectangular pen. Beside it, a campfire crackles in a low barrel, with logs surrounding it for seating. Once they finish taking pictures enthusiastically, everyone settles in, grabbing blankets from a wicker basket to drape over their laps. There's even a basket going around with all the makings for s'mores, and a bundle of roasting sticks propped next to the fire.

I drift over to Parker's side, taking it all in. "When did you do all this?"

But when I turn to face him, he's already slipped away. The women make themselves comfortable, smiling and laughing.

"This is just like that summer at camp!" Lucy squeals. "That was the best summer ever."

"Yeah, remember they had that spooky old barn, but it was empty and haunted? I heard a ghost in there once."

"You did not, Abby. You heard the camp counselors going at it."

"Oh my god, *nooo*! Do you think so?"

They all erupt in laughter.

Abby looks scandalized. "People *did it* at camp?!"

"People definitely did *stuff* at camp," Veronica says slyly. "Or so I heard."

They all scream and demand the details, but I get distracted by the sound of hooves clomping through the barn. I whip around, thinking maybe a horse has gotten loose, but it's Parker guiding Zeke outside, tacked up with an oversized Western saddle.

He winks at me as he passes by, and it sends my intestines somersaulting again.

"Happy?" he asks, his voice low.

I nod. "Extremely," I murmur back. "And I owe you. Seriously, you will be thanked profusely for this."

His gaze heats, and a ripple of excitement goes through me.

"I like the sound of that," he says in a low voice.

I don't know where he found that cowboy hat, but I think it might have magical powers.

"Alright, who's first for the ultimate cowgirl experience?" Parker says, standing at my elbow with Zeke on his other side. The beat of silence is deafening before they burst into a collective squeal that nearly bursts my eardrums. Zeke, true to form, doesn't even flinch.

"Wow, that sounded so incredibly dirty," I whisper under my breath.

"Shut up," he hisses back. Then he raises his voice so the others can hear him. "And by that, I, uh, of course, mean a completely innocent ride."

"That too," I mutter above barely contained giggling.

Even in the firelight, I'm sure I can see the tips of his ears going pink. "No, I meant—ugh. Never mind. Who wants to sit on the horse?"

The group positively howls. Parker tosses his hands up and turns to leave, but I stop him. I steer him by the shoulders over to the riding paddock, Zeke trailing steadily along.

"Don't worry, it's not your fault, everything you're saying has a double meaning," I say with my hands still on his shoulders. "You're talking about *riding*. At a bachelorette party. I can't say I blame them."

"Excuse me for thinking we were dealing with adult women and not a bunch of twelve-year-olds."

"My friend, at a bachelorette party, we're the same thing."

I give him a pat on the back, my eyes greedily cataloging the way his hard muscles ripple as he checks everything over. As much as these women seem to want him, I've come closer to any of the fantasies guaranteed to be running rampant through their minds right now. It makes it all the more difficult not to imagine how his bare shoulders would feel under my curious, exploring fingers.

"We should start with our guest of honor!" I announce, clapping my hands together and turning to the group.

Veronica tugs Lucy forward, who is practically bouncing with excitement. I don't know if it's because it's her bachelorette party, or if it has anything to do with her opinion of the workshop so far, but it's enough that more than a tiny part of me believes a good review could be coming my way. Lucy is wearing dark-wash skinny jeans that are shredded on the thighs, paired with a wide belt around the waist of her gray-and-white plaid top, and cowboy boots that appear to have never been worn.

"That's me! The future Mrs. Keith Cooper, at your service!" she says, adjusting the plastic tiara and short veil adorning her club-worthy blonde curls.

Not for the first time tonight, a collective *oooooOOOH* rises from the girls like a fight song at a high school football game. The bride's sister, Molly, doesn't join in. She hasn't left her sister's side all night, and I've been watching her the closest. She's the only one who doesn't seem to be having quite as good a time as the rest of them and has barely cracked a smile since they arrived.

Before she follows me, Lucy pulls Veronica into a bear hug. "This is all *perfect*," she gushes, waving at the fire, the barn, the horse. Or maybe it was Parker she was pointing at. "Nobody knows me like you do. I honestly couldn't have asked for anything better."

I glance at Molly, who wears a pained expression on her face before she tips her head back to down the rest of her drink.

"It was nothing, really," Veronica says. Though she's beaming, I catch her sneak a sympathetic glimpse at Molly too; I then recall that she was the one who was supposed to organize the party.

"No, it's not nothing," Lucy insists. "It's everything."

She turns to Parker, but hesitates when he extends the reins to her, looking a little sheepish. "Oh, um ... I know this might come as a shock, but I'm not much of a horse girl."

"You don't ride?" he asks, surprised.

"Sure, if you count the pony ride at the county fair when I was nine."

"Aren't you the one with the country blog?" Parker asks bluntly.

I wince, but thankfully Lucy laughs. "It's more about the country *aesthetic*. Lifestyle, fashion, home décor, etc. I'm happy to be on the farm so long as I don't have to get too close to the *smells*, if you know what I mean."

I have to give Parker points for not rolling his eyes.

"I guess this experience includes a lesson then, too."

I turn away as Parker gets Lucy on the horse and talks her through where to put her hands and feet before leading her around the riding ring. He's obviously got his part covered, and I don't want to intrude on the rest of the group, so I hang back awkwardly, away from the fire, doing my best to blend in.

"Sloan, get over here! You look like you're freezing," Veronica calls, patting the empty log beside her.

I try to decline politely, but cave when they all join in, if only to get them to stop yelling. It has gotten cooler, a crispness to the fall air that makes me wish I had a coat. The women look comfortable, but they have the added benefit of booze warming their veins.

"Thank you for making tonight so special," Veronica says, handing me some of her blanket. "She loves it."

"I heard."

"You get full credit for it. This is ... so much more than I even expected."

"I know, can we stay and have the wedding here?" Abby jokes, waving towards the lights strung up all around. "This is like, the absolute cutest little place."

I cast another glance over at Molly, staring sullenly into the fire. "I think your marshmallow's burning," I tell her.

"Whatever," she mutters, stabbing the flaming marshmallow into the coals.

"Are you going to tell us what your deal is with that guy, or what?" Veronica asks, pulling my attention back to her.

The girls around the fire exchange knowing looks, a couple of them leaning over to get a better view of him in action.

"Uh, nothing?"

Veronica rolls her eyes, amused by my lame deflection. "Puh-lease. We're not blind. Besides, chemistry like that doesn't lie."

There's a murmur of agreement from the others. My cheeks warm, but it has nothing to do with sitting closer to the fire. The women are all leaning toward me now, literally on the edge of their seats. Probably hoping they can live vicariously through me with a vivid description of Parker's ... private talents. I can't deny that sparks have been flying tonight, though I didn't think anyone else would notice. It turns out that drunk women are pretty observant. I don't get a chance to brush them off with another lame answer, though.

Before I can open my mouth, a scream pierces through the night air.

Chapter 21

I'm up in a flash.

I don't look back to see if the blanket I toss aside lands in the fire. I'm on autopilot, ignoring the clamoring heartbeat drumming in my ears, the adrenaline coursing through my veins. I yank open the gate and dash across the paddock, cursing as the soft dirt sucks at my feet, slowing me down. Up ahead in the shadows, outlined in the haze of the string lights, Parker is crouched on the ground beside Zeke.

Oh shit, oh shit, oh shit.

"What happened? Is everyone okay?"

"He tripped. Easy boy, it's okay," he mutters. Despite the soothing words as he strokes the horse's neck, I can hear the waver in his voice. "He couldn't get up when he tried. I don't know what's wrong."

The tremor in Parker's voice scares me even more, but Zeke isn't the only one I'm worried about. As the others catch up, I rush towards Lucy, standing a few feet away, cradling one arm with the other; her eyes are wide and distant. *Fuck.* I should have been here, not indulging in girl talk like I was attending the party instead of hosting it! How could I have been so irresponsible? There isn't time to freak out, though. Parker is focused on Zeke, who is still on the ground, and Tabitha is out with Jim, and Lyla didn't want to be here. I'm in this alone ... failing alone. This situation is entirely on me, and I have no idea what to do.

Calm down, I tell myself with a shaky exhale. *This has to be handled. Handle it.*

Unlocking an inner reservoir of calm, I shut down the emotional side of my head entirely as I gently gripped Lucy by the shoulders and asked her to explain what had happened.

"I landed on my wrist."

With her slight nod of permission, I pull it tenderly away from her body to get a closer look, which causes her to hiss in pain.

Molly blows up like a fuse. *"You broke my sister's arm!"*

I immediately turn into the mediator, maintaining a calm but firm tone I didn't know I was capable of. "We don't know it's broken, and none of this is Parker's fault."

"Not him, her!" Molly jabs a finger at Veronica, who balks. "We wouldn't even be here if it weren't for you!"

Her face goes from shocked to furious in a matter of seconds. "I wouldn't have even planned this if you had done your job. *You're* the Maid of Honor, but you couldn't even be bothered to make the reservations for her bachelorette party!"

"Stop! Just stop, both of you!" Lucy wails.

The sight of tears streaming down her face silences them both, and their anger melts into concern. I want to cry too. How did things go so wrong so fast?

"Everybody, calm down!" My no-nonsense voice surprises even me, and once I get their attention, I make the most of it. The situation is barely within my grasp, and I need to do everything I can to keep it that way. "Molly, there's a first aid kit hanging on the wall in the office," I say, pointing towards the barn door. "First door on your left. Get it and bring it back here for your sister. Veronica, take the girls and grab your stuff from the loft. Get the limo to take everyone home. Parker—" The moment my eyes make contact with his, I stutter. My chest gets tight, and every shallow breath feels like an effort to pull in, while something thick and heavy fills my throat. I feel it coming, the slight tremble of my hands, my bottom lip, the prickle of tears behind my eyes. He sees it all, and I'm sure he can see the panic behind my eyes. But then he gives me the tiniest nod. That subtle motion pushes the fear back enough that I can hear myself think and realize that he's silently waiting for my instructions—waiting for me to take charge.

Because he trusts me.

I swallow. "Do you have your cell phone on you?"

He nods.

"Call the emergency vet and stay with Zeke until they get here."

Molly appears at my side, extending the first aid kit to me. It was mostly a task to keep her distracted, but I want to make her feel useful, so I open it and find an instant cold pack. Placing the kit at my feet, I twist and squeeze the pack, then give it a quick shake before pressing it carefully against Lucy's wrist. "Come on. Let's get you to the hospital."

Boot heels click on the barn floor. Before I even see him, I can tell by the gait that they belong to Parker. He finds me huddled in the corner, knees tucked up to my chest. Like me, Parker's still dressed in his clothes from last night.

"I couldn't sleep after I got back from the hospital," I explain, my eyes lingering on the wraps around Zeke's legs. "Wanted to see for myself that he was still okay."

"Yeah, me too." He steps towards Zeke, eyes ringed with dark circles, and strokes his long nose before doing another once-over. Settling in next to me, back against the wall, he drapes his forearms over his knees and tilts his head back, letting out a sigh.

"What did the vet say?" I ask, rubbing my tired eyes.

"He needs his legs wrapped for a few days to give him extra support, but he's not seriously injured. He's just getting old, and his joints are weak."

I nod, relieved it's nothing more serious. If anything had happened to Zeke on my watch, I'd never forgive myself.

"You should go try and get some sleep," I say, pulling my eyes away from Parker. "I'll stay with him."

"I'm not sitting here for Zeke."

I turn my head slowly to look at him, not trusting that I heard him right. I sink into his gaze, the sympathy in them enough to make my throat squeeze. Too tired to say anything, we let our eyes do the talking. The air around us turns heavy, until finally I turn away, afraid I might see his expression change. Afraid he might look away first.

"You know it's not as bad as it seems, right? It was a close call, but in the light of day it won't seem so bad."

I let out a humorless laugh. "I doubt Veronica and her friends will think so."

"Are you kidding? You gave them a hell of a night to remember. They'll be telling this story for years."

"That's what I'm afraid of." I can feel his eyes on me, but this time I don't return the look.

"It was going so well," I mutter, thinking back to how the evening began. "They were having a great time. And then with the campfire and everything you did ... it was the cherry on top. I never imagined it ending this way."

"Nobody did. That's why they call them accidents."

"Right, but this was my first time out of the gate. I just ... couldn't afford this one." I realize what it sounds like I'm saying, and quickly backtrack. "Sorry, I'm not blaming you," I say quickly, turning to look at him now. "You were trying to help, and it was perfect."

Until it wasn't.

"I guess I have my answer," I say miserably. "I was never meant to be a business owner. My bad luck is going to haunt me forever. I swear, it knows how to lull me into a false sense of security, making me think things are finally going right for me. But it's just waiting until the moment it can do the most damage." I drop my gaze, plucking at a rip in my jeans with a sniff that I don't care if Parker notices.

"People face setbacks all the time, Sloan," he reasons. "If you want this, you shouldn't let what happened last night get in the way."

I shake my head. If it wasn't Lucy's fractured wrist last night, something else would have happened—just like if Adam hadn't lost his job, there would have been another reason why Lyla had to pull out. "Even if I could get a business up and running, I don't think I'll ever trust that it won't disappear overnight. I can't put everything into something when I know it's not going to be permanent."

I feel his gaze on me again and let it linger. Not pausing long enough to think about what I do next, I tilt my head sideways and rest it on him, his shoulder warm and comforting against my cheek. I barely have a chance to appreciate the musky scent of his aftershave mingling with his green apple shampoo before he pats my knee, his hand lingering for a second longer than it has to on my jean-clad thigh.

"Come on, Princess. We've got work to do."

"We? Since when is the union strike over?"

"Since you're not the only one running on a few hours of sleep. Besides, you could use the distraction."

"I'd rather stay here and let my world implode around me while I wait for Lucy to post whatever horrible review is coming for me."

Zeke lifts his head, staring at me while he munches loudly on a mouthful of hay.

"I know." Parker rises gracefully to his feet and reaches out a hand towards me. "Too bad the horses don't give a shit if you're having a bad day. They still have to eat." When I still don't move, he gently tips my chin up with a crooked knuckle. "Trust me, on the bad days, it doesn't hurt to have something to take care of other than yourself."

I try to ignore how his skin feels in my hand as he pulls me up, his palm warm and rough. But I have a few extra seconds to enjoy it, because he doesn't release me right away. Slowly, I lift my eyes to his. We're standing close together, almost as close as yesterday when his hands were on my hips, when he looked hungry for me.

He doesn't look hungry now, though. There's something else there in his eyes, deep, imploring. But he doesn't leave it there long enough for me to decipher it. Instead, he drags me up and puts me to work. I hadn't realized it before, but in the past few weeks, we've developed a quiet synchronicity. Side by side, we fill and distribute feed pails to each of the stalls, the barn growing loud with the sound of twelve rousing horses chomping on grain before we start turn out. The whole time, Parker is a steady presence beside me, pressing me forward when I start to slow with a light touch on the base of my spine, or a tap on my elbow to keep me from getting lost in my thoughts when they threaten to sweep me away from the present. It turns out that being distracted isn't the best idea when dealing with animals several times your size, with twice as many feet. I'm trailing him out into the bright morning light, leading a twelve-hundred-pound horse, when her big hoof pinches the side of my foot painfully.

"Ouch, Buttercup!" I mutter, stumbling.

I look down to get my footing back and make sure I don't get stepped on again. The only problem is, looking down prevents me from looking up, and when Parker stops at the paddock, I smack right into his horse.

"Sorry! Sorry!"

"I thought you used to do this all the time?" he says, shaking his head at me, his lips tipping up.

"I guess I'm out of practice," I lie.

He unloops the chain and pulls the gate open, leading his horse into the grassy paddock and releasing him with a gentle pat on the neck, before sending the horse trotting away. He turns to hold the gate open for me. "Make sure you hold on—"

His following words are lost as my arm is nearly ripped out of its socket. Buttercup takes off, running after the other horse before I can unclip the lead rope.

Meaning, I'm *still attached.*

Not for long, though. I stumble, my legs instantly tangling up beneath me as I'm flung to the ground, landing hard with a face full of dirt. *"Owww,"* I groan, pushing up onto my hands.

Parker skids to his knees beside me, eyes wide as he grips my shoulder.

I peer up at him, glaring. "Tight? Is that what you were going to say? Hold on tight? Great advice, thanks. A-plus for timing, by the way."

His face relaxes instantly, the tight lines around his mouth giving way to a teasing grin. "Come on, let's get you cleaned up."

I get to my feet while Parker catches up with Buttercup to remove the lead rope before guiding me back to the barn office by the elbow.

"Sit," he says, pointing to the desk. "Does anything hurt?"

"Just my pride. Seriously, I feel fine."

He gives me a look, then returns to searching the cupboards for the first-aid kit. "You might be sore in the morning."

"Perhaps. Or maybe I'm getting tougher. I've been spending so much time with you in the barn that I can handle being thrown by a wild horse."

He locates the first aid kit and turns back to me, setting it on the desk beside me. "That horse is hardly wild, and you weren't riding her, so you weren't thrown. Thrown *down*, maybe."

"What are you talking about, not wild?" I cry, feigning outrage. "She galloped away with no warning! She's out of control."

The legs of a chair scrape against the floor as Parker drags it in front of me and sits. With the height difference, I'm now looking down at him for the first time. His smooth skin is deeply tanned from working outside, and I itch to run my fingers across the dark scruff on his jaw. I stop myself from leaning forward.

"She barely broke a trot. Now hold still."

"What are you—ow!" My right knee stings as he wipes it with rubbing alcohol through a rip I hadn't even noticed in my jeans.

"Get over it, Princess." He glances up, the hint of a smile pulling at the edge of his lips.

Heat pools in my core, reminding me what I want. How badly I want it. It takes me back to the last time he had me in here like this, taking care of my blistered hands. "If I didn't know any better, I'd say you were getting me into these situations on purpose so you can play doctor," I murmur.

"I planned that the horse would run off, did I?" he asks in a low voice.

His smile deepens, but he keeps his eyes on my knee as he cleans my scrape. It gives me the chance to admire his face, the smooth line of his nose, the soft bottom lip. Almost involuntarily, I imagine what it would feel like between my teeth.

His eyes flip up to mine, and I'm busted.

My cheeks go pink. While he wasn't looking, I've been leaning closer, but instead of shifting back, I hold my position. "Could have. You spend a lot of time in the barn. How should I know if you're working or plotting?"

Resting his elbows on his knees, he crowds even further into my space. His eyes are locked on mine, but somehow, I remain hyper aware of that perfect mouth of his, that sly smile doing strange things to my insides.

"Are you still holding me responsible for tearing up your own hands because you refused to take a break?"

"If you hadn't called me a princess, I wouldn't have had anything to prove."

"I guess I should stop calling you that."

I lift one shoulder in a shrug. "I don't mind so much anymore. Depending on the context." The way the word rumbled out of his mouth a minute ago, though ...? I think I'd let him call me anything if he promised to say it like that.

His throat bobs in a hard swallow, and his voice has a slight rasp to it when he asks, "How are your hands, by the way?"

I lift my hands in front of me, palms facing out. "All better. See?"

Slowly, he reaches past me to set the cotton swab on the desk. His rough fingertips graze my palms as he slides his hands up, mirroring mine, and my brain goes fuzzy like the static on the upstairs TV as he eases his fingers between mine in one gentle, slow movement, completely ensnaring me. This is nothing like yesterday, when he was all over me. He's only touching my hands, but my whole *body* is on fire.

We both struggle to steady our breathing. His chest rises and falls beneath his navy T-shirt, and his gaze drifts dangerously low. Sensing me watching, his eyes drag up. They brush over my chest, my neck, my face, as if they were his actual fingertips, and when they finally reach mine, it's like a high-powered magnet is turned on. We're laser-focused on each other, and there's no question about what he wants. What *we* want.

I arch my back slightly, easing closer, and that's all it takes.

His lips are on mine before I can close my eyes. Somehow, his hands untangle from mine and find their way to new homes, one on my neck, the other wrapping around my lower back. Mine move on their own, drifting up and around his neck, pulling him into me.

It's intoxicating.

I'm drunk on him; his smell, his taste, his touch. I can't get enough. His lips—impossibly softer than I'd imagined—trail across my cheek and halfway down my neck before I pull him back to my mouth, demanding more. And more is exactly what I get. His tongue grazes my bottom lip, so warm I almost moan. When his tongue slides over mine, I'm absolutely done—I can no longer be held accountable for the noises I make.

Our movements grow frantic, no longer exploring but grabbing, insistent, desperate. His hands—which I guess have worked their way down from my face at some point—settle on my hips, gripping hard over my jeans. I gasp as his fingertips slip up beneath my shirt, grazing my skin. Even with so little contact, the sensation is overwhelming.

So overwhelming it's dangerous.

I'm about to make a stupid decision, and we're out in the open, in broad daylight. As much as we both might want to, we *cannot* go at it in the barn. Gently, I lay my hands on his chest and ease him away as my brain screams, *'What the hell do you think you're doing?!'*

With a couple of inches of space between us, Parker shakes his head like he's physically clearing the fog from it. "Sorry. I've been wanting to do that for a while," he says breathlessly.

We're still tangled up in each other's arms, my knees gripping his hips at the edge of the desk.

"Oh really? I couldn't tell."

"Ha, ha," he says flatly. "I guess we should ..."

"Get back to work?"

His gaze drifts to where I've pulled my bottom lip between my teeth. "Yeah. Work. That's what I want to do right now. I'm so excited about work. I could work all day long."

He sighs heavily, vocalizing the sexual tension that I feel in my bones. In the space he makes as he steps back, I slide down to my feet, straightening my top as I slip past him, heading for the door.

"Let's get back to work," I say. "You've got a lot to do. It's going to be a long day. Long and *hard*." My smile turns devilish when his chuckle comes out as a groan. "Come on, cowboy. Someone once told me horses don't give a shit if you're having a bad day."

He calls after me as I leave the office, my boot heels clicking on the concrete floor.

"You're killing me, you know that? You are *actually* killing me."

Chapter 22

I feel like I deserve an award for dousing that fire. As hard as Parker found it to get back to work, I've found him equally distracting after he gave me quite possibly the best kiss of my life. Escaping up to the loft is only partly to clean up the mess I didn't bother to deal with last night, but mostly it's to keep my hands to myself. It's not an easy task when he's in the barn making manual labor look easy. Truthfully, I thought it would be fun teasing him a little—but the looks he keeps shooting my way are enough to make me feel like I'm about to combust.

The sight of the loft brings me crashing down from the cloud I've been drifting on all morning. Lo and behold, the leftover desserts are—well, leftovers no more. Mid-morning light, shining through the slats in the walls, illuminates the dust floating in the air, landing on half-eaten cake and on remnants of champagne and cocktails in plastic cups. Flies buzz around the food scraps, and I try to ignore what looks like pawprints in the sticky smears of icing spread across my formerly perfectly decorated dessert table. At least the raccoons enjoyed the party. I stand for a moment with a trash bag in hand, wondering where to begin, before it all feels like too much.

I ignore the mess, though, because seeing it makes me realize that there's one person I need to talk to about this, someone I should have remembered much earlier than I have. I pull out my phone.

"I have to tell you something," I blurt when Lyla picks up. "Last night went horribly. And not like someone got food poisoning, this was well and truly a disaster."

Lyla's quiet for a beat, and I can picture her face rearranging into big sister mode. "Start from the beginning."

I tell her everything, from how well it started, even though almost everything was slightly different from how I pictured it would be, Parker's surprise campfire and cowgirl experience, and how it ended with me and the bride-to-be at the hospital.

"*No*," she gasps. "Pumped stomach?"

"Fractured wrist."

"*NO*."

"She'll be in a cast for her wedding next weekend."

"Okay. There's ... a lot to unpack there. Let's start with the fact that I'm guessing you're probably beating yourself up over it, am I right?" She takes my silence as her answer. "Accidents happen. I'm sure she doesn't blame you."

Maybe not, but that doesn't mean she won't tell the whole world about what happened under my watch. I keep that bit of intel to myself, though. Rightly or otherwise, I decided not to tell Lyla when I discovered Lucy's online persona. I was stressed out enough without Lyla knowing the stakes of taking *our* business on a test run without her. Now that I've royally screwed things up for both of us, I know I need to tell her the truth. What I don't know is how to bring it up.

"It never would have happened if you were here. I don't know why I thought I could ever do this without you." Lyla's presence alone is enough to keep people in check, which she attributes to being a Leo. I think it has more to do with growing up as the oldest of five siblings and practically helping her working parents raise her brothers and sisters. But Lyla likes to believe in the power of the universe, and who am I to take that away from her? It takes me a beat to realize she's gone quiet. "You still there?"

"Would you ever?"

"Would I ... what?"

"Open the business on your own. You could do it, you know. You don't need me."

I press the phone closer to my ear. "Whoa, where is this coming from? I thought we were pausing the business. Why does it sound like you're pulling out completely?"

"No!" she says quickly. "It's just ... we should probably talk about what happens if Adam gets this job in New York."

The unexpected rush of emotions catches me off guard. I'm happy for Adam, but I hate the thought of even *more* change coming my way. A month and a half ago, I was about to start spending every day with Lyla. I hate even to think it, because I've been the one hiding from my life here at Salem Stables, but the idea of so much distance between us, *permanently*? It scares me. At the same time, I'm conflicted by the thought of going back myself. I hadn't planned on leaving anytime soon, but now I realize I may let myself ignore the fact that eventually, I'll have to. I can't stay here forever ... can I? It is starting to feel like home in every sense of the word. And if Lyla is telling me she can't be part of the business, I'm not sure what I have to go back to. Parker's face floats through my muddled mind, and it's enough to prove that whatever is going on between us is so much more than a simple distraction.

"We don't have to decide anything right now." I'd prefer if we didn't. "How do your parents feel about all this?" I know how much they rely on her for the family business.

"They'd be more than fine with it if they could see how well Billie's stepped up," she says, and her younger sister's mischievous face pops into my mind, deceptively sweet with that dusting of freckles on her nose. She's in her mid-twenties now, but I will forever see her as the wild child drawn to every thrill-seeking risk she could find; the girl was single-handedly responsible for Lyla's first frown lines. "Billie wasn't thrilled with being part of the family business at first, but she seems to have come around, for whatever reason. It's Billie, though, so I'm not convinced it's a genuine change of heart."

Her words are spoken with a weight I've grown used to hearing but have never questioned before. I've always viewed Lyla as the older sister who *likes* getting involved in other people's problems. After this brief conversation, I'm wondering if she sounds so tired because she's been dealing with other issues, and the weight of responsibility is finally catching up to her. It sounds like she might *want* the distance from it all. I only wish I knew where that left me.

I think of Sam, and how he's still fighting to convince his father that he wants to work at his garage after taking some time to explore other options. His dad might not understand, but Sam needed to step away to gain that perspective and make sure he was there because he was *choosing* to be, not because it was the path chosen for him.

"Maybe it is genuine," I say, letting myself be optimistic for a change.

"This is my sister we're talking about. Do you remember what she told me when I started working for my parents? That I was settling in the worst way because I was dedicating my life to perpetuating someone else's dream instead of my own."

I wince. "Yikes. That sounds ... harsher than I remember."

She laughs, sounding more tired than bitter. "You're telling me. Of all my siblings, she's the least likely to sugarcoat things. Which is why it doesn't make any sense that she's back and leaning into this."

This time, when I picture Sam, I also think of myself and how naïve I used to be. I took the world and my life at face value; I didn't ask questions because things were exactly the way I wanted them.

"She's older now. Maybe she sees things differently."

Lyla scoffs. "Billie can't commit to a hair color, let alone a career path."

"People change their minds, Ly," I say gently.

She's quiet for a long beat. Eventually, she says, "Yeah ... yeah, they do."

We chat for a few more minutes before we end the call, and I stand there for a long while afterwards, staring at the phone in my hand, unsure what to do about the unsteady feeling brewing inside me.

At the sound of his voice, my head snaps up to find Parker standing in the doorway, leaning against the frame.

"Sorry to interrupt the moment you're clearly having with your phone, but I'm starving and couldn't tell how much longer you were going to be. I had to take matters into my own hands."

How does a person make a T-shirt and jeans look so damn good? Honestly, the thought dances a conga line through my head at the same time I realize Lyla's sudden departure came in time to stop me from gushing about making out with Parker while he was standing right behind me. Though the thought of him standing behind me is not exactly an unwelcome one.

"How long have you been lurking there?" I demand, my cheeks growing hot.

"*Observing* is not the same as lurking."

"It's the same as *spying*," I shoot back, doing my best to ignore the intoxicating smell of him.

Ignoring me, he steps through the door and walks around the room, looking past the mess and focusing instead on my sample art around the loft. There are a few pieces on each table and a whole bunch that I put up on the walls as inspiration for the group. But a bunch of drunk, giggling women at a bachelorette party is a much different audience from a thirty-something, stone-cold-sober man, and I suddenly feel incredibly self-conscious. It's an odd sensation, because I've never been shy about my work before.

"Did you do all these? By hand?"

I nod, trying not to squirm as he continues around the room, sauntering like he's at a gallery. He stops to look at each one like they're masterpieces, while I, in turn, study the slope of his nose, the upturned end that gives him a slightly boyish look and which cranks up when a grin pulls at the edge of his mouth.

My stomach drops when I realize what he's looking at. "Oh my god!" I lunge for him, covering the sign with my body.

"What was that about a G-spot?" he says through barely contained laughter.

"Nothing!" I say, dodging his grab for it. "You misread it. Clearly, you can't read. Or you need glasses. Or all of the above! Hey, why don't we take you right now to get that checked out? I'll drive."

"Absolutely *not*—ha!" He fakes left and his arm darts past me before I can stop him, and I am so mortified I think I might die.

"I read that wrong, huh?" he says, turning the sign around so I can see my own stupid words staring back at me. I grab for it again, but he lifts it easily out of reach. "Funny, I didn't see anything like this on your Instagram page."

Normally, I would be thrilled at the idea of someone scrolling through my feed, but imagining Parker judging me based on those tiny square windows into my life makes me feel anything but happy. It's unsettling. The woman inside those boxes is the furthest thing from the one standing in front of him now. But I don't know how to explain that to him without sounding insane.

I cringe inwardly as I remember one of the last photos I posted was of me wedged between him and Sam at the bar. I'd done it even before we got home that night, when I was drunk and not thinking clearly, before I talked more with Parker, the unfamiliar flutters of attraction began, which have only strengthened their hold on me since then. By the next morning, I'd already felt weird about it. I'd posted it, hoping that Caleb would see it and realize I wasn't sitting around in a dark room with a pint of ice cream pining for him like he thought I was. But less than twenty-four hours after posting the picture, it felt wrong. I'd stared at that picture more than once, with my thumb hovering over the delete button, though I could never bring myself to do it. Because what did *that* say about me? Instead, I'd tried to bury it under other photos of the farm, aesthetic and balance be damned. Too bad Parker seemed to be combing through my page as if he were looking for evidence and he had no doubt seen it regardless.

"That's because I've never done anything like that before."

"Why not? It's funny."

I roll my eyes. "Maybe for a bachelorette party. But now, in the light of day, I'd like to burn it. Could you get that fire going again for me?"

He frowns. "You're not serious?"

It's my turn to laugh. "What else am I going to do with it? Nobody wants to buy this."

"Maybe not your usual clientele, but around here, I guarantee you somebody would pay for this."

I tilt my head sympathetically like he's a small child who thinks they can make bank on a lemonade stand. Cute, but utterly misguided.

"People like my stuff because it lets them show off how happy they are." I move around the room, pulling down cardstock samples as I go. I hold them up for him to see my best sellers. "'Good vibes only.' 'My happily ever after starts here.' 'Eat, pray, love.' That's the bullshit people want."

It's also the kind of crap I'm not sure I can fake anymore. What does that mean for my business, for me ... I have no idea. But since the inaugural event crashed and burned, the ashes still clinging to my shoes, any plans for that might be up in smoke regardless. I thought I'd be relieved, knowing I at least tried before giving up. But I know now I didn't only want this for Lyla and me. There was a part of me that wanted it for *me*. Realizing I can't keep doing this ... feels like saying goodbye—something I've been doing more than enough of lately.

Still, knowing this makes me realize how much I haven't missed my social media job —or any of my clients, for that matter. Even though

I could continue creating custom calligraphy on the side, producing wedding pieces, gifts, and cards until the day I die, I truly enjoyed the process of hosting an event. Selling something I've created is one thing; what I love—*really* love—is creating an experience for people. That's probably why I was so successful in my social media job: the campaigns I created and the platforms I managed were all about shaping how people expected to experience a product or brand. I'm positive now that I don't want to do that for other people anymore. After a month and a half of procrastinating at Salem Stables, it's suddenly glaringly obvious that no part of me wants to go back to that. It's time to cut ties—officially—with my clients. I deserve to have something I'm passionate about, and they deserve someone sincere and engaged. The idea of stepping aside without a safety net is scary as hell, but maybe it's the only way I'll stop feeling stuck and finally move forward with whatever comes next for me.

"Maybe they want the bullshit because that's what you're offering them," he says, stepping closer. "Give them something real. They might surprise you."

I give a sad smile. "I've been doing this long enough to know people only want my help showing the shiny snapshots of themselves that make their lives look like something everyone else wants. It's what I'm good at," I add with a shrug.

Parker is studying me closely. I try to ignore the feeling that he can read every thought that's crossing through my mind and toss the handful of samples onto a table unceremoniously, crossing the floor to pull the one out of his lowered hand. *I might be bad with directions, but at least I can find my way to my G-spot.* God, what was I thinking? I cringe, thinking about Lucy's friends making fun of it in the back of the limo on their way home.

He shakes his head as he looks at me with an expression I've never seen before. "You don't even see it, do you?" he asks quietly, eyes soft.

My eyes land on him again, and I blink. *See what?*

He steps closer, his hands drifting up to cup my face, tilting my chin up to his.

"What don't I see?" I murmur, letting myself get lost in his sweet brown eyes.

"You're talented, Sloan. You think you need to go along with what everyone expects of you, but you could do so much more than that if ..." He frowns down at me as he struggles to find the words. "You have all the right instincts, Sloan. You need to trust yourself to follow them."

I'm still absorbing this when he slants his lips over mine, overwhelming my senses with the slow sweep of his tongue over mine. Electricity shoots up my spine as he catches my bottom lip between his teeth, tugging gently with just the right amount of pressure before he pulls back.

He drops his hands from my face and laces his fingers through mine, steering me towards the door.

"Where are we going?" I ask, following without even a second of hesitation.

He turns to face me, continuing to walk us both backward towards the door.

"You can wait here for forest creatures to feed you and braid your hair, Princess, or you can try your luck with my cooking."

"Sure," I say, holding back a smile. "Food sounds good."

Chapter 23

In the hearth, a small fire crackles, casting a happy glow over the sitting room of the cabin, tucked in the trees on the back half of Tabitha's property. I stand close to the flames, relishing the warmth after spending the morning outside in the brisk fall air. The smoke mixes pleasantly with the scent I've come to associate with Parker —a clean, musky, and spicy fragrance that I can never seem to get enough of. If I could, I would bury my face in it and never resurface.

I stand awkwardly as Parker busies himself in the basic kitchenette, taking in my surroundings. The cabin is exactly as it has always looked. No photos on the wall, the same quilt and sheets on the bed that have always been there. The furniture hasn't even been rearranged to his preference. The only evidence he's even here is a stack of books on his nightstand, a spare pair of boots on the mat at the door, and the edge of a military duffel bag that I can see poking out from under the bed. There's nothing personal because every spare dollar this man earns is shared willingly with the people in his life who need it, whether they deserve it or not. And from the sounds of it, that's nothing new.

"I have an idea, and I want you to hear me out without getting mad, okay?" I say.

He grunts from across the room, and I shift on my feet as I steel myself to voice the idea I came up with earlier, when I was trying to think of anything that would keep me from jumping on Parker in the middle of the barn in broad daylight. I talk to his back as he moves around the kitchen.

"What about doing a Halloween event here at Salem Stables this week for Tabitha's last farmers' market of the season? There's more than enough space in the front field for all the vendors, plus tables for pumpkin carving. The kids can put on a costume fashion show on the porch. I could set up a photo opportunity by the barn, and you can take the kids for a walk around on one of the horses. Not Zeke, obviously," I add quickly. I'm speaking to his back, which shows no reaction. "We'll have hot apple cider, and people can roast marshmallows at the fire like they did last night, and we can even let people pick apples from the little orchard. And we'll sell pumpkins, of course. Whatever money we raise, we'll use to cover what Ray asked for."

Parker, who has been still this whole time, slowly turns to face me, a blank, unreadable expression on his face. But I don't let that scare me. I know he might be screaming at me internally to stop talking, to leave this alone, but like it or not, he needs my help, or somebody is going to get hurt. I don't want that to be his dad, but I'd hate it even more if it turns out to be Parker. Knowing what I know now about the selfless, strong, brooding man in front of me, he would take a beating if it meant protecting someone he cares about. His dad might not be perfect, and he certainly doesn't deserve his son's protection, but if Parker cares about him, then that means something to me. And whether he wants me to or not, if he's stepping up to protect someone else, there's nowhere I'd rather be than by his side while he does it. I'm not about to let him handle anything like this alone ever again—not if I have anything to say about it.

"I know you don't want my money," I press on, keeping my shoulders square and my voice steady as he walks towards me slowly, eyes locked on mine. "Think of it as a job. If we pull this off, the market gets to go out with a bang, *and* you earn the money you need to help your dad before Ray comes back with a baseball bat. Everybody wins."

He's quiet as he closes the distance between us, stopping within arm's reach.

"If you won't do it for me, at least do it to make sure Mason and Cass don't get pulled into this mess too."

We stare at each other for a long moment.

"Here." He hands me a steaming mug. "Sit. Drink."

I let him place the mug in my hands, but I don't sit. Not yet. I won't let him change the subject so easily, not before we finish this conversation. "You're reverting to your caveman speech patterns," I murmur, hoping he's in the right headspace for a joke right now.

The fact that he hasn't immediately changed the subject is progress, so instead of pushing, I leave him enough space to think about it without me backing down. I tip my head to sniff the cup, my nose wrinkling.

"What is this anyway?"

"Peppermint tea."

I cut my eyes back to him, unimpressed. "I've been awake practically all night and you're offering me peppermint tea?"

He chuckles softly, then walks away. "Yes. I've seen you caffeinated."

I follow him into the tiny kitchen, my heart swelling with hope at the sound of his laugh. "So?" I venture, my heart thudding in my throat. "What do you think?"

"I think ... you're amazing," he murmurs, his voice smooth and low. "I can't believe you'd do that for me."

I'd do anything for you.

The words echo inside my head, but I don't voice them. It's *way* too soon for that, but that doesn't stop it from being a truth that runs deeper than I ever expected. His hand ghosts down my arm, his grazing fingertips sending an electric current running through my body. I swallow, trying to stay focused as he eases closer, his eyes darkening with the same hot want that's brewing in my belly.

"Stop changing the subject," I whisper.

"Who said I'm changing the subject?"

His hand threads loosely through my hair, and a dull pulse stirs between my legs. He tugs me closer, turning us so my body is pinned between him and the counter. With the distance between us effectively obliterated, I can feel his hard length through his jeans, and he holds my gaze as he presses into me, making no attempt to hide it. My heart hammers in my chest, my throat going dry with the lust I can feel overtaking me. I do nothing to resist when he grips my chin gently between the thumb and forefinger of his left hand, tipping my face up to look at him. His other hand is still tangled in my hair, the pads of his fingers massaging as he alternates between tightening and loosening his hold on me.

"Are you going to answer my question?"

His voice is thick gravel in my ear as he says, "I'd rather do this." Dropping his head towards me, his tongue trails over the curve of my ear once, twice, before he bends his knees to work his mouth over my throat. With a whimper, I tip my head back to give him better access, but instead of giving me more of what I want, he draws back, dragging his nose over my jaw, up my cheek until our foreheads are pressed together, and the only sounds are our breathing and my heavy heartbeat.

"I brought you here because I want you, Sloan. Not because I want something *from* you."

The words play back on a loop as I let them soak in. He wants me. He wants *me*.

This time, when he reaches for me, there's nothing slow about it. Our lips crash together frantically, our hands everywhere. I whimper against his tongue, and he grabs the back of my neck, holding me there while he continues to devour me. My fingers tear at the buttons of his shirt, stopping only to tug my own over my head. His lips reconnect with mine in an instant.

But I need more.

My hands around his neck, I let him dip enough to grab my legs and lift me against him, pressing my chest against his torso. Every part of me is touching him. And it's still not enough.

His lips drag down my throat and I feel his teeth nip at my bare shoulder while his hands work the other way, slowly pressing up my waist, my ribs, fingers splayed against my burning skin. He stops at the cotton band of my bra and I arch into his touch. Another moan escapes me as his mouth trails lower still, pausing on the curve of my breast, rising and falling with my heavy breathing to lick and suck. My head is spinning. It's too much. But it's not enough. The frantic energy between us from all the near-kisses and failed starts has reached a breaking point. I know it's not just me—we didn't trust what this connection was between us before, but we do now. I can feel it in the way he touches me now without restraint, the way I ask him for exactly what I need.

"Parker," I pant, head tilted back as he sucks and bites at my breast. "*Please.*"

It's all the permission he needs. He carries me easily across the small room to the bed and lowers me to the mattress. My legs, still locked around him, drag him down with me. I relish in the feel of his weight on top of me, the ripple of his shoulders beneath my fingertips as he moves. I arch my hips toward him, desperate. He responds with a groan, a deep, throaty sound, as he rocks against me. Hard.

Oh my god.

We're both panting now. Hands clinging, desperate, frantic, pleading. I never want to stop kissing this man.

But he's not a multitasker. His lips stop moving when I reach for him, feeling him through his jeans. His forehead drops to my shoulder, like he can't even hold himself up anymore. I fumble with the button and hear him swallow hard when my palm makes contact with him.

"*Fuck,*" he breathes.

Raking my fingers through his hair, I tug him roughly to my lips, desperate to taste him again. My hand keeps working and I roll my hips, telling him what I want. I stop kissing to look at him, begging him to listen. The heady look in his eyes tells me what I need to know: message received. Loud and clear.

He rolls off me, rummaging around in his bedside table while I wrestle off my jeans. Foil rips, and I smile.

"I guess you do live here after all," I say to his back, propping myself on my elbow.

"What?" he asks, panting.

"Just saying, Tabitha never kept the place stocked with condoms when I stayed here."

He rolls me onto my back again, placing his hands on either side of my head. "Can we *please* not talk about Tibby right now?"

"Right, sorry." My fingers drift up to cover my lips, as if to keep them closed.

His hand closes around my wrist, gently pulling them away. "I think we're going to need that," he mutters, in what's possibly the sexiest voice I've ever heard.

I pull my bottom lip between my teeth, feeling suddenly shy now that he's looking at me, acutely aware of how naked I am. He leans in closer, trailing a series of sensual kisses up my jawline in slow, purposeful movements.

"Do you have any idea how badly I want you?" His growl tickles my ear.

I squirm in anticipation beneath him before I murmur my answer. "Show me."

Another curse falls off his lips and he settles himself between my legs. His mouth is on mine when he presses against me, but he pauses. Through my barely coherent thoughts, I wonder if he's waiting to see if I'll change my mind. I tilt my hips up, wrapping my knees around his waist to pull him into me, dispelling all doubt.

He eases inside me in one slow, steady motion. His forehead falls against my shoulder and he lets out a guttural groan. The pressure of him lets something loose inside me and I pull him deeper, fingers grasping at his skin. He's everywhere, it seems, his hands, his tongue, his teeth, filling my body and soul. I don't think I've ever known pleasure before this moment. Not like this. When he pulls back and slides slowly into me again, I see stars.

"You feel incredible," he mumbles, his teeth chasing his words against the shell of my ear. "So much better than I imagined."

"Daydreaming about this, were we?"

"Every day. All fucking day."

There's no hint of teasing in his voice, only brutal honesty. His hand finds my hip and his fingers dig into me as he repositions my angle. I gasp at the contact it gives us.

I can feel him holding back, his body coiled like a spring that's about to release. He's deliberate and slow, but after a few minutes, I can barely take it anymore. My hips are moving on their own, and I'm squirming beneath him for more friction. I drag my fingernails along his back, causing his hips to buck with more force this time, making me practically whine.

"*Yes.* Parker, please. I need more," I whisper.

He grunts but gets his movements back under control and I'm losing my mind.

"Sloan, baby, I can't." He sounds pained. "Not yet. I want to get you there."

The strain in his voice is clear. I don't want this to be over either, but this slow, tender touch is torture after all the thoughts I've had about this moment, about him moving over me like this. He thinks if he picks up the pace, he'll come. What he doesn't know is that I will, too.

"Trust me, you will," I promise. Or maybe beg. At this point, they sound the same. I drag my hands up the smooth plane of his muscular back, gripping his shoulders.

He swallows and for a second, I'm afraid he won't listen. I'm wrong. Propping himself up on one elbow, he pulls back enough to look at me. Chest heaving, I go still. His eyes burn with an intensity I've never seen before, and when they darken, lighting my insides on fire, I know he's made his decision.

Reaching above us, he braces one hand on the headboard and rocks into me. Hard. My mouth falls open, and a string of unintelligible words comes tumbling out, all of them some form of encouragement or praise. Pressure builds inside me with each thrust. His body tightens and I know he's holding back.

I'm so close.

I don't know if I say it out loud or not, but a few more and I'm there, like I promised. I can't be held responsible for the sounds I make. All I know is that I'm glad the nearest neighbor is half a mile away.

Chapter 24

"Aren't you glad you decided to like me?" I tease as Parker presses kisses against my shoulder.

I don't know how long we lie tangled in the sheets together. I'm on my side, Parker curled around me. His arm folds over me, wrapping me in a protective cocoon, his fingers intertwined with mine. I have no issues holing up in this tiny cabin for as long as we can. Away from the world, away from our problems. The world shrinks until it's just me and him, and I feel safe. Whole.

"There was no decision, Sloan. It was inevitable." I pull our hands towards me and kiss each one of his fingertips. "I am sorry, though," he says, and I love the way I can feel his voice through my entire back. "For being such a jerk. Even if you were a total pain in my ass, sometimes, I've been told I have issues trusting people."

"Is that why you're so afraid to take my money?" I ask, the dim cabin feeling like a confessional.

He takes a deep breath before he answers. "It's not that I don't trust you. I'm afraid of becoming like my family. If I don't owe you anything, then there's no chance of me ever hurting you."

I roll over to face him, my fingers tracing the curve of his cheek. "But …"

He stops me, a finger brushing over my lips. "Haven't you ever been scared of something that doesn't make sense?"

I swallow, sudden tears pricking the back of my eyes. "I'm afraid I'll never feel like I belong somewhere."

He blinks. "What?"

I squeeze my eyes shut and let out a long breath.

And then I tell him everything.

The whole complicated mess comes spilling out, along with the emotions I've been suppressing around it all. I don't know how much time passes, but when I finally finish, Parker's expression is mixed. "That's … I can't even imagine how that must have felt to find something like that out. My family is far from perfect, but at least I've always known where I come from. You must be so angry with them for keeping that from you."

I shake my head. "I keep waiting to feel angry, but that's not it. Did I wish I wasn't the last one to find out? Yes, but I understand why they chose not to tell me. Honestly, what makes it so hard is that nothing is changing. Regardless of how I got here, he's my dad. He always will be. I love him, I just … don't know how to act around him right now. It feels strange to go back to talking about everyday things after finding out something that should be monumental, you know? I think maybe with a little time, I won't feel so awkward about it all."

"Is that why you haven't returned his calls?" he asks gently, drawing light circles on my shoulder.

How much did Parker notice about me before I even realized he was paying attention?

"I haven't even talked to him since I got here. I wouldn't know what to say."

He turns his unfocused gaze forward, deep in thought. "He might," he says eventually. "Maybe all you have to do is give him a chance to say it."

"I'm scared," I admit. "We've already talked about it, but now it's like there's this concrete before and after, and I'm not sure I'm ready to be on this side of it. And it's about more than my relationship with my dad; it affects Tabitha, too. We've always had this special connection, and ... I'm not ready for that to change."

"Hey." He sits up, pulling me with him, swiping a thumb across my wet cheek. "You don't have to worry about that, okay? Never. Tabitha loves you. Nothing is going to change that. Trust me, being related by blood doesn't mean shit. Look at my family. My mom and brother took off to get away from my deadbeat dad, who spent so much time in the casino that he barely noticed, unless it was for long enough to blame me for everything." He sighs. "Dad gambles a lot. Growing up, he'd sometimes be at the casino for days. Lost more than a few jobs because of it." Other than shame, there's barely a hint of emotion in his voice.

"You've never mentioned your brother before," I say softly. "Do you want to tell me about him?"

I'm not sure if he does, and I don't mind if he'd rather not talk about this. I only want to offer him the same support he's showing me; in whatever way he'll accept it.

"Luke was a year younger than me. When my mom left, I ended up trying to take care of my dad and him. He always talked about getting out, like we'd be able to walk away from him one day. He had a plan for us to join the military and see the world. But when he finished high school, I couldn't go through with it."

"Why not?"

He stares at nothing, his jaw tight. "If we left, my dad would have no one looking out for him. I couldn't wash my hands of him, knowing that." He scoffs. "Hell, even now, I can't even leave him for a week without wondering what shape he'll be in when I check on him. He wouldn't survive on his own. But Luke's biggest fear was turning into him. He didn't want to get stuck. Turned out that mattered more to him than Cass, even after she told him she was pregnant."

I smooth my hand over his bicep, frowning as I realize something.

"You keep talking about him in the past tense. Did he ..."

"He's alive. He's just ... not around anymore. He got out of this town and decided he wanted to stay that way. Didn't think he could be a good father, so he never bothered trying. I guess he thought it was best to leave that to me, and suddenly I was taking care of Cass and Mason too. He's never coming back, so there's no point pretending there's still a chance of that."

An apology catches in my throat because I know it won't change anything. Instead, I try for something that I hope means more.

"They're lucky to have you."

He gives me a tight smile, like he doesn't fully believe me.

"Why are you telling me all this now?" I ask, my fingers brushing the hair at the base of his neck.

"Because you asked. And because, despite everything, I ... trust you." As he watches me, I get the distinct feeling that he might have been about to say something else. His chocolate eyes drop to my mouth. "Don't break my heart, okay?"

I fold into his arms and breathe him in, trying to leech some of what I feel for him back into his skin. "You don't have to handle this alone," I whisper instead, letting my free hand drift up to the center of his chest, resting there.

His muscles contract beneath my fingers, like his body is physically trying to keep me out of his heart. But I can tell from the look on his face that it's not working.

"Let me help you, Parker."

Let me in.

I can't explain why the need to bypass all his walls is suddenly so consuming, but it's the only thing that matters to me right now. The line between his eyes deepens, but there's no anger there. His shell is cracking, finally, and instead of patching up the weak spots, he's choosing to let them come down. Even though he's unnerved, he nods, and my chest constricts with a tight squeeze of relief, happiness, and gratitude rolled up into one.

I wake, eyes sandy with sleep. The sheets beside me are rumpled but empty and I look up to see Parker emerge from the bathroom.

"You're dressed," I complain.

"Sadly, yes."

I burrow deeper into the mattress, pulling the covers up to my chin. "What are you doing out of bed?"

"It's late. I have to go turn in and feed the horses."

I sit up, holding the blanket against my bare chest as I look out the window; pale, late-afternoon sunlight illuminates the open-concept cabin. I reach for the nearest piece of clothing, which happens to be one of Parker's hoodies, and stretch as I get out of bed before following him to the kitchen.

"I'm guessing you can't play hooky? I'm keeping this, by the way," I add, the sweatshirt coming down enough to cover all the parts that need covering, washing me in Parker's scent and fleecy softness.

"If I don't show up, I *will* be missed. And yes, please. It looks much better on you anyway."

He plants a kiss on my head and turns back to the fridge.

"You want some eggs?" he asks, slipping bread into the toaster with capable hands. "I never did feed you earlier."

"No thanks." I toy with the long sleeves that dangle past my fingertips as something strikes me. "Hey, why do you have so much food here? I thought you always ate at the house with Tabitha?"

He scratches the back of his neck with the handle of the spatula. "Oh, right. That's kind of ... kind of a new thing?"

I fight the smile tugging at the edges of my lips. "How new?"

I let him squirm for a few seconds longer than I have to before I put him out of his misery, grinning. "You're adorable when you're embarrassed."

His ears turn red as he dishes the eggs onto a plate.

"Whatever. Point is, Tibby might not miss me for dinner, but I can't say the same for you. You gonna talk to her today?"

The toast springs up with a loud pop, and I spread peanut butter on it with a knife and take a generous bite. "Yes. I think she'll be on board with my idea for the Halloween event, even though it's short notice."

He puts a hand on my shoulder, drawing my attention to him.

"That's not what I meant. You need to tell her the truth, Sloan."

I let out a breath. I know he's right. So why does the thought of telling her make my stomach turn queasy?

"She cares about you, no matter what."

"I know. I care about her too."

"Then you need to trust her. Caring about someone means being honest with them, even when it's not the easy thing to do."

I set my toast back on the counter. My call with Lyla rolls around in my head along with the conversation I need to have with Tabitha, and I'm not sure which one is making me feel worse—Parker's right. I need to be honest with Tabitha, and with Lyla. Going home to open our business isn't as important to me as it was a few weeks ago, and I'd be lying to her if I pretended it was. No matter what my final decision is, I need to let her know where my head's at so that she can make her own decision with both eyes wide open. And once I've spoken to her, I can fill Parker in too. It doesn't seem right anymore to keep something like this from him, even if I'm not planning to take Lyla up on the offer. I'll tell him everything. I care about him too, so I'll take his advice and be honest with him about the situation, even if that means he'll leave entirely. I know how important honesty is to him, and I want him to know that whatever is happening here between us, I'm all in.

But I owe it to Lyla to have that conversation with her first. Whatever I choose, the decision needs to be mine and mine alone. The second I ask other people for their opinions, the decision stops being mine. And I know myself well enough now to know I need to act before I give anyone else the chance to influence my decision, or make Lyla feel like I'm choosing someone else over her. If things have a hope in hell of working out between Parker and I, like I hope they do, I need her not to resent him for taking me away from her.

Parker rinses his now-empty plate in the sink and dries his hands before he moves to me. Just being near him sets my equilibrium back in balance and makes me feel stronger for the tough conversations I need to have. Somehow, in a few short weeks, he's become the anchor I didn't know I needed.

"I've gotta run," he says, wrapping his arms around me long enough for me to try and memorize his smell. "Call your dad, then talk to Tabitha. You'll feel better." He tilts my chin up to place a tender kiss on my lips, tugging on the sweatshirt of his I'm still wearing. "And please, *please* be wearing this when I see you tonight."

He wishes me luck, hitting me with a lingering look on his way out the door that somehow steels me with the courage I need to gather my phone off the couch where it ended up earlier. In the quiet confines of the cabin, heart pounding, I pull up my dad's contact and make the call I've been putting off for weeks.

Dad picks up on the second ring. "Sloan?"

My breath catches in my throat. Suddenly, I'm shaking, because I don't know what to say, but then Parker's voice reminds me that I don't have to do everything alone—all I have to do is be here.

"Hi Dad," I say, my words trembling.

An exhale rushes out from the other end of the line, and I hold my breath through the silence that lasts a beat, then two, three.

"It's so good to hear your voice, sweetheart."

The tears welling in my eyes break free, rolling in waves down my cheeks, and I don't bother hiding my sobs. When I first found out the news, I was so shocked and numb that I didn't cry at all. But I can hear the relief in his voice, and it tells me everything that I needed to confirm—he still wants me. Dad soothes me as I cry into the phone with words of comfort, until eventually I calm down enough to talk.

"I'm sorry I didn't call you sooner," I tell him. "I've been so scared of how things would change."

"Oh, honey, they don't have to change. I've told you that."

"It's okay, Dad. Different doesn't have to mean worse."

As I say it out loud, I realize it's the truth. And it gives me the confidence I need to have the other difficult conversation I've been putting off. Dad and I talk for a while longer, eventually moving on to catch up on what we've each been up to over the past several weeks— the kind of things we would talk about before everything changed. We finally hang up through tearful I love yous after making firm plans for the timing of our next call, and then I clean myself up and let myself out of Parker's cabin, heading up to the house in search of Tabitha.

The air is crisp, a sharp, cool breeze cutting through my thin layers as I hike through the forest beneath the canopy of bright yellow, orange, and fiery red leaves. Despite the wind, the late afternoon sun is warm on my face, though as the temperature drops with the incoming cold front, it's a reminder that the change of seasons is officially here, and soon we'll be trading long sleeves and vests for heavy sweaters, coats, and hats. Most of the clothes I brought with me are about to be useless. It would be nice to go home to visit my parents and collect more of my things—if Tabitha is still okay with me staying, that is.

As I kick off my muddy boots and head inside the main house, an invisible grip tightens around my throat, but I push my feet forward and follow the familiar sounds of the whirring pottery wheel to the studio. I want to stay, but only if Tabitha knows the truth.

About everything.

She looks up, beaming at me as I rap lightly on the door so I don't startle her. She calls me in enthusiastically, beckoning with her head since her hands are busy. I'm grateful that she'll have a slight distraction as I say what I need to say. Still, my timing is off since she stops working almost immediately, sitting back on her stool and cocking her head like she does with every finished piece to decide if she's happy with it or needs to start over. She nods, then stands to wash her hands at the sink in the corner. It's nice to see her confidence back, but as much as I want to ask her about it to deflect from the real conversation, I steel myself and blurt, "I called Dad."

She looks at me over her shoulder, turning to face me fully as she dries her hands on an old rag.

"That's great! Hopefully, he'll stop bugging me about you every two days."

"That was the first time I spoke to him."

She frowns. "Since you got here, you mean?"

"Yes. And ..." I swallow hard around the marble in my throat, my fingers clenching and unclenching at my sides. I take a final look at her, mentally capturing the image of this version of Tabitha—the one I might be saying goodbye to forever in mere seconds. "Since I found out he's not my biological father."

Tabitha's hands go still. Her entire body freezes as her expression goes blank, trying to process my words. "Wh-what?" Her voice is shaky. "Are you ... I can't tell if you're joking."

"I found out by accident," I press on, a crack carving its way through my heart at the sight of Tabitha's crestfallen face. "I was never supposed to know. Nobody was. The DNA test was Lyla's idea, for my birthday."

"Yeah, I remember ..."

"We thought we might be connected to a celebrity, or a member of the Royal Family. Worst case scenario, we thought we'd fill in some DNA gap that would help catch a serial killer." We'd been so naïve, thinking about problems that were so unlikely to touch us, never considering for a second that we were about to unravel my entire identity. "What I learned instead is that Mom and Dad had trouble conceiving and decided to use a sperm donor." I gulp down some air. "I'm not Dad's biological daughter. Which means ... I'm not your real niece."

I have to look away as I say the last part. I can't watch her change the way she sees me, because if Tabitha doesn't know who I am anymore, I'll be lost all over again.

"Oh, Sloan."

Her voice is closer now, right in front of me.

"I've known this whole time, but I've been too afraid to tell you because I don't want it to change anything between us," I rush, still not looking at her. "I don't want to lose what I have with you, and I don't want to lose this place because Salem Stables is the *only* place I've ever really felt like I've belonged. But I still don't even know how I feel about this, and I've known for weeks. So, I understand if you need some time to process, and—"

"Wait, what do you mean? Process what?"

My eyes snap to hers, and some unknown feeling swells in my chest. "... well, you might not have agreed to let me stay here indefinitely if you'd known."

She stares at me, confused.

"I lied to you," I whisper.

"You were processing this, like you said. I don't need time for that. I know how I feel."

"You do?"

"Yes." Her eyes bore into mine, imploring me to listen, so I do. "Because the way I feel hasn't changed since you walked through that door, or since the first time I watched you ride a horse, or graduate from college, or when you dressed up as me for Halloween when you were eight. How I feel about you right this second is the same way I felt about you the first time I held all six pounds, twelve ounces of you when your parents first brought you home from the hospital, Sloan. I was your aunt then, I'm your aunt now, and I will hold onto that title tomorrow and the next day and the next, until you pry it out of my cold, dead hands, got it?"

A watery laugh bursts out of me as she wraps me in her arms in a hug so fierce it hurts. I cling back just as tight as a fresh wave of tears rushes out of me because it's the exact same hug she gave me when I showed up on her porch six weeks ago.

She wipes away a tear from her own cheek before placing tender hands on my cheeks.

"You're my Sloan. You will *always* be my Sloan. Got it?"

My lips quiver. I know I wouldn't be able to speak even if I had the words, so instead I nod vigorously and let her pull me into another hug. I cling to her, my tears pouring down my cheeks like a river of every emotion I've been holding onto. Fear, sadness, and uncertainty drain away, making room for a deep sense of relief. My heart swells with the kind of happiness I'm not sure I've ever felt and a grounding sense of calm that I've only felt with Parker earlier today. My life is still a mess, but even though I don't have everything figured out, I know that I already have what matters most.

Chapter 25

Tabitha falls instantly in love with my idea. The more I tell her about the things I'd thought of to make the final farmer's market of the season special, the more her face lights up, until she's practically bouncing in her chair in the yellow kitchen. I tell her about raising money for Parker, but I don't tell her why. It's his private business, and it's up to him whether he wants to share it with Tabitha. It's a testament to how much she trusts him, because even though she seems concerned when I tell her it's for Parker, she nods and doesn't ask questions. She probably already knows about Parker's father. Who knows, maybe he *has* come to her for help before. But this time, he's letting me be the one to help him. And I won't betray his trust, even if there's a chance she already knows the details. Not unless I have to, for Parker's safety.

Having a project quickly becomes a central force in my life, but this time I don't feel any of the stress of event planning that I did when trying to pull the bachelorette party together. This time is different. I have help, a team of people rooting for me, and I don't want to let them down. But I also don't want to let myself down. I have a vision for this event, and I know I can make it work with Parker and Tabitha's help. The last market is this Thursday, a few days away, and we have enough time that

I'm actually letting myself have fun as I prep some decorative elements around the barn doors to make the spot more picturesque. Every so often, though, I lift my head long enough to remember that it's not going to erase the damage I did with the bachelorette disaster.

"Stop torturing yourself." I jump at Parker's voice behind me, nearly dropping my phone onto the driveway in the process. He strides past me into the barn with a horse on either side of him, leading them each into their stalls. "I wasn't kidding when I said I'd chuck that thing into the pond."

"I was checking the forecast," I lie, though there is some truth to it.

A hurricane is set to make landfall on the East Coast in the next few days, and though we're mostly protected here, a massive rainfall would do a pretty good job of keeping people away from the market.

"It's not going to rain. And you're full of shit."

Ignoring him, I go back to arranging the hay bales, stacking them to create layers and scattering pumpkins of various sizes on top, leaving enough space for someone to sit for a photo op. With the barn as a background, a picture in this spot would look like something from a catalog.

I make it five minutes before sneaking my phone out again to check *The Country Bumpkin* blog for Lucy's review. Still nothing. I know it's coming, though, it has to be, and if it's taking this long, I'm sure it won't be anything good.

Parker deposits the last two horses in their stalls and hangs the lead ropes on a hook before leaning against the wall to spear me with a pointed look.

"You'd be having a lot more fun with this if you stopped worrying about what other people think," he says, nudging my side with an elbow.

I know he's right, but this bad review won't just affect me. I put Lyla's reputation on the line, by association.

"I'm sure a world without other people is your idea of paradise, but that's not the one we live in."

He stays serious, refusing to let me joke my way out of this one. "All I'm saying is don't let something bad that happened once ruin everything good in your life you still have coming."

I drop my gaze. His words are the arrow that hit the bullseye of my heart, and I think he notices because his tone is gentler when he speaks again.

"You're putting a lot more pressure on yourself with that thing," he says, pointing at my phone. "Would you spontaneously combust without it?"

"Absolutely not! I can be without my phone, thank you very much."

"Oh yeah?" he says, eyes dancing with amusement. "Prove it."

I roll my eyes, tucking it into my pocket and giving him a pointed look. "See? All gone. Happy now, Grandpa?"

"Nope, not good enough. I dare you to keep it off all day on Thursday."

"But that's the day of the market," I say.

"Exactly."

"But what if—no, you know what?" I say, stopping myself at the superior look on Parker's face. No way am I going to let him be right about this. "Thursday it is."

"That's the spirit." He grins.

"What do I get if I win?"

"Accomplishment for the sake of personal gain."

"Otherwise, it would be an accomplishment for the sake of people-pleasing, and I'm not doing that anymore, remember?"

"Fair enough." His tongue forms a bump behind his stubble-covered cheek as he thinks. "I know, if you win, you can spend the night at my place."

"That sounds like a prize for you."

"Fine, you pick then."

"Anything?" I ask, an idea popping into mind.

"Yeah, whatever you want."

"You take me out."

"On a date?"

"Yeah," I say, trying not to let my face crack too soon. "Deal?"

He steps towards me, slipping his arms around my waist.

"Deal. Although that's kind of a prize for me too."

I let my hands glide up his chest, enjoying the solid feel of his body under my palms. "Aw, it's sweet that you think that. But I haven't told you where we're going yet."

"And where is that?"

"You're taking me shoe shopping. To replace the ones you ruined, remember? And maybe an extra pair for my trouble."

He tips his head back and groans as he laughs.

I pat him on the chest and turn away to make a final adjustment to the decor.

Laughter catches my attention, and I find the source across the yard. From the barn door, I shake my head at my aunt and Jim, who Tabitha swears is still 'just a good friend.' As if I'm blind. The two of them are huddled together, giggling like teenagers in love as they work on painting the photo op with face holes cut out for the kids.

"I swear, if I catch them necking out behind the barn, I can't be held responsible for my actions."

A pair of arms slinks around my waist from behind, and this time, I lean into the solid frame they're attached to.

"I don't mind," Parker says, nipping at my ear. It sends electricity zinging down my spine, landing with a flutter in my belly. "The more they distract each other, the more I can get away with doing stuff like this."

Instead of untangling myself, I walk backwards, pushing us both further into the barn where we'll be out of view. I turn around to face him. He brings my arms around his neck, swallowing my sharp gasp as he captures my mouth in a deep kiss. His tongue flicks over mine and a tiny whimper escapes me as the sensation causes my entire body to tingle, heat and heavy want pooling rapidly between my legs.

"Wh-what are you doing?" I say, gasping as he runs his tongue along the sensitive skin on my neck.

"Pushing my luck," he murmurs, his teeth following the same path his tongue traced.

"Don't tease," I complain, trying to put some space between us to clear my head.

He lets me push him but comes right back to me like a boomerang. His mouth hovers at my ear and he holds my head in place while his other hand caresses my waist. "Who said I'm not planning to follow through?"

"*Here?*" I hiss, laughing against his mouth. "Are you crazy?"

Grabbing my hand, he yanks me into the feed room, closing the door behind us and dragging the wheelbarrow in front of it to keep it that way. If I wasn't already wet, the look in his eyes right now would be enough to get me there. It's everything that I love about him—heat, focus, humor and want—all wrapped up into one pair of beautiful brown eyes, trained on me like I'm the only other person in the world.

Eager anticipation buzzes over every inch of my skin as he stalks towards me slowly, backing me into the worktop against the opposite wall. But when I bump it, he doesn't stop coming. With strong, capable hands, he lifts me swiftly onto it, stepping into the cradle of space between my thighs and pressing into my core. I gasp. We're nose to nose, my eyeline a fraction of an inch higher than his at this level. His hands slide over my legs, my waist, then around, dropping until he has two fistfuls of my ass and he's pressing me into him even harder.

"Would it kill you to agree with me, just once?" he growls against my lips.

"It might," I whisper back, enjoying the strain of his flexing jaw as I irritate him further. "I wouldn't want to risk it."

"You love driving me crazy, don't you?"

It's not a question, and my smile widens. Because it's true. I've never felt more in control, more brazen, more ... myself, than when I'm pushing Parker. Because this push-and-pull we have is everything to me. I've spent my life letting myself be pulled around by other people's priorities, their plans, and often their ideas of what my own should be. Pushing against Parker has been about so much more than him from the beginning. It's about going against all of it, carving out my own space to finally hear myself think, and claim whatever tiny piece of this world that's mine for myself.

"Shut up and kiss me."

The world outside these four walls ceases to exist. He pounces on me like a starved lion, and I don't mind one bit. I match every lick, every bite, every grab with one of my own as we fall into a kiss that's as desperate and natural as the need to breathe. His tongue slants over mine, claiming my mouth. It's rougher than it was yesterday when we gave in to this thing between us, finally.

Last night, while I lay in my bed, wishing I were in his, I wondered if it was the not having it that made us want it so badly. But if my wildly flipping stomach and the hard thing pressing into my leg are any indication, the flame hasn't faded at all. It's only burning stronger than before. He's being firmer, his movements more assured, knowing that he can ask for what *he* wants this time, more confident that I'm not about to change my mind. And my wanting him back just as badly seems to be doing something for him.

He presses against me, rock hard inside his jeans, and I press my lips together to keep from moaning.

"God, Parker, you feel so good," I pant instead.

His hand tangles through my hair, pulling my mouth back to his so he can devour me in another kiss.

"I might be able to resist you if your ass didn't look so fucking good in those jeans."

I arch my back, lifting my hips and giving him better access to grab the part of me he seems to like so much. *So, he's an ass man*, I think to myself, making a mental note to show him just how good I can make a pair of jeans look.

A groan slips out of him as he palms me through the denim, and suddenly my hands are moving of their own accord, clawing and tugging his belt.

"Please tell me you have a condom."

He stills, and I pause too, looking up through heavy lids at this man that I love and hate so much in this moment.

"Shit."

"You're kidding. You're the one who started this out there!" I say, frustration etched in my voice. "What happened to 'who said I'm not going to follow through?'" I shove his chest. "You really are a tease."

A square foil packet appears in front of my face, along with his devilish grin.

"I hate you," I deadpan.

"I think by now we can safely say that's not true."

I press my fingers to his lips before he can kiss me. "Nope. You had your chance, mister. You blew it. Which means that now I won't be." He tips his head back and lets out a laughing groan before he drags a hand over his face. "I should get back to work, since you don't need me."

"Oh, I need you," he rasps, his voice gravelly. "I've needed to be inside you ever since yesterday."

I do my best to keep my fake glare in place as he trails his hand down my cheek, along the curve of my throat, ghosting over my chest.

"Come on, Sloan. Let me change your mind."

His hand continues to carve its gentle path down my belly before he trails his fingertips from the top of my thigh to my knee, then back again. "No?" he says, his tone light and teasing, and I know he's turning the tables on me before he does it. "Alright. Beat it, then. Go ahead. There's the door."

I scowl at the smirk on his face, but deep down, I don't care if he wins this round. We both want the same thing. Decision made, I'm still glaring when I reach for his belt again and watch desire overtake his features again. Before I can finish my task, he pulls me off the counter and drops me on my feet, wheeling me around and working my jeans and underwear off my hips to my knees. With a firm push on my shoulders, I'm bent over, my palms braced against the surface as he finishes unbuckling his belt without my help.

I'm panting and squirming by the time he tears open the condom wrapper, and the three seconds without his body in contact with mine are agony. I bite on my shirt sleeve to keep from moaning when he presses himself against me from behind, one arm wrapped firmly around my waist while the other slips down over my bare ass. Every inch of me is on fire, so much that I don't even notice the cold air in the unheated barn. My knees buckle when his fingers slide over my wet slit, and my head falls forward as I relish the feeling of him touching me.

His warm breath hits my ear before his lips do. "Still think I'm a tease?" he asks.

I lift my head, smiling as I turn my head towards him over my shoulder. "That depends on what you do next."

His finger disappears, and the next thing I feel is the head of his cock dragging over my wetness. My mouth falls open, all playfulness gone. There's no room for games anymore, not while the desperate need I have for him is claiming so much of my headspace.

"Yes, Parker, please. *Please.*"

With a booted foot, he nudges my feet as far apart as they'll go with my jeans still around my knees, and I'm sure the pause is him checking the door with one final glance before he sinks into me with one slow, purposeful thrust.

"*Ohmygod.*"

"*Shhh,*" he murmurs into my ear. "We have to be quick. Can you be quick, baby?"

I nod, mouth clamped shut—while I can keep it that way. I've never done anything like this before, never had sex anywhere but in a bed.

Where we are, coupled by the fact that there's a slight chance we could get caught, while horrifying if I think too long about it, is also exhilarating.

He moves then, slowly dragging in and out, and it's so tight and good I could scream. Instead, I grip whatever I can hold onto, focusing on breathing through my nose to keep quiet. Or, at least as quiet as possible. There's nothing I can do about the whimpers of pleasure tumbling out of me at every thrust, and there's nothing he can do about the grunts and stream of curses he's whispering for my ears only. They intensify as the pace of his thrusting builds, and as if that didn't feel good enough on its own, he reaches around my waist and lets his finger toy with my sensitive bud.

Our heavy breathing fills the air, but outside of this, nothing else exists. I rise onto my toes to tilt my hips upward, and the angle instantly hits the perfect spot. I told him I could be quick, but I didn't realize how fast I could be until I had him inside me, driving into me over and over again with such delicious pressure. His fingers continue toying with my clit and he lays a claiming bite on the base of my neck, exposed under my collar, and that's what does it.

My mouth falls open again as my release reaches its peak, but this time, he's prepared for it. He moves the hand that was on my waist to my mouth, gently muffling the sound I can't capture on my own. As my climax erupts and my walls tighten around his cock, I sink my teeth into the palm of his hand.

"Fuck. Oh *fuck*." His hips stutter to a stop at his release before he curves forward around me. As we both sink to Earth, we're quiet for a few seconds, listening to make sure there isn't any movement outside the door we might have missed. Then he turns his head, laying a tender kiss on my cheek. "I don't know how I'm ever going to get any work done around here."

Far too soon, he pulls away. The metal of his belt tinkers gently as he rights his clothes while I slide my jeans up over my hips with my back still to him. I should be deliriously happy right now, but worry is working in overdrive to take root in my brain. And it's painted across my face because as I turn, Parker's face falls, turning instantly serious.

"Sloan? Everything okay?"

I'm halfway through nodding when I remember who I'm talking to. I don't lie to Parker. He's the one person in my life I've ever been comfortable speaking my mind with, the one person I've never worried about being the people-pleasing Sloan with. And, since we've already had that conversation, I know that it's part of what he likes about me. So I shouldn't be worried to ask the question that's on the tip of my tongue for fear of making him uncomfortable.

"What are we doing here?"

"In the feed room? I was minding my own business when your horny ass dragged me in here." As he talks, he finishes fastening his belt and looks up as he tugs his flannel shirt back into place over his hips.

"That's not what I—hold on, that's not how it happened. *You* dragged *me* in here."

"Not how I remember it."

"Then you must have had a brain aneurysm in the last five minutes, because that *is* what happened. Whatever," I say, trying to regroup while he smirks in amusement. "That's beside the point. I meant—"

He grabs my chin, his eyes locking on mine. "I know what you meant. I just like to see you all fired up."

"Oh good. That's what I'm here for, to keep the people entertained."

My flat tone does nothing to dampen the amusement in his eyes. His fingers trace my cheek. "You're not entertainment, Sloan."

"No?"

He shakes his head once, his nose brushing against mine as he does. Laying a kiss on my lips, he backs away, leaving some space between us. I lean back against the counter, hardly able to believe what we just did up against it.

"I don't want to make assumptions," I say after a breath.

Before I go planning my life around you. I've already done that once because Caleb and I couldn't figure out how to have an honest conversation with each other, and I am not going down that road again.

"Look, Sloan. I'm not asking you to marry me or anything, but you should know I don't do anything casually. Least of all, dating. I've got enough going on in my life without adding that layer of complication or dragging anyone into bullshit they don't need to be dealing with." He pushes the wheelbarrow that was blocking the door out of the way, and even though I get the sense that none of this is easy for him to say, he keeps talking. "I wouldn't be doing this if I didn't think there was something here."

Something warms inside me as I realize what he's saying. He doesn't usually date, and he wouldn't be doing this with someone he didn't trust. I know how important his family is to him. He wouldn't let anybody into his world by accident. As my insides hug at the realization, his face grows serious.

"But if that's not how you see this, if this is just ... I don't know, fun for you, I need you to tell me now."

"It's not," I assure him quickly, stepping forward until I'm in his arms. "I know this is all new, but ... I'm not going anywhere, Parker."

As the words come out of my mouth, I realize the truth behind them, a sense of relief washing over me like warm sheets from the dryer.

I'm not going anywhere.

I couldn't see how much I don't want to go home until I decided to stay right where I am. For the first time in weeks, everything finally feels right.

The beauty of a small town is word gets around.

Fast.

It didn't matter that we changed the location of the last market with only a week's notice; a few strategically placed posters and designated gossips spread the details faster than a fire in a paper factory. By the time the vendors start arriving early Thursday afternoon, we'll have managed to transform the yard at Salem Stables and bring my vision to life. It's exactly how I pictured it—and even better when I see the tents popping up around the perimeter, the vendors buzzing with excitement as they set up their wares. I knew it looked good before, but just like with the bachelorette, seeing the people enjoying themselves is what makes me realize it's working.

Surprisingly, I'm not itching to take my phone out and capture the moment. I've held to my deal with Parker and haven't checked my phone all day. The nagging feeling persists at the back of my mind that the blog post could be up right now, and the *Country Bumpkin*'s hundreds of thousands of followers could be reading all about my epic failure and inability to run an event as I stand here, in the early hours of another one. But I made a promise to Parker, and I intend to keep it, so I push the thought back to the back of my mind—or at least as far as my back pocket, where my phone is safely tucked away and ignored—and try to stay in the moment. Everything might not be perfect, but so far, this event is going smoothly.

The signs I made are staked firmly in the ground at each activity station so they won't blow away in the growing wind. The pumpkin patch, costume runway, photo ops and marshmallow roasting are all set up, the front field designated for parking. Parker's busy saddling up Bailey for the horseback rides in the sand ring, so I light the fire in the pit on the lawn and arrange the roasting sticks and basket of marshmallows on the plaid blankets laid out around it on the log seating. People will be arriving shortly, and this way, the delicious campfire smell will greet them as they do. Booths are set up around the perimeter of the large gravel driveway, and as more people arrive, the space fills quickly.

At first, I think it only looks busier because the area isn't as open as the baseball fields where they usually have the farmers market, but I quickly realize it's more than that. The side field is fuller than I expected with cars, and each vendor seems to have several families milling around their booths. Better yet, people are buying things. They're also snapping pictures at the photo ops like I'd hoped, and the cutout that Tabitha and Jim made for them is a hit. There's also a line of excited kids waiting for their turn on the horse. I check on Parker, who gives me a wave as he leads a little girl with blonde pigtails around the ring, then head over to Tabitha's stand.

"How's it going over here?" I ask, pulling her attention away from Jim, who seems to be spending more time at Tabitha's booth than his own.

"Do you see all these people?" She pulls me into a fierce hug. "You, my darling niece, are a genius!"

"This is fantastic, Sloan, really," Jim says, flashing me a kind, grateful smile. "Far better than we would have been able to put together without your help. And looks like we got lucky with the rain holding out."

I glance back up at the clouds I've been keeping an eye on all day. With the phone ban in place, I haven't been able to check the forecast, so I'm going with good old-fashioned meteorology. I've been nervous all day, especially as the clouds turned darker, but there's only an hour or so left before we wrap up and I think we'll be okay until then.

"We haven't had a turnout like this all year, not by a long shot," Tabitha gushes, moving back towards Jim, who nods.

"Most of the vendors have already confirmed they're coming back next year. And there's some interest in having it here every week, now that they've seen what we can do."

"Is that what you want?" I ask, surprised.

Tabitha shrugs. "I'm thinking about it. Jim said he'd help. And maybe you'd consider it too, Sloan?"

The idea sounds great—in principle. After our talk, Tabitha made it clear that I'm welcome to stay here until Christmas, like I planned, and beyond. We didn't make any concrete plans, and with things between Parker and me still so fresh, I was worried about jumping in too quickly and freaking him out. He'd surprised me with his admission, though, and then again, when, instead of panicking when I made my promise to him, he looked relieved.

I'm not going anywhere.

What Tabitha's suggesting now is more permanent than that, but it feels right, and something tells me Parker would be happy about it, too.

Technically speaking, though, I'm not in a position to accept the offer. Not until I talk to Lyla.

"Would you mind watching the booth for us for a little while? Jim's neglecting his, and I want to make sure he has a chance to sell some of his produce before we lose this crowd."

I nod, waving them off. I've been buzzing around the market for over an hour, so it feels good to take a breather and be still for a bit. But I'm not alone at the booth for long, which is set up with Tabitha's art and my own, leftovers from the samples I made for the bachelorette and a few other signs I made in preparation for today.

Sharp laughter drifts closer and I turn to see a pair of women approaching me, their eyes on the table. I don't interrupt their easy conversation as they inspect Tabitha's pieces on display. They appear to be in their fifties; their hair is slightly graying at the temples, and they have laugh lines around their bright eyes.

"Diane, look at this," the brunette says, holding up one of my signs.

Smiling politely, I try to catch a glimpse of which one has caught her eye.

Oh my god.

"Oh—uh..." Words fail me, and I can't think of a valid reason to rip it out of her hands.

The second woman moves closer, leaning in to read it out loud. "I might be bad with directions, but at least ... oh!" The two share a surprised look—and then burst out laughing, clutching each other's arms as they double over.

I smile awkwardly, cheeks flaming. "I'm so sorry, that's not supposed to be there. I don't know how that got in there."

I know exactly how it got there, though. This is Parker's doing. Why won't she put it down so I can hide it before anyone else sees it?

"How much?" asks the one still holding it up, wiping a tear away.

My mouth falls open. "You … you want to buy it? *That* one?"

Before I can question her again, she's pressing a twenty into my hand and asking if it's enough. I'm almost too stunned to answer, but somehow manage a jerky nod. Their laughter carries as they wander off and I stand there, staring at the money in my hand. But it's Parker's face I see. His eager eyes as he told me I could do this, that someone would want to buy this. Though I'm reluctant to admit it, as much as I tried not to let him in, he seems to know me better than I ever wanted him to. And I don't hate the feeling.

In fact, I love him for it.

It hits me like a sucker punch to the heart, bubbling inside me to the point where I feel I'm about to overflow. I've never fallen for someone so fast before, and though the physical chemistry between us is undeniable at this point, I know it's so much more than that. My feelings for him run deeper than I ever expected them to.

Suddenly, I'm not on the fence about staying anymore—I'm firmly on one side. This side. The one where I stay put at Tabitha's, the place where I've finally been able to stretch my legs and start running events, even if they're not the kind I used to picture myself running with Lyla. Staying here to keep trying to get something going on my own feels like the right place for me, even more so—but not only—because of Parker.

Which means that I need to call Lyla. I have to explain the situation to her and hope that she'll understand that this is the right decision for me, even if it's not the one she wants to hear. And I can't wait until she calls with an update about Adam. He's not guaranteed to get that job, so part of me knows that I could wait and see what happens. If he doesn't get it, I won't have to have this conversation at all, and I wouldn't be risking hurting my best friend's feelings. But Parker's right—being honest with Lyla is more important than making her happy. I have to trust her not to hold this against me, to be the friend that I know she is.

Across the yard, Parker's helping a little boy down from the saddle, and a swell of hope that I haven't felt in a long time rises inside my chest—like I'm finally doing something right.

I turn my back, pulling my phone out of my pocket, knowing full well that I'm breaking the rules of my deal with Parker. But even he would agree it's for a good reason, and it can't wait until Lyla calls me. Luckily, she answers quickly.

"Don't you have your hands full with the market right now?" she says after a quick hello, but she doesn't wait for an answer. "Whatever—I'm glad you called, because I have news. Adam got the job!"

I still, but the roller coaster in my stomach doubles in speed. Oh no. I should have called sooner. I do my best to sound cheerful.

"Wow ... you must both be so relieved."

"You have no idea."

She sounds happy, but there's a heaviness to her words that makes the joy feel forced, somehow. But I can't dwell on that when I still have to be honest with her about my secret.

"I guess this means you're moving, right? So ... we should probably talk about what happens next—"

"I can't do it!" Lyla shouts. "I'm sorry, Sloan, I can't do this to our friendship."

"Slow down—what are you talking about?"

Lyla breathes a heavy sigh. "I'm sorry. I should have been honest with you sooner. When we couldn't open, I kept waiting to get sad, but honestly? All I've felt this whole time is relief. The idea of moving to New York was scary at first. I've never been away from my family. But I've found myself wishing for it anyway. I need a break from being the one everyone depends on."

"Have I been stressing you out?"

"No, the opposite!" she says. "You've kept me sane these last few weeks. But if we spent every day together, I worry that might change. I take charge by default, and you *let* other people make decisions for you. You don't need that from me, and I worry that changing our dynamic would affect our relationship like it has with my siblings."

"Where is this coming from, Lyla?"

She lets out a heavy sigh. "Something is going on with Billie, but she won't talk to me. When I tried to get her to open up, she said I don't get to be her parent *and* her sister. I'm about to rebuild my entire life in a new city; I need to know my best friend is going to be there when I need her."

My shoulders dip, the anger leaving as quickly as it came. "How long have you been feeling this way? Since Adam got laid off, or before?"

She's quiet for a beat. "Before. I'm so sorry, Sloan. I wanted to tell you weeks ago, as soon as I realized I was relieved we didn't get the shop. But you've had so much going on, and I didn't want to pile on. I never meant to change the plan like this."

"Change isn't always a bad thing. It does sound like I've been stressed for nothing about deciding to stay, though."

"Wait, you're staying at Salem Stables? As in ... *permanently?*"

"Tabitha wants me to help out with some things, and ... Parker and I have started something."

She pauses. "Are you staying for you, or for him?"

I almost give her a hard time trying to parent me right now, but I know she can't help it. It's who she is. It also makes me see she probably has a point about us spending every day together. I can roll my eyes lovingly at her now, but maybe I would start to tire of her making all the decisions. Especially now that I've seen how much fun it is to plan events.

"For me," I tell her, then, more firmly, "I'm doing this for me, Lyla, I swear."

She sounds unconvinced. "There isn't a teeny *tiny* part of you that's hiding?"

"What do you mean?"

"I saw your Instagram post. And I saw right through it. You were trying to make Caleb jealous."

I groan. His name smacks me like a sucker punch to the gut, and it takes my brain a few seconds to catch up. It feels like months, not weeks, since I posted that picture. "That was a stupid mistake. It didn't mean anything."

"Really? Because when he broke up with you, you couldn't get to Salem Stables fast enough. Now, it seems like you might be throwing yourself into another relationship with someone you actively hated a few weeks ago ... are you sure this isn't a distraction? I'm worried you might be looking for reasons to stay."

"I'm not looking for anything," I assure her. "I was always coming home, Lyla."

"So, you making Caleb jealous means—"

"Nothing!" I throw some extra conviction into my voice. "He doesn't mean anything to me anymore. Like I said, it was a stupid mistake. I wasn't thinking clearly, but I am now."

"If you say so. What does Parker have to say about you staying?"

I chew my bottom lip, nerves fluttering in my belly. "Parker doesn't know yet. Obviously, I never expected anything to happen, and I was never planning to stay longer than a few months."

"By all means, feel free to fill me in."

Parker's voice startles me, and I turn to find him standing a few feet behind me, a hard scowl painted on his face.

Chapter 26

Anger radiates off Parker's stiff frame, his eyes cold and hard. "Anytime, Sloan."

"Lyla, I'll call you back."

"Of course," she says quickly, and from her tone, I can tell she heard Parker interrupt. "We're okay, though, right?"

"We're good. Promise. I really have to go." We hang up, and I turn my attention back to Parker for damage control. "I promise that wasn't as bad as it sounded."

"Which part?" he asks flatly. "Me meaning nothing and being a mistake, or the part about you leaving?"

Okay, so it's as bad as I feared, and Parker did hear most of that conversation, or at least my half of it. I know how bad it probably sounded, and I can see the hurt in his face. I immediately want to wipe it away, to explain.

"None of those things are true, Parker. Let me explain—"

His face twists as he barks out a laugh. "You just said you were always going home. Were you planning on telling me before you had me drive you to the bus station?"

A flash of annoyance breaks through my need to comfort him. "That's some hell of timing you have. Did you miss what I said right before that, about how you and I are starting something?"

"Something you called a mistake two seconds later."

"No, I didn't! *Caleb* was a mistake. Lyla wanted to know if I posted that picture of us to make him jealous, but—"

"Did you?"

I press my lips together. "It was a mistake. That's why I told Lyla that *he* doesn't mean anything to me anymore."

He dips his head, shaking it at the ground beneath his boots, before he pulls his eyes back to me. And they're nothing like the ones I'm used to. Where there's been warmth and humor, now there's nothing. They're closed off, and I can feel the rest of him following suit. The realization sets my heart skittering as my mind races, too, trying to figure out how to fix this.

"That's not what I asked."

We stare at each other, cold wind biting my face. *Be honest,* I tell myself. *He cares about you, he'll find a way to understand.*

"Well, yes, but—"

He's moving away before I can finish my sentence, brushing past me and making his way around to the other side of the barn. I don't even think twice before I bolt after him, leaving the booth unattended. I catch up with him quickly, but don't manage to drag him to a stop for several steps, stepping in front of him so we're toe-to-toe.

"Don't storm off like a five-year-old who just got told he's not getting ice cream," I fume, angry with him for not hearing me out. "Speak, Tarzan. Why are you mad at me?"

He glares at me, but I don't shrink back. This is good, I think, for a second. This is familiar, this is *us*. But then he does what I asked. He talks. Turns out I'm not prepared for what he's about to say.

"I'm mad at myself," he says, his voice rising, "for letting myself think this was anything more than a detour for you and your perfect image."

"Excuse me?" I demand. My feelings shift from anger at him for jumping to conclusions, to being defensive of myself. I haven't done anything wrong here. Why am I under attack? With anyone else, I would probably let it roll off my back in a moment like this and focus on the bigger issue of sorting out this misunderstanding. But with Parker? There's no way I'm letting him get away with that. Hell, he's the one who taught me not to.

He leans towards me as he lifts an arm, jabbing a finger towards the barn.

"We stood right there two *days* ago, and you practically begged me to tell you that you were more than just a fling. But that's all this ever was to you. You used me."

My skin grows hot, anger boiling inside my veins. My emotions are still running high after my conversation with Lyla, and the fight-or-flight response in my body has been completely obliterated. "That's what you think? Based on half an eavesdropped phone conversation?"

Somehow, it's worse than him fully glaring at me. He feels further away than ever. I can feel him slipping away, wrenching free of me. Already prepared to stop trying. The walls around my own bruised heart start to rise, but I keep them from locking into place. Not now. Not yet. There's still a chance that we can figure this out. And even if I'm reaching for someone who won't be there to catch me, I can't help but try.

"I meant what I said when I told you how I feel about you," I say, my voice catching as the walls of my throat constrict painfully, tears pricking the backs of my eyes. "Do you honestly think I would lie about something like that? And for what? What could I possibly get out of that?"

"What do you get out of any of it?" he snaps back, his voice sharper. "Validation for five seconds that you matter. That *everybody* loves you." His words sting like a slap, but he doesn't stop. "I have enough to deal with without being your freaking puppet to go along with your games."

"It's not a game, Parker!" I cry, furious and hurt and hardly able to believe what I'm hearing. "None of this has been, I swear!"

"Well, whatever it is, it's too complicated for me."

I choke on a sob, though I'm still glaring at him through my tears.

He rakes a hand through his brown hair, over and back, then shakes his head like he's trying to clear something from it that won't budge. "This is exactly why I don't date. I don't have time for this. Not when I have people depending on me."

Right. *Other* people. As in, not me. Cass, Mason, his dad—they're all that matters to Parker. He's anchored to them so deeply that he'll never budge so much as an inch in any direction. Not even to make room for me.

No matter what I say, Parker will find a way to turn it around and throw it back in my face. There's no point even trying to explain any of it. I'd be screaming into a void, and I'd still end up heartbroken. I can already feel the crack forming right through me. Despite Lyla's warnings, it's too late for caution. Parker already has my heart. I realized it before as I watched him across the yard, imagining a future with him. One better and more real than any other dream I've ever had. And I know it to be true as that image shatters into a million tiny pieces that fall through my chest, cutting me once, twice, a thousand times until I'm ripped completely open.

We stand for a few moments in silence, my hammering heart ringing in my ears.

"Here."

I blink, then look down at his hand, holding out a handful of bills.

"Cash from the ticket sales so far."

My voice is raspy, coming out like gravel. "Keep it."

"I can't take your money, Sloan."

"It's not mine," I snap, my voice suddenly firm. Because if there's anything that matters right now, it's this. "It was never mine. This," I say, waving my arm back towards the market, "was a job, and that's what you earned. You can think the worst of me, Parker, there's nothing I can do about that. But I won't let you give me that money to prove a point when your dad's safety is at risk. When *your* safety is on the line. You never have to accept anything from me again, but just ... *please*. Pull your head out of your ass long enough to do it this *once*."

His hand drops to his side and he stares at me now, his mouth set in a grim line. For several beats, we're both quiet, the sounds of the crowded farmer's market still drifting around from the other side of the barn like nothing ever happened.

"What now?"

"I'm going home, remember?" I say, my words cold and empty, realizing it's my only option. I'm not going to drive him out of a job, nor am I about to put Tabitha in the middle of this. Though why should he believe me? I'm not trustworthy. No, worse than that. I'm not real about anything. And any fight left in me to prove otherwise has entirely drained after this. The tears are still burning my eyes, but I refuse to let them fall in front of him. If he wants to hurt me, fine. But that doesn't mean I have to let him see how much. "But I guess you won't believe me until I'm gone, huh?"

The muscle in his jaw tenses, and his eyes bore into mine one last time. But this time, I know he's looking at a stranger. His eyes pull away, and he nods before turning his back on me and walking away.

Chapter 27

Whatever was going on between me and Parker is over now; that much is clear. It's time for me to leave Salem Stables. Sticking around will only put Tabitha awkwardly in the middle, and I'm not prepared to do that to either one of them. I'm the one who doesn't belong here. Tabitha was adamant that I was acting rashly, but even though I can't prove I'm cursed, she can't prove I'm *not*, either. Salem Stables is the happiest place on Earth for me, and I somehow found a way to taint this too. I'd rather leave before I have a chance to ruin things more than I already have. So that maybe one day ... I *can* come back. Even though she's letting me go, my heart breaks a little at having to say goodbye before I'm ready. Making sure I didn't lose her was the whole reason I came in the first place. Now that I know we're on solid ground, I'm still not quite ready to let go. She won't let me leave until the bad weather clears, though.

All night I toss and turn, replaying the day's events over in my head. The knot in the pit of my stomach ferments overnight, and no amount of coffee the next morning will settle the sickening feeling. The further away I get from Salem Stables, the better. But the steady rain and dark skies don't let up.

"I know this is the last thing you want to hear, but it looks like you might be here a little while longer, yet," Tabitha tells me the next morning. "There's flooding on some of the roads around here and the buses are cancelled. But don't worry, the forecast says the rain should stop today." She pours herself a cup of coffee and sits down next to me at the kitchen table. "It's days like these I'm grateful for living here, I tell you. With our elevation, everything runs away from the house, and we really only get flooding in the back fields, so the horses can still go out safely."

I give a noncommittal grunt, but I'm only half listening.

"On the bright side," she adds, squeezing my hand and drawing my attention to her. "It's a little more time together. There's a new true crime documentary on TV I recorded for you."

Halfway through the first episode, Tabitha seems to notice I'm hardly paying attention and excuses herself to make some popcorn. I pause the show and curl my legs up under me on the couch to burrow deeper under the blanket I'm wrapped in. Closing my eyes, I lean my head back on the sofa, trying not to let my thoughts wander. As Tabitha bustles around the kitchen, my phone chimes and I reach for it automatically, expecting to see a text from Lyla, whom I updated last night to let her know I was coming home after all, without going into too much detail.

The little red notification makes me drop my feet to the floor and sit up straight. The blog post is live.

I have to swipe three times to pull up the browser to read it. Maybe I'm a masochist, but I need to see it for myself, even if I already know what it's going to say. I skim read the whole thing, my eyes jumping ahead as quickly as possible. But it doesn't mention the disaster from last weekend at the bachelorette party. It doesn't even mention the bachelorette at all.

Tabitha comes back into the living room and sets the bowl of popcorn down between us.

"Lucy's wedding venue got flooded," I say, holding up my phone. "It's supposed to be tomorrow at her parents' property, but the whole place is under six inches of water."

"Yikes. I guess she's looking for a plan B right about now."

"Yeah, for her and two hundred of her closest friends and family," I say drily, scrolling back through the post again. "According to this, there's nowhere around that can accommodate a group that size on such short notice. Everything is booked."

Tabitha gives a knowing nod. "This time of year is popular for weddings around here. Everyone loves having their photos taken with the beautiful fall colors. You saw how much people loved that yesterday, and that wasn't even anything special, it was just my front yard!"

She grabs the remote and turns the show back on.

"Yeah." The words taking a moment longer before bouncing back into the forefront of my brain and registering. "Yeah ... except unlike Lucy's parents, your yard isn't a giant puddle."

Slowly, she turns to look at me. "I don't like that look," she says, her lips angling with apprehension.

I grab the remote from her still lifted hand and press pause again, setting it down as I stand. She watches me pace around the living room, the idea gaining steam like it's its own being inside my head.

"Sloan, no," she says, not needing me to voice it out loud to understand what I'm thinking.

I smile. "Yes."

"Absolutely not."

"Hear me out!" Energy is suddenly coursing through me, relieving the weight that's been sitting on my chest since yesterday. "She didn't post about the disaster she experienced because of me—*yet*. But that doesn't mean she won't next week. Or next month, or next year, even. And even if she doesn't, it's always going to be in the back of my mind. That could ruin everything, and I'll never be able to stop waiting for that other shoe to drop. *Unless* I can undo some of the damage."

"You know, you could send her some flowers, maybe a nice edible arrangement as an apology. This? It's..."

"A lot. I know," I say, rushing forward and perching on the coffee table in front of her. "And it could be an even bigger disaster."

"Exactly! The guest list is twenty times bigger!"

"But all they need is a space where they won't be ankle-deep in water," I say, talking myself through it as much as her. "The wedding is supposed to be tomorrow, and since it was already planned as an outdoor event, they'll already have the tent and tables and chairs rented—all they'll need to do is change the delivery address. I reach for her hands, gripping them tightly on my knees while my eyes implore her with every fiber of my being to say yes. "Lucy is in a cast for her wedding because of me. If I can make sure the wedding happens, there's a good chance she'll forgive me. Not just for me, but for the sake of my business."

It's something I want to fight for again. Because even if it hasn't been flawless, I know suffering through the growing pains will be worth it to give it—to give me—a fair chance. Just because something doesn't get off to the right start doesn't mean it's worthless.

My thoughts flash back to Parker and our rocky beginning. Despite that, we somehow managed to get close. Even though it didn't start or end that way, for a few days it *was* perfect. I'm not stupid enough to think that it would always be like that between us. Parker's damaged in a way I'm only beginning to understand, and I have a laundry list of my own issues I need to work on. Neither of us is going to change overnight. Fighting would be inevitable, as it's in our nature. But we fight because we care, because we're pushing each other to be better versions of ourselves—the glimpses we see in each other, even when we can't see them in ourselves. Being with Parker would mean embracing the ups and downs, but knowing that those moments of perfection are waiting for us is enough to believe that it's worth fighting for too. That *he's* worth fighting for.

Leaving isn't the answer. That word is too generous; I'm not leaving ... I'm running, like a coward, giving up because it's easier than trying and failing, easier than letting Parker see the other parts of me, the flawed ones—the *real* me. He wanted to tell me that, and I wouldn't listen. Well, I'm listening now.

Tabitha groans and pulls her hands away, and I can hear the conflict in that one sound. She's close to giving in. She gets up and pads to the kitchen, me trailing close behind.

"Come on, Tabitha! We must have had at least two hundred people at the farmer's market yesterday, if not more."

"Yes, but that was spread out over the course of a few hours," she counters, reaching into the cupboard for a glass. "Not all at once, and not for an eight-hour event."

"True, but they'll be more contained, so you'll hardly notice." I infuse my voice with as much confidence as I can muster as I sweeten the pot. "They probably even have one of those fancy portable bathroom stations ordered, so no one will go in the house, or the barn, if you don't want them to. And no riding this time, promise."

She fills the glass with water from the tap, gulping before she turns back to me.

"How much of this has to do with Parker?" she asks, eyeing me closely.

I let out a long breath, seriously considering my frame of mind right now. "Everything. Nothing. Honestly, I don't know. It feels like this is the right thing to do. Like this is what I'm supposed to do next. And for whatever reason, I want to trust that feeling."

The glass hits the counter with a thud and Tabitha shakes her head. "I can't believe I'm saying this, but fine. Call Lucy. If she's open to it, her guests are going to need the new address sooner rather than later."

Squealing, I rush over to her and wrap her in a giant hug.

"All two hundred of them," she grumbles into my hair.

The day of the wedding arrives with blue skies and sunshine and—mercifully—not a drop of rain in the forecast. I've been up for hours, showered and dressed before the first truck arrived at seven a.m., kickstarting the flurry of activity.

Tabitha agreed to host, under the express condition that the barn and the horses remain absolutely, one hundred percent, off limits. If she hadn't met the bride-to-be herself, I'm not sure she would have agreed at all. But Tabitha truly does have a big heart. She cares about people and does what she can to help them, and I'm trying to take after her more in that way.

I only hope it's not too late to make things right with Parker.

Tabitha's done her part to help me with him. He grudgingly agreed to help, but only because Tabitha lumped it into his job description for the weekend, so technically, he's getting paid to do it. Meaning he's treating the whole thing as purely a business transaction and refuses to take instructions from anyone but Tabitha.

I'm not surprised. When he first saw that I was still here, he couldn't get away from me fast enough, and he hasn't been back to the house since.

I try not to dwell on it, though, focusing instead on a few special touches to the wedding that will make Salem Stables a memorable venue, not some second-rate backup location.

"We'll be back tomorrow at eleven for the teardown, once the tables and chairs and everything are cleared out," the guy in charge of the tent delivery crew says.

He hands me a clipboard and I sign on the line, deciding not to worry about how tired I'm going to be by then. If everything goes according to plan, it'll all be worth it.

I keep reminding myself of that, just like how every time the anxiety tries to bubble over inside me, I tell myself that I don't have to pull this off on my own. Tabitha has rallied Jim and her friends to help set up and direct traffic in our makeshift parking lot in the side field, and the wedding coordinator is helping remotely, working on rerouting all the food, linen, flowers, cake, alcohol, and five thousand other moving pieces that go into an event like this. Once Lucy was on board, she connected the two of us to sort out the logistics over FaceTime, and Sarah, the coordinator, was mainlining coffee the entire time, talking a mile a minute. The poor woman has to be more stressed than I am right now, and I make a mental note to send her a thank-you card and one of Tabitha's custom mugs after we make it through this weekend.

I spot Parker exiting the barn, marching towards the white wedding tent with his hands shoved deep in his pockets. I thrust the clipboard back and thank the delivery guy, rushing off to catch Parker.

"Hey," I say, suddenly timid. My heart races standing a few feet away from him.

"What do you need me to do?" he asks, not meeting my eyes.

"Parker," I say softly, willing him to look at me. "Can we talk first?"

"I'm here to work."

"But if I could just—"

"Work. Not talk."

I try one last time, but he cuts me off short with a hard gaze.

"If you don't tell me what to do, I'll just go. I'm not here to waste my time with you again."

He shrugs his hands out of his pockets as he turns back towards the barn, but this time, I'm not giving up so easily.

"Is that what you think it was between us?!" I shout, chasing after him. "A waste of time?"

"Wasn't it?" he demands, rounding on me so fast that I stumble to avoid bumping into him. He closes his eyes for a second. "Don't answer that. Do you need my help or not?" he says, impatience creeping back into his tone.

I pull the seating chart out of my back pocket and hand it to him. He snatches it from my grasp. He nods in my direction without looking at me, then heads back towards the tent. After a few brisk steps, he stops cold. For one heart-skipping beat, I think he might turn around and give me another chance, but his neck and shoulders are stiff, and his head stays pinned forward, sights locked on something in the driveway. There's enough unusual activity that I don't immediately spot the problem. When I do, my body reacts before my mind has a chance to catch up, and the hairs on my neck below my ponytail stand at attention.

Ray.

With all the excitement of the last twenty-four hours, I'd forgotten about him entirely. Knowing that Parker had the money he needed to cover the debt owed to him, I'd pushed it out of my mind like it was taken care of—a checked-off item on a to-do list. I guess Ray hadn't left a business card, though, so Parker must have been waiting for him to show up to pay him. His feet unstick from the ground, and he starts for the truck, growling over his shoulder at me to stay put.

As if.

I'm right behind him the entire way.

"Guess my invitation got lost in the mail," Ray drawls, tipping his chin at the white tent on the lawn. He's leaning against his sleek black pick-up truck, no doubt paid for with other people's money.

"Sorry, we're full up," I snap.

Parker's hand reaches behind him to rest on my arm, effectively silencing me.

"Here's your cash," Parker says, pulling out an envelope from inside his jacket and tossing it to Ray so he doesn't have to get any closer. "That clears my dad's debt. You're square."

Still smiling, Ray peels open the envelope and counts the money inside.

"Not quite."

In front of me, Parker bristles. "Fuck that," he growls between clenched teeth. "That's every penny that he owes you."

Ray tuts. "You're forgetting interest, Junior." His face turns cold. "Price is double."

"What the hell?!" I shout.

Parker's so furious he doesn't even try to shut me up this time. "You said I had six days," he says to Ray, leveling him with a glare. Despite their height difference, Ray doesn't seem intimidated.

"I did. Day six was yesterday."

"It's not his fault you didn't show up to collect," I argue.

Ray turns his dark eyes on me, and Parker shifts once more to position himself in front of me, like he's trying to shield me from him. "No. But he could have come to me."

"Tried to find you, but all the dumpsters in town were empty," Parker says through gritted teeth.

His anger only seems to make Ray more pleased. He grins again, pinched fingers smoothing the edge of the envelope in his hands. "Not my problem."

Parker drags a hand over his face, exhaustion setting in. "I don't have another two grand."

"Again, not my problem, boy."

"Fucking lowlife," Parker snarls.

Ray's face hardens. "No, that would be your old man. He's the scum who took my money knowing full well he had no intention of paying it back."

A beat passes while they glare at each other, before Ray seems to cool slightly.

"I could come back if you prefer, but you know how unpredictable my interest rates can be."

Parker turns to pace in a small circle and brings both hands to his head, clasping his fingers together at the base of his skull. His cheeks puff as he lets out a long exhale, his eyes flashing dangerously as he wrestles between figuring out a solution and breaking this guy's nose. I remember the look on his face when Ray left the barn after the first visit, how hopeless he looked. I know what it feels like—that sense of loneliness, despair. Like, no matter what you do, it won't matter. When I felt like that, Parker proved to me that it wasn't true. And he was right. What if I can do the same for him?

"I have the money."

Both sets of eyes flash to me, but my voice doesn't shake. My hand doesn't either when I reach into my vest pocket and pull out my phone.

"What's your email?" I say to Ray, keeping my eyes on my device. "I'll e-transfer you right now. Whatever it takes to get you out of here immediately."

Ray laughs, a harsh barking sound that cuts through the brisk air. "How stupid do you think I am, woman?"

I don't fully suppress the urge to give him a look that tells him exactly what I think of him. In two steps, Parker closes the distance between us and grabs my elbow, pulling me sharply away from Ray.

"What are you doing?" he hisses, leaning towards me.

"*I'm* not doing anything," I say, meeting his eyes. "*We* are putting an end to this. Together. I'm not going to let you drown in this alone, Parker. No matter how badly you want to."

"Isn't that sweet?"

"Shut up," we both say at once.

Something else shutters over Ray's ragged face. "I could go and ask your other lady friend instead," he says, tucking the envelope of cash into the inside pocket of his leather jacket. "She must have a fair bit of cash lying around, from all those tips working at that bar."

Parker and I both tense.

Ray turns, moving to get back into his truck. "Maybe I'll swing by her place now, say hello to that kid of hers."

"You son of a bitch," Parker snarls, emotion cracking his voice as he lunges for him. I grab him, yanking him back.

"Parker, listen to me, *please,*" I beg, grabbing his face and forcing him to look at me. "This guy is not messing around. The only way out of this is to give him what he wants. Let me help you, and this will all be over."

"Sloan, I can't let you do this. Especially after yesterday, I—" Words fail him.

I place a hand on his arm, trying to comfort him. To make up for the strength he's lacking right now, like he's done so many times for me.

"Yes, you can."

He stares at me for a moment longer, the war he's fighting in his head evident in his brown eyes. I give his arm a reassuring squeeze, silently begging him to let me help. Finally, he nods.

Dropping my arms to my side, I turn back to the rat standing a few feet away, watching us closely.

"You can follow us to the nearest ATM."

Ray's lips pull back over his teeth, but he shakes his head no. "I don't think so. You'll ride with me, darlin'. I need to make sure you're not going to make any unexpected detours."

I bark out a laugh as Parker grinds out, "Like fucking hell she will."

I've seen about a thousand too many true crime specials to consider getting in a strange man's truck, especially one with a known track record like Ray. Still, I have the sinking feeling that now that he's voiced it, he's not going to accept anything less. Immediately, my mind races, but I keep my face carefully neutral as I try to come up with a plan.

"It's funny," Ray says conversationally.

"What's that?" Parker growls, his jaw clenched so tight it's twitching, hands balled into fists at his sides.

"You seem to think the rates aren't climbing while you're standing here wasting my time."

The air escapes from my chest in a wheeze, and I know we have to move. It's now or never, and if we don't get this over with, who knows what the consequences could be.

I turn to Parker and grab his face, forcing him to look at me, imploring him to see the apology in my eyes for what I'm about to do.

"Follow us," I say, before darting around to the passenger side of Ray's truck before Parker can stop me.

Chapter 28

"S*hit*. Sloan!" Parker bellows.

I lock the door of the truck, hating that I'm doing this to him, but knowing there's no other choice. Parker's eyes flash as Ray jumps into the driver's side and revs the engine, and I crank my neck around to watch him sprint for his truck so he can follow us. My stomach drops out of my throat when he flies up behind us before we even make it out of the driveway. A glance at Ray shows he's smiling, as if this is all a fun game.

I don't notice my phone is still clutched in my hand until it rings, Parker's number flashing on the screen. The rest of my plan clicks into place.

I answer it and lift it to my ear before Ray can react. "I'm sorry."

Ray yells in protest and Parker's shouting at me through the other end, but I keep the phone where it is as I turn my fierce eyes on Ray.

"I talk to Parker or the police, your call."

I'm proud of the fierce, steady tone of my voice. He works his jaw, scabbed knuckles flexing on the wheel before he grudgingly accepts that this is the better of the two options.

"What the *fuck*, Sloan?" Parker yells across the line over the sound of his truck engine. "Are you insane? This guy could be dangerous!"

"We didn't have a choice. I'm fine. And you'll be there as soon as I get out of the truck to bring me home."

He lets out another string of expletives, and his figure tenses in the reflection of the side mirror as he stays inches from our tail.

"Parker, this will all be over soon. Trust me." I put as much weight as I can into the last two words.

The breath hisses out from between his teeth before he grants me his clipped consent. "Fine."

As subtly as I can, I slide my thumb over and press the end call button, severing our connection. "Stay on the line with me, okay, Parker?" I lower the phone, pretending to fumble with putting it on speakerphone. But instead, I swipe to open the camera and quickly set it to video recording, angling the phone so the screen faces the window, out of Ray's view. I can't see, but I'm pretty sure the angle will capture him in the driver's seat from here, and it's far enough from his reach that he can't snatch it unexpectedly.

"You want to tell your boyfriend to back up?" he snaps.

I cast a glare in his direction, letting my anger distract me from the reality of how dangerous this situation could be.

"What did you expect? You're blackmailing him, remember?"

"I'm collecting payment owed to me, girl. You're lucky I'm only interested in the money."

His dark eyes skim over to my side of the cab, dragging up my legs. I shrink back against the door, fighting the nausea that climbs up my throat. We drive the next couple of country blocks without speaking. The closer we get to town and an ATM, the more my lungs begin to fill with air again. We don't seem to be going in an unfamiliar direction, and I'm pretty positive that, despite how hard he's working to intimidate us, all Ray really wants is the money.

"God, it's freezing in here," I say, quickly reaching for the heat and cranking the dial, turning the fan on and adjusting the vents to face me. I'm not cold. In fact, I'm sweating under my arms like a motherfucker. However, phase two of my plan is to touch as many things in this truck as possible. I hit the radio next, turning it on and quickly punching my way through all the preset stations before he smacks my hand away and shuts it off again. I slump back and fold my arms with a huff, pretending I'm more annoyed than scared. I mean, it's not like he's armed. That I know of. Checking to make sure Parker's still behind us, I let out a long, bored breath, drumming my hands on the dashboard.

"You have terrible timing; do you know that? I have like a million and one things I need to get done today, and this is not on the list."

He doesn't respond.

"So, are you the brains behind this operation, or just the goon who collects the money?" I say, breaking the silence.

"I'm a one-man operation, sweetheart. The clients are all mine. Including the repeat customers like your boyfriend's daddy."

"Riiight, so by clients you mean addicts you take advantage of by loaning them money for illegal gambling and then charging them triple to pay it back?"

"They know what they're getting into."

I chew my lower lip, arms crossed, as I look out the window, pretending to think hard.

"Look, I'm not sure I have all of it in my bank account. I'll give you whatever I can."

"You'll give me all of what I'm owed."

"I can't help it if my bank has a limit on withdrawals! Look, what if ... *ugh*. Forget it," I mutter, glaring out the window.

"What if what?"

I sigh, as if this is the last thing I want to admit.

"Look, I know I don't look like it, but I'm a decent poker player."

His eyes slant sideways at me, and I hold my breath, knowing I need to play the next bit extremely carefully.

"And?"

I lift one shoulder in a tiny shrug. "And ... if you happened to know where a game was happening, I could give you the money that you're owed, plus enough to keep you from needing to come back to Parker's dad ever again."

I watch him for a minute, then pretend to dismiss the idea as stupid by turning back to the window. "Never mind."

"517 Murphy Avenue. Midnight tonight."

With a guarded look at him, I nod once. We're quiet for the rest of the ride, but a few minutes later, we're arriving at our destination—time for phase three of the plan. I unbuckle my seatbelt and grip the handle as we pull into the gas station's parking lot, which has an ATM around the side of the building. Parker is still right behind us, and I hop out as soon as Ray jerks to a stop.

Parker flies out of his truck while it's still running, but Ray steps between us before he can get to me, the slippery man faster than either of us gave him credit for.

"You good, Sloan?" Parker calls tightly, his eyes cutting to me over Ray's shoulder, relief and anger warring in them.

I nod, then go to the ATM with trembling fingers and withdraw the maximum amount. My phone in one hand, I thrust the money at Ray with the other.

"Here. That's the extra two thousand. We're done here."

Smiling, Ray puts the cash in his pocket and backs away from Parker, keeping his eyes on him until he's halfway into his truck, speaking over the door.

"Change your mind about tonight, sweetheart? Afraid you won't be able to handle it?"

"Handle what?" Parker growls.

"Oh, Ray here invited me to an illegal poker game. I can't remember the address, but don't worry. I can play back the recording." I smile sweetly at Ray as I lift my phone, which has been rolling this whole time. His face falls slowly as understanding dawns on him.

"You think that gives you anything on me? I didn't say shit that the cops would give a fuck about."

"No, but they will if I tell them you kidnapped me," I say, closing the distance between me and Parker.

His surprised eyes bore into the side of my face as he tries to catch up.

"I don't know if you realized this," I say, "but I touched pretty much everything in your truck. Do you have any idea how far forensics has come in the last five years alone? If anyone so much as breathes inside your truck, they can tell who, when, and for how long. It might be my word against yours, Ray, but scientific evidence is indisputable. And the amount of it in your truck right now means that if you know what's good for you, you'll leave Parker and everybody he knows alone. For good. Got it?"

"You think I don't know how to wipe for fingerprints, you little bitch?"

I laugh. "That's cute. Honestly, if you're going to be a criminal, you should keep up with what the good guys are doing. You could drive that truck into a pool full of bleach and they'd still find something. But by all means, be my guest. And keep talking, while you're at it," I say cheerily, circling my finger in the air. "Tell me more about how good you *think* you are at destroying evidence. Honestly, this is all gold."

I anticipate his next move before he finishes taking his first step towards me.

"Destroying the phone won't do you any good. I've already uploaded this as a draft to Instagram. Say the word and this puppy goes live. I'm thinking, hashtag thug life. Do you have a handle you want me to tag?"

I'm bluffing, but I took a calculated risk that this middle-aged criminal isn't up to date on his social media platforms, and it pays off. Maybe I'd be decent at poker after all. With an impatient suck of his teeth, he casts both of us one final glare before slamming himself into the truck and peeling off.

Before I know what's happening, Parker's arms are wrapped around me and I'm collapsing into him, letting him hold up the weight on my wobbly legs, useless after forcing them to stay solid under me until now.

"What the *hell* were you thinking?" he breathes into my hair, one hand around my waist and the other gripping the base of my neck as he clutches me against him. It feels great to be back here again.

"I'm sorry," I squeak, though it's difficult to speak when he's squeezing me so tight.

A humorless laugh escapes him as he pulls away. "Come on, let me take you—back."

I would bet another four grand that he almost just said 'home.' And he would have been right. Salem Stables is home to me now, more than anywhere else I could ever hope to be. I thought Parker was anchored to this place in a way I never would be, but I was wrong. This is where I belong. Not despite him, but because of him.

Without looking at me, he walks me towards his truck, closing the door behind me after I climb in. The weight of the silence is heavy in the crisp air between us as we drive back to Salem Stables, his discontent almost enough to fog the glass. He has every right to be angry with me for getting into a vehicle with someone like Ray, especially without first informing him of my plan. What I did was risky and shortsighted, but he wouldn't be so upset if he didn't care about my safety ... if he didn't care about *me.* Would he? The hope blossoming in my chest encourages me to break the silence as we pull into the driveway.

"Parker, I'm sorry," I say again, twisting in my seat to face him.

He pulls the keys out of the ignition, staring at the steering wheel for a beat before he climbs out of the truck, rounding to my side and opening the door. Quietly, I unfasten my seatbelt and slide down into the space between him and the truck, waiting for the words I know he's building up to.

"Do you have any idea how stupid that was?" he asks, but the wild emotion I heard earlier has faded.

"I know. But I couldn't think of anything else to do. And it worked, didn't it? It was worth it."

"It wouldn't have been if anything had happened to you." His thumb brushes my cheek. "Sloan, I swear, if he so much as laid a finger—"

"He didn't," I'm quick to assure him. My hand comes up to his, holding his palm against my cheek.

His eyes are so warm and familiar, pulling me into them. I shift up onto my toes, my lips brushing softly against his.

"Sloan." There's an apology in his tone as he pulls away.

I keep my eyes pressed closed for a second longer, so I don't have to watch the rejection I know is coming. I sink back down until my heels hit the ground and lift my lids so I'm looking at his chest, unable to meet his eyes.

"Nothing's changed for you, has it?" I whisper, the cracks in my heart deepening with every word. "Even after all that."

Defeat weighs his neck forward, and even his words come out heavy. "We were never in this together, Sloan. None of it. If we were, you wouldn't have even thought about leaving me."

I flinch, realizing the implication of what I almost did. Leaving is what his dad did to him when shit hit the fan, when Parker needed him. And I'd gone and done the exact same thing.

"I was never trying to string you along. That phone call with Lyla, I can explain—"

"No." He takes a step backward, distancing himself from me. "No more explaining, I get it. Believe me, I get it. I was a distraction for you. Until things got complicated, and then I wasn't worth the trouble."

My mouth opens and closes like a fish, wanting so badly to explain but not knowing where to begin. Both of our heads turn at the sound of my name being called. Across the driveway, Tabitha is standing underneath the white wedding tent, looking frazzled.

"Where have you been?! We have a big problem on our hands."

"Uh ... sure. Give me a sec?"

"I'd love to, hon, but this is time sensitive. We could use your help over here."

Of *course,* this is happening right now.

"Go. It's fine," Parker says, taking a step back. "It doesn't matter."

"It does matter," I say, reaching for him. "*You* matter to me. We can fix this, can't we?"

His fingers circle my wrists, and my heart rises in my chest as I prepare for him to pull me in.

Gently, he removes my hands from his chest and steps back. "I can't," he says, his voice low and thick with emotion. "That's my problem. I give people too many chances. You were right. This is too complicated, too messy. I'm sorry, Sloan, but I don't have room for messiness in my life. And you've got two hundred people waiting for you, remember?"

My heart is back on the floor, the treads of his boots leaving their mark.

"I don't care about the wedding," I say, meaning it—more than I've ever meant anything.

He presses his lips in a line. "They will, though. And they're not going to care what the reason is if their day doesn't go perfectly."

I don't blame him for being cautious. He's been let down by the people who were supposed to take care of him too many times, hurt so bad that it seems the only way to make it through is to play it safe. Proving to him I'm worth taking a chance on is going to take something more ... something big.

One grand gesture, coming right up.

Chapter 29

The early evening air is buzzing with music and laughter, the formerly empty tent now crowded with bodies in formal wear, and by some miracle, everything has gone without a hitch—at least since the guests arrived.

Lucy moves effortlessly around the maze of tables, glowing more radiantly than the elaborately beaded trumpet gown that makes her look like a movie star from the twenties, even with the cast she's wearing on her left arm, which has been bedazzled to match her gown like an extra accessory. When they finally make it to their seats at the head table, I give them a couple of minutes to themselves before I interrupt.

"Congratulations, you two. So? What's the verdict?"

Lucy beams up at me. "Everything is *perfection*. You're a miracle worker, Sloan. I don't know how you did it!"

"Honestly, we can't even begin to repay you," Keith adds, slinging a suited arm across the back of his wife's chair. "We owe you."

"I wanted to do this because *I* owed you. Let's not forget I'm the reason you're wearing a cast," I say, nodding towards the white, bling-covered fiberglass on her arm.

Lucy's face softens. "Don't worry about this," she says, touching her fingers to the cast. "The photographer said they might be able to Photoshop it out. And Veronica bedazzled the crap out of it, so I'm trying to think of it as a statement piece for today. Honestly," she looks over at her new husband, love filling her eyes, "I'm too happy right now to be mad about anything."

I'm not sure which photographer she means, since she hired a whole team, in addition to the magazine photographer who was here earlier for the exclusive event coverage. Still, I ignore that in favor of seizing the opportunity in front of me.

I let out a nervous exhale and take the opening. "In that case, maybe now's a good time to request a small favor?"

"Oh no," Lucy winces. "Is my sister still giving you a hard time? I swear, she's more upset about me being in a cast for my wedding than I am. I love her more than anything, but that girl would rather rig up a bridge with explosives than mend a fence, you know? I keep telling her it's not worth the frown lines, but she won't listen. I guess it's true what they say; you can't choose your family."

I laugh. "No, it's nothing like that. She's been great today."

It's a slight exaggeration, which Lucy must suspect because she exchanges a look with her new husband. "I doubt that. But if this isn't about Molly, what's this favor that you need?"

Having rehearsed this part, it doesn't take me long to explain. I step away after getting the green light, then scan the room to make sure Parker's still here. He's standing politely while Veronica talks his ear off about something, just as we planned. Veronica spots me and I twirl my finger to signal that she needs to keep talking. A few minutes later, Paul steps up to the podium and grabs the microphone. The guests cringe as a screech of feedback rips through the speakers, followed by a ripple of polite laughter. Paul looks annoyed until a passing groomsman moves him a few steps away from the speakers and gives him a reassuring, if somewhat patronizing, pat on the shoulder.

I down half a glass of champagne as the guests take their seats, thanks to Paul's semi-coherent instructions, but it does nothing for my dry mouth. As the first course is served, I can't ignore the thumping in my chest as I wait for my opening. When it looks like Paul is about to go for the mic again, I rush to beat him to it.

"Don't worry," I say, pushing him back into his seat and patting his shoulder like the other guy did. (It seemed to work when placating Paul.) "You eat, I got this. Read this for me after, would you?" I pass him a folded napkin.

"This your number, beautiful?" he says, sounding overly pleased.

I roll my eyes and head for the mic, clearing my throat into it tentatively to make sure it doesn't do that awful screech again. The conversation quickly hushes and people turn in their seats to face me, no doubt wondering who the hell I am. There's still a gentle clinking of cutlery, and I'm grateful for the background noise.

"Um ... most of you don't know me," I start, gripping the mic to keep my clammy hands from shaking. "My name is Sloan Sanders, and on behalf of the staff, I'd like to welcome you all to Salem Stables."

There's a smattering of applause, and I'm bolstered by how professional I'm sounding.

I finally see the one head that matters—Parker's—turn towards me, recognizing my voice, which I'm sure he didn't expect to hear over the PA system. Especially after he'd flat-out refused to play along with using walkie-talkies during the setup. Something about not wanting to talk to me any more than he had to.

I swallow. Grand gesture, I remind myself. He won't trust me until I can prove how much he means to me.

"I'm glad to see that everyone managed to find the place, given that it wasn't exactly what was listed on the invitation..." There's laughter, the kind that only happens after a chaotic turn of events is resolved. "Though if there is an empty seat beside you, please let us know. We'll make sure that nobody is sitting in a dark, swampy field wondering when the signature cocktails will arrive."

The rumble of laughter this time is genuine, and the crowd roars again when someone calls out, "Where's Aunt Millie?!"

Underneath the white canopy, the barn door is framed with the Edison bulbs we repurposed from the loft, the pasture ringed with the ones we never bothered to take down. Against the darkening sky, it appears to be a genuine wedding venue, not a backup plan.

"I think it's safe to say that the happy couple has gotten the beautiful day they deserve. Thank goodness they're willing to roll with the punches, so to speak. You'd never know to look at them that two days ago, they had no place to have their wedding. Lucy was here last week for a bachelorette party—"

There's a cheer from the bridesmaids that makes me chuckle.

"That's the reason behind the cast she's wearing, if you haven't heard the story yet. The short version is, I wanted to do something to make up for it and somehow talked Lucy into giving Salem Stables—and me—a second chance."

I take a deep breath, lifting my eyes to the span of faces looking up at me. "I'd love to tell you that things went smoothly this time around—which is what I told the bride and groom earlier—but that would be a lie. I would *not* be lying if I told you the truck that delivered the tent got stuck in the driveway this morning. Or that I had to bribe one of the delivery guys to make sure everything was set up in time. Oh, and that I was still wearing sweats when the first guest pulled in. Everything looks great now, but getting here was nothing short of disastrous."

There's a smattering of hesitant laughter, though most people are wondering where the hell I'm going with all this.

"My point is, life doesn't always go according to plan. Today certainly didn't. If you don't believe me, you can see for yourself. The messy behind-the-scenes reality is online with the wedding hashtag." I chance a look towards the bride, whose curious expression has been replaced by a frown. With a sharp inhale, I look away, plowing on and hoping I'm not making a terrible mistake. "Lucy's trip home for Christmas six years ago didn't go to plan either. Her flight was canceled, the trains were booked, and she ended up in a car, squished in the back seat between two jocks she'd never met before. One of them is sitting beside her tonight."

I turn, and the audience looks with me, heads tilted in collective appreciation and admiration. "How's that left hand feeling, Keith?"

He leans over to kiss Lucy on the cheek. "Light as a feather."

A ripple of laughter titters through the crowd.

"Life rarely works out the way we expect it to," I continue, my eyes finding Parker at the back corner.

He's growing restless, and I'm afraid he might leave before I make my point. Veronica is hovering near him, but she won't be able to stop him if he decides to go now. I need to wrap this up, and quickly.

"More often than not, neither does love. It's messy and chaotic and terrible and wonderful, everything you want and don't want to feel all wrapped up into one person."

I hold my breath as Parker looks up, our eyes locking across the tent. Clutching the microphone tighter, I keep talking.

"I'm not married, but I have been in love. So, I'll share the single most important piece of advice I've ever gotten. Embrace the mess. Be real with each other. The memories you'll make along the way won't be the perfect moments you capture on camera; it'll be everything in between. If you're lucky enough to find that person you belong with, the one you can be completely real with, you have to jump. No chute, no backup plans, no exit strategies. Jump with both feet, even if it takes you somewhere unexpected, even if it throws off your life plan. Because life isn't really about plans, it's about love ... family. Everything else comes second." I look away from Parker to the crowd again, trying to stay steady on my trembling knees. I might be used to putting myself on camera for social media, but there's something so much more vulnerable about being in the same room as the people watching me.

Or maybe I'm only this nervous because Parker's here. His is the only opinion I care about.

"A few minutes ago, the bride said to me that you can't choose family. I'm not sure I agree with her." I think of Tabitha, and my parents, and how they chose me. Chose to bring me into their lives, to love me, and to give me a family I could be proud of, no matter what. "Lucy and Keith chose each other, and—as of today—they're family."

"Here, here!" rises from the crowd.

I now turn to Keith and Lucy, who are watching me curiously.

My voice wavers, but I push through the emotion that's threatening to break it as I speak directly to them. "Anyone lucky enough to find the family they belong with has everything they'll ever need. Blood is one thing. But the family you choose? The family that chooses *you*? That's something special. So, Lucy, Keith, now that you've jumped in with both feet, hold on as tight as you can. And *never* stop showing each other that no matter what happens, no matter how much time passes ..." I break away and my eyes find Parker's one final time, speaking only to him now. "You still choose him. You'll *always* choose him."

I enter the barn through the people door at the side entrance, in search of Parker, and find him sitting with his elbows resting on his knees, behind a rope draped across the wide doorway, a no-entry sign swaying in the gentle evening breeze. It's bright in the barn, and it takes my eyes a minute to adjust to the light. He doesn't turn, but I can tell by the set of his shoulders that he heard me coming. My heels aren't exactly conducive to sneaking up on anyone.

"You left," I say, at a loss for words. After pouring so much into the microphone, I think maybe I've run out.

"I'm supposed to make sure no one comes in here, remember?"

I nod, and awkward silence hovers over us. He eyes me closely, his expression unreadable.

"What you said back there..."

"I meant it," I rush, stepping forward.

Nodding slowly, he keeps his eyes trained on me. "Will you still mean it tomorrow?"

He looks deep into my eyes, his dark ones masking a hurt I know I don't fully understand yet. When I don't answer, he stands and disappears into the office. I stand, my arms dangling limp at my sides.

Is that it? I wonder. *Is it over, just like that?*

My heart lifts when he reappears, setting an overturned bucket on the ground to sit on and leaving me the chair. I perch on the seat, placing my hands in my lap. The air is cold, and though I can't do anything about my bare legs, I pull my blazer tighter around me.

"I get why you're scared, Parker. I've given you every reason to be. But people can surprise you. You're the one who made me realize that. I don't want to throw away what we have because it took me too long to figure it out."

He's frowning at his boots, his expression frustratingly impossible to decipher.

"If you believe anything I've said tonight, please believe me when I say the last thing I ever want is to hurt you."

He rubs the back of his neck as he struggles to find the right words. "I don't like owing people a debt—especially ones I can't repay. When you got in that truck with Ray..." he drags a hand over his face. "Sloan, if you'd gotten hurt, I never would have forgiven myself."

"I wish I could apologize," I say, my voice soft. "But I'm not sorry for what I did."

His eyes lift, catching mine in the dim glow from the string lights over the door.

"You aren't?"

I shake my head. "I know this might be hard to believe, but I kind of like you, Parker. You were in trouble. And every time I've been in trouble, you've been there to help. I just … wanted to do the same." I pause. "No. That's wrong." I look back up, catching his eyes in a frown. "I don't like you. I love you."

I marvel at how easy it is to say, even when I'm pretty certain he won't say it back. Because at this moment, I don't need anything from him. I only want him to have this one thing from me. This one, simple, real thing, that means nothing and everything.

"None of this happened by accident," I say, gesturing between us. "It wasn't luck or fate or destiny. I chose you then, and I'm choosing you now."

I stand, knowing that I've said everything I have to say. Choosing someone doesn't always mean they'll choose you back. But if you only love what you know will never go away, then you'll spend your whole life never loving anything at all.

And he can't tell me not to wait for him.

I walk past, hoping that he'll reach for my hand to stop me as I duck under the rope to head back to the tent. But he doesn't. I take a few more steps, then pause, turning back to him one last time.

"If you're asking me to promise that I'll never hurt you again, Parker, I can't. Nobody can." If I've learned anything lately, it's that the only way to avoid getting hurt is to be alone. "But when I'm with you, it feels like I've found a piece of myself I didn't know was missing. And I wish you would give me the chance to be the same for you."

I fight the lump forming in my throat as I walk away, tears stinging behind my eyes, but I will them not to fall. Not yet. I'll wait until the darkness swallows me, somewhere between the barn and the tent.

I'm almost there, my throat tightens painfully when gravel crunches behind me. Parker calls out, and I turn as he reaches me, far more out of breath than he should be for the distance he ran to get here. Before I can say anything, his hands tangle through my hair, pressing his forehead to mine.

"What was it you said about both feet?"

My face threatens to split in two, but I don't care, because right now I have everything I'll ever want or need. I reach for his chest and gather his shirt in both hands, not caring if I wrinkle the fabric.

"Hold on tight," I whisper.

Standing in the driveway, framed perfectly by the lit doorway of the barn, beneath the stars, with crickets chirping in symphony all around us and the music playing in the distance, he kisses me like he's never wanted anything more, and I can't help feeling like I'm the luckiest woman in the world.

Epilogue

Ten months later

Summer sunlight pours onto the pale hardwood of the now-familiar space as I take it all in. Scraps of newspaper are still stuck in places on the large windows that wrap around the front and side of the corner unit. The glass could use about a bucket worth of Windex, cobwebs are visible in the ceiling corners, most of the light fixtures are missing bulbs, and the floorboards desperately need to be reacquainted with a mop.

I link my fingers under my chin and take a deep, solidifying breath.

It's wonderful.

This is the fourth time I've seen the space in person, not to mention the light stalking I've done through photos of the online listing, and every time I fall more in love with it. Windows wrap around two sides of the corner building, old enough to have a hint of charm without being stuffy.

By now, Sharon, the realtor, is used to my process. Once she lets me in, she settles in at one of the wrought iron tables left over from the days when this place was a café to answer emails on her phone while I look around some more, visualizing everything this place could be. At least having another person here means I'm not talking to myself.

It's dusty and unloved, with muddy footprints on the floor and a broken window in the back, but I can work with this. The last owners were going for a cabin vibe. I imagine the wood walls painted white, with black tables and sleek chairs accenting the space, creating a chic and cozy atmosphere that combines traditional and modern elements. The twinkle lights in the window will be adorable inside and out, with a neon-pink sign featuring the store's name—*Start Here, With Love*—surrounded by mismatched frames in different colors to showcase my own hand-lettering pieces that people can buy. I have a flash vision of Veronica, Lucy, and their friends laughing over a bottle of rosé as they paint raunchy signs to give each other as gifts. (I'll put Lucy's sister down as a maybe, since she still doesn't like me much.) The glass dessert case at the counter will be filled with colorful cupcakes; instead of a business partner, I'll have an employee handling that.

Even though she's not directly involved, Lyla has been very invested in the success of this shop as a solo venture for me. Apart from Parker, she's been my biggest cheerleader, and is already planning to tag along with my parents for the grand opening—despite how many times I've tried to reassure her that she does not need to travel with a small baby to be supportive.

Like my relationship with Tabitha and my parents, things are different now—but not for the worse. We all have a different understanding of each other now, and Lyla and I have a healthy respect for the parts of ourselves that will be forever linked, as much as the separate ones. We're not inseparable like we used to be, but we also have so much more to talk about, and I am so grateful to know she's in my corner, no matter where our paths take us. It turns out, our friendship hasn't unraveled at all—it's just been woven into something brand new, and possibly even stronger.

Everything is ... *almost* perfect.

"Sorry, I'm late!" Parker says as the bells above the door jangle with his arrival, making my head turn. "Did I miss it?"

I shake my head. "I told you I haven't made a decision yet."

He sets down the moving box he's carrying on the flat counter, moving through the space like it's already mine. "Sharon, would you mind giving us a minute?"

She excuses herself with an amused smile, closing the door softly behind her as she steps onto the sidewalk out front.

"What is it this time?" Parker asks with a knowing smirk.

Steepling my fingers at my chin, I take a slow spin around the space in my tank top and cutoffs, ignoring the mental note that my brain tries to make to get the air conditioning in here sorted out asap. *It's not mine yet. I don't know if this is the one.*

"I'm not sure," I admit.

"You've described what you would do with this place to me fifty times. Trust me, it's perfect for you."

He's right. Even before we found it, it was almost exactly what I had described when I first toyed with the idea of expansion. Salem Stables is an amazing venue, but without any heat, it's only available for five or six months of the year. It's been the perfect place to start small, but lately I've been noticing that something is still missing.

I think it's the risk factor. It's hard to put it all on the line when total failure wouldn't have much of a consequence at the end of the day. I love Salem Stables, and I love sharing the cabin with Parker—a welcome change that *nobody* complained about after Jim started spending a ton more time at the house last winter. But I'm ready to carve out a little more independence, to see if I truly can do this on my own. I want to build my own brand-new happy place from the ground up.

That doesn't mean I'm not nervous as hell.

Parker's been helping me all summer, scouring online listings and driving all over town to check out any space that might work. Something's always felt just a little bit off, though. Even now, with a shop that fits my specifications perfectly. Today is different, though, because I'm finally able to put my finger on why I haven't been able to commit.

"I don't think it's the space I'm not sure about." I turn to face him, letting him bear witness to all my doubts and insecurities. In the same way, he's witnessed *Start Here, With Love* blossom and flourish over the past ten months. "What if I can't manage a whole business on my own? It's a lot of moving pieces. If I am cursed, maybe my bad luck is waiting until I'm nice and complacent before it strikes again?"

Parker closes the distance between us and places his calloused hands firmly on my shoulders, amusement playing at his lips. "You *can* manage it, and you are *not* cursed. You find problems and face them because you're capable of solving them. You've been that way since I met you."

I snort. "I was a mess when you met me."

His smile widens, his chocolate brown eyes watching me fondly as he does what he does best and disagrees with me. "I promise you, I didn't see a mess. I saw you putting your life back together after several major setbacks and still making time to help Tabitha with her creative block, throw a party for some woman you'd never met, and help me with my dad. You went out of your way to solve one impossible problem after another, Sloan, and you didn't even realize you were doing it. You're pretty incredible."

I feel my cheeks turn pink at his praise and lift my hand to touch the dark stubble on his cheek. Things between Parker and his dad are still complicated, but he's slowly learning to find a balance between being there for him and keeping his boundaries in place when he needs to.

"You're pretty incredible, too," I tell him, meaning it.

He smiles. "Can I show you what I brought?" He tips his chin towards the box on the counter.

I eye it suspiciously. "It doesn't *look* like champagne, unless that also comes boxed, now?"

A soft chuckle escapes him. "It's better than champagne. Go take a look."

Moving to the counter, I reach inside the box and pull out one of a dozen or so mismatched picture frames.

"When did you do this?" I murmur when I find my voice, tracing a finger delicately over my hand lettering inside the frame.

"This is why I was late." He steps up behind me, peeking over my shoulder. "I hope it's okay that I snuck into the loft to steal some of your work. I had a feeling you might need a little push to see this place as your own." He reaches into the box and pulls out a hammer and nail, trading them for the frame I'm holding, then jerks his chin at the wall to the right of the front door, the only one not covered by a massive window. "What do you think, Princess? Ready to try your luck at something new?"

Grinning, I make my way over to the wall and pick a spot roughly in the middle, not bothering to make sure it's perfect. Perfect isn't the point. With three quick drives of the hammer, the nail is in. I hold my hand out without looking back, and Parker is right there behind me, passing the frame to set in its new home.

The soft jingle of bells announces her as Sharon pokes her head inside. "So? What do we think?"

I turn my face to meet Parker's eyes and watch as he waits for my answer, lifting a brow in question.

"I'll take it."

THE END

Acknowledgements

If I've learned anything from the process of writing and publishing my first book, it's that it does not happen alone.

Nicole Payne, my agent extraordinaire, I will be forever grateful to you for taking a chance on me. Your time and insight made this story and my writing stronger (I promise I'm working on starting less sentences with "And", even if it doesn't seem like it). Thank you for everything you have done to bring my story to readers. I would not be here without you.

To Alexandria Brown, Tina Beier, and the entire team at Rising Action Publishing. Thank you for trusting me, and this story. You've made a lifelong dream come true, and I am incredibly proud to have found a home for my debut at Rising Action. Thank you to Lucy at Cover Ever After for bringing this book and the characters to life.

A lot (and I mean a *lot*) of work goes into writing before an industry professional even gets a whiff of your book, and just like my agent and publishing team, I truly believe I wouldn't be here without any of them.

Annie McQuaid, I can honestly say my luck was running high when we crossed paths online, and your chance response to a post about swapping opening chapters turned into steady critique partners, then writing buddies, and now a years-long friendship. Going through this process with you has been wonderful and rewarding. You are a steady rock in the raging rapids that is the world of publishing. Thank you for not letting me give up on this book when I was ready to throw in the towel, and for always knowing how to fix it. For the record, you were right. You're always right. You truly are the best in the biz.

Thank you to all my fellow romance writers on the Smutfest 2.0, Tortured Writers Department, and 2026 Debuts Discord groups for providing such a supportive writing community. Huge thanks to Judy Penz Sheluk for your guidance, encouragement, and insight on the publishing process, to Meredith Schorr for your SmoochPit feedback which was instrumental in shaping this book, and to Michelle Hazen for your support with my query letter which helped find a home for it. Your kindness and generosity are appreciated more than you know.

What many people don't know about the publishing process is how long it takes to go from "I started writing a book," to "I got a book deal!" to "Okay *now* you can buy my book."

I am forever grateful to the friends who have held my hand—both literally and metaphorically—through this process. The Bookettes—Alex, Anna, Brittany, Karly, Kelly, and Vicky. You've been asking for book updates the longest, and I love you all for it. My forever reading buddy, Rachel Mayo, thank you for always being my earliest reader, and for telling me I could do this. Brooke, for getting your book club on board to read this about two years too early. I hope it was worth the wait. Thank you all for being the biggest cheerleaders a girl could ask for, and getting excited over every milestone, big and small, along the way (even when you had no idea what the heck I was talking about.)

Lindsay Lou, your enthusiasm (aka borderline impatience) makes me work harder when I start to lose steam. I will never get tired of talking about books with you.

To my family: Mum, Dad, Amy, Alan, Alex, Marguerite, Mary-Ann, and Larry. Your encouragement means the world to me. Mum and Dad, sorry for the sex scenes. I *sincerely* hope you followed the strict instructions to skip those chapters. Thank you for your love and support. As far as I know, you are my biological parents, but I can say without a doubt that a DNA test wouldn't change a thing.

Tash and Scott, if there is anything you need to tell me, now would be a really good time. Thank you for loving me as fiercely as if you were my own parents, and for letting me spend countless hours writing on your dock, a kindness I will never be able to repay.

Poppy, I know this isn't your kind of book, but I also know that you'll read it anyway, and I love you for that. Tell Gran about it when you see her one day. You have both always inspired me with your ability to create beautiful things; I hope I made you both proud. (Minus the kissing chapters.)

There are too many extended family members, friends, coworkers, and fellow writers to name individually, but bear with me as I extend a blanket thank you to anyone who has ever asked me how the book is going. Every time you ask is a tiny nudge of encouragement to keep working.

My heartfelt thanks to any librarians, book sellers, and reviewers who may have played a hand in getting this book into your hands. If I could hug you all, I would.

To the future writers, in case you don't have anyone already telling you this—you *can* write that book. This is my first published novel, but it's far from the first thing I've written. What you hold in your hands is the product of years of learning, and it wouldn't exist without the team of people I've mentioned already. This novel is the result of a lot of time, hard work, setbacks, patience, and yes—a healthy dose of luck. So write that story that won't leave you alone. Do it now. Do it scared. Do it before you know how. Do it before you understand how to write a query letter or find an agent—those are the details that come with time. Just start writing. The only permission you need is your own.

Finally, to my real-life book boyfriend. Tyler, words always fail me when I try to describe how special you are to me. Who knew one chance meeting (thank you, Karly!) would turn into spending the rest of our lives together? You are my biggest cheerleader of all, and the reason I know what love is. Thank you for reminding me to believe in myself when I forget how, for making time and space for me to write, and for forgiving me when I spend our vacations accidentally starting new book projects. I love you more.

About the Author

Emily Wood was born and raised in rural Southern Ontario, Canada where her days were spent as a stereotypical horse girl and her nights as the quintessential bookworm. The former journalist and newspaper editor now works in library services by day, and spends her nights spinning stories that will make you blush (and which she desperately hopes her family won't read). When she's not writing, she enjoys reading, crafting, hiking with her husband and golden mountain doodle, and being lakeside with a blank page and a cup of tea.